TEA AT SAM'S

Sue Cross

Dedication

To Peter, without whose patience this book would not have been possible.

With best from

Sue Crost

1

CELINE

Celine checked her watch. She had another hour to wait before her plane would leave. As usual she was too early. Unable to concentrate on her novel, she sipped a coffee, her eyelids heavy with tiredness. Closing her eyes she thought fondly of her father and then her husband. Dear Dad, darling James. She could not wait to get home. Home was important to her. All that Celine had ever wanted from life was a contented, settled family life.

'Hope James has missed me. Can't wait to see him again. And I wonder if Holland will ever feel like home. Did I pack my black dress - think I did? Hope Mum will be all right.' She bit her bottom lip as she recalled the past few weeks and fought back the tears.

It was a mercifully short flight from England to Holland.

Schiphol Airport was packed that day, the pervading smell of continental tobacco and coffee not unpleasant.

Standing at the luggage carousel she spotted her suitcase and reached out for it but was interrupted by a strong tanned hand that lifted it and placed it at her feet like a trophy.

"Thank you." She glanced up at the stranger. He had a practised smile that revealed perfect teeth.

"Don't mention it." The man's accent was thick, Italian perhaps. In his late thirties or early forties, he was drinking in Celine's appearance. Starting with her wide hazel eyes, his gaze travelled downwards, past her slim waist and hips and then back up to her fine featured face which was framed with a mane of chestnut hair. Feeling embarrassed by the intensity of his gaze, Celine averted her eyes before hurrying away, pushing through the pressing crowds towards her goal.

Scanning the sea of faces, she spotted her husband, staring into space as he so often did. Deep in thought no doubt as he waited for her, his dark hair and tall stature making him stand out in the crowd. How she loved this quiet, good-looking man. Still mourning her father, she could not imagine life without her husband and wondered how her mother was coping now that she was alone in the house. It was 1969 and Celine had taken it for granted that her father would be a part of her life for at least another decade but a cruel stroke had snatched him away.

Almost running, she dropped her suitcase, flung her arms around James's neck and relished the relief she felt to be with him again. It would be their fourth wedding anniversary the following week and she was content that they had fallen into a comfortable routine as a married couple. She had already planned the special meal that she would cook for him to celebrate the occasion – Coq au Vin was one of his favourites. Her mother had taught her to be a good cook and, a product of growing up in England in the 50's and early 60's; Celine never questioned her role as a dutiful wife.

Although she would have liked children, he had insisted that this was not going to happen and so she had forced herself to be content just to have James. Always malleable, she did not object when he told her that she would have to give up her job as a fashion buyer and move with him to Amsterdam. Devotion had made her resigned to the fact that her career was a thing of the past. Her husband was ambitious, so she supported him in his chosen career. Accountancy bored Celine and they rarely discussed James's working life.

Celine was a creative and intelligent girl, but whatever she achieved she never felt that she had quite made it - perhaps because she never had affirmation from her critical mother or perhaps because she expected too much from herself. Or both. James rarely complimented Celine but her vulnerability was deep seated and not entirely due to his lack of attention. But she had a generous, kind spirit and a conscientious attitude by nature. People were drawn to her unselfconscious charisma, something that James, always a loner, discouraged. It was a paradox that whilst wanting to keep her to himself, when alone with her she was often ignored; like a costly ornament – at first cherished but soon unseen by its familiar presence.

From an early age her main ambition was to find love and marry. She was steeped in unrecognised maternal instinct and practised it by cherishing her husband and Persian cat, Sasha. Celine was a mother without children.

"Darling, I've missed you so much," she held him close as the announcements were made at first in Dutch and then English over the airport loud speakers.

6

He mumbled something inaudible against the buzz of the crowd and she wondered if he was embarrassed by her affection in such a public place.

Lifting her suitcase with ease, he walked purposefully to the exit while she scurried behind him across the terminal. Glad to get into his car she closed her eyes, aware of the familiar smell of the leather upholstery and enjoyed a moment's quiet before they set off home.

Once on the highway he drove fast, overtaking each vehicle in the slow lane. She glanced over to him, aware of an uneasy feeling between them which she found hard to decipher. Her senses were acute with spent emotion and she jumped as a leaf fluttered onto the windscreen. Weariness and the stress of the past few weeks had finally caught up with her. Her father's sudden death and the need to help sort out her mother's affairs had taken its toll.

James drove in silence along the thoroughfare that led them to the outskirts of the city.

"What are you thinking?" she asked him before she could stop herself, knowing that this question always irritated him.

"Nothing. Why do you always presume I'm thinking something?"

"Sorry. You just looked deep in thought, that's all."

"I'm concentrating on the traffic."

Wondering what was wrong, she tried to lighten the atmosphere, "You look well. Like the new shirt – where did you get it?"

He paused before replying. "Can't remember. How's Veronica coping?"

"Mum's not bad considering. I don't know whether it's sunk in yet. But I think she'll be all right. Of course she never stops talking so that hasn't changed. She still takes a paranoid interest in the neighbours and is as nosy as ever. I wish we got on better but we don't seem to have anything in common. Dad didn't leave a will, which made things a bit complicated. Janet and I spent ages looking for it but Mum said he never made one. She would have known if he had. But I found out something when I was looking for the will. I'll tell you about it later." She smiled a weak smile across at him as he drove into the grounds of their modern apartment block, relieved to be home at last. James looked bored. He was preoccupied and had not been listening.

Living in Amsterdam was to be their first base abroad and, although Celine had pined for her job and work colleagues for the first few weeks, she had forced herself to settle down quickly. The couple were adjusting to a new life, unfamiliar surroundings, alien language and different life style. She was resigned to the fact that theirs would not be a settled life and that they would have to move from country to country if James was to climb the corporate ladder.

They had got to know other expatriates through James's work and had a busy social life, although James was only involved for career purposes and not in search of friendship. When alone in the quietness of their apartment she often felt empty inside and longed for some direction and purpose that cocktail and dinner parties did not provide. James, on the other hand, seemed to be relishing their time abroad and was unaware of Celine's disquiet. If she tried to communicate her feelings to him he would chide her for being a complainer, or worse – a nag. Wasn't he providing her with every luxury? What more did she want?

As he carried her suitcase into the bedroom Celine put the kettle on for some coffee and noted that the place looked clean and tidy. She liked everything to be just so and became irrationally agitated if her home became messy. The cat, which had greeted her with almost canine abandon, had followed her into the kitchen.

"Want a coffee?" she called out as she reached for a mug, glad be away from the confines of her mother's house and her constant chatter but feeling guilty for thinking it.

"No thanks. I'm going to have a proper drink. It's been a busy week." She heard him opening the drinks cabinet in the sitting room and, feeling herself becoming tense at the sound of the bottle opening, picked up Sasha and breathed in the sweet smell of its fur. Switching on the radio, the poignancy of the song Homeward Bound moved her to tears as she thought about her father.

"Let's have an early night if you're tired." She had dried her secret tears and taken her coffee into the sitting room where she flopped onto the ultra modern sofa. She longed for him to take her to bed and hold her close in his arms, but experience had taught her to play it cool. If she were too keen he would inevitably reject her advances.

"Blast, I forgot to change the sheets!" he muttered.

"What's this sudden concern with things domestic? I'll have to go away more often. It hardly matters about the sheets – we've been married for a while now." She teased him.

Sasha was purring loudly on Celine's lap in blissful ignorance of the tension in the room.

"I'm going to have a shower and go to bed. Don't be too long darling." She got up, straightened the cushions and placed the cat on an easy chair, but the animal followed her faithfully into the bedroom where it jumped on the bed, stretched and settled down to another snooze.

Showered and feeling refreshed, Celine fell into bed alone and luxuriated in the pure cotton white sheets which felt soft next to her bare skin – quite a contrast to her mother's yellow nylon easy care bedding.

Eventually James joined her, his breath sour with whiskey. She waited for him to reach out for her but instead he kicked the cat off the bed and fell into a deep slumber.

Tears of rejection pricked her eyes as the pent up grief that she had hidden from her mother in order to be strong ran down her cheeks and soaked the pillowcase. Reaching out for Sasha, she fell asleep holding the animal close to her face.

The next morning James left early for work, without explanation. As an executive accountant for a city stockbroker, his work was always a priority.

"Goodbye dear. Have a nice day." Celine muttered to the wall before getting up.

She felt disorientated to be back in Holland and thought she would busy herself to take her mind off the events of the past few weeks. Checking the laundry basket, she took out the shirt that James had been wearing the previous day and decided to change the sheets before unpacking. As she was peeling off one of the pillowcases her heart started to thud and she felt sick. A long black curly hair was stuck to it like a thin snake. She removed it and examined it closely, feeling breathless and so lightheaded that she found herself clinging to the bedstead to keep her balance. Then she remembered his words the night before "Blast, I forgot to change the sheets." His words resounded in her head like a ghostly chant.

Then suddenly her mind became sharp and clear. She now felt certain she knew why he looked different. His hair was unusually long and he was wearing new trendy clothes. He had a mistress. But he couldn't. He loved her. Just as she could not countenance the thought of betraying James, so she believed that he would feel the same way.

Looking again at the long black hair, she placed it carefully like a rare specimen under a perfume bottle on the dressing table. Then she stood back and stared at it in disbelief.

'There must be a logical explanation,' she thought.

But the only explanation that she could imagine was that James no longer loved her.

She wanted to scream "NO!" Feeling as if she was in a dream and not able to wake up, a sudden panic engulfed her. Should she speak to her husband? If she confronted James she knew that he would deny it.

Then she wondered if she should question her neighbours in case they had seen a girl with long black hair entering the apartment.

'I only know them to nod to, how can I ask such a personal question?' she reasoned.

Going to the telephone, she started to dial her mother's number, longing for her familiar voice to offer comfort and advice, but when the phone started to ring she slammed the receiver down. She could not upset her mother at such a difficult time in her life.

Taking a deep breath, she took control of her wayward emotions and planned her strategy. Starting in the bedroom, she worked her way through each drawer, at first methodically and then frantically, looking for evidence. A scarf or item of clothing, maybe. Rummaging through James's pockets the only thing she found was a receipt from American Express. It seemed that he'd been on a spending spree whilst she was gone. She sniffed his jackets for any tell tale signs of perfume and thought she detected Aramis. James never wore aftershave or cologne even though she tried to persuade him to use it for her benefit.

'He was probably standing next to someone in a lift,' she rationalised.

Thinking that there may be some evidence in the sitting room, she proceeded to throw the sofa cushions onto the floor and ran her hand along the back of the upholstery. Nothing. Just the dark hair and a premonition. She wandered about the flat in disbelief, pausing at the sideboard to gaze at their wedding photo as if somehow it could restore her to sanity. The couple in the picture looked carefree. She was gazing up at him as a wry smile played across his mouth, his dark good looks heightened by the suit and white shirt that he wore with such elegance. What had happened to them? Lifting the photo, she held it to her breast and remembered her wedding and the hopes that she had for a future with James. She had never imagined that this could happen to her. This sort of thing only happened to other people. What had she done to deserve this? Celine had always thought of herself as a good wife who put her husband's happiness before her own. Where had she gone wrong? The couple in the photo were strangers. She placed it face down on the sideboard as if to dismiss the events of the past hours from her life.

Robotically, she dressed in her best trouser suit and studied her reflection critically in the mirror. She knew that she had good dress sense – hadn't she been told innumerable times by colleagues at work when she was a fashion buyer? What had she done to drive him to another woman?

She took a taxi to the heart of the city where James's office was situated. The normality of the city's activities affronted her as she watched cyclists, shoppers, young mothers with prams and business people going about their daily routine. A brass band played on a street corner and Celine felt as if it were mocking her. How could life go on like this? She paid the taxi driver and ventured into the tall, modern block that housed his office. It was a long shot but worth a try. Feeling strangely empowered, she strode out of the lift on the eighth floor. She had planned what to say to the young blonde receptionist but the desk was empty and so she walked straight into his office, not knowing what she would say to him if he was there. Good, the office was empty. She had to act quickly.

Nothing in his desk drawers. Except a bottle of Aramis.

"What the heck? He hates aftershave!" She thought in fury, now convinced there was another woman.

Her hands shook slightly as she moved with rapidity, opening the tall filing cabinet. The third file she opened held the evidence that she had been looking for. Holding her breath she withdrew a package that was bundled together with an elastic band. The photographs, about a dozen in all, showed a young, attractive girl with olive skin and slanting eyes. There were poses of her standing outside what looked like a club or café and the rest were taken in her apartment. There was one on the small balcony that led off the sitting room and others sitting on the sofa in the living room. There was even a picture of her holding Celine's Persian cat. She was drawn to the girl's hair. It was dark, long and curly. Feeling a mixture of disbelief and triumph that her plan had born fruit, she stared at the pictures for what seemed an eternity until she heard a noise in the corridor. Jumping, she knew she had to escape before she was discovered. Enraged that this stranger should be usurping her in her own home, she rammed the pictures into her large leather handbag and headed for home. She would confront him tonight.

"Good morning Mrs Smedley, are you looking for your husband?" the receptionist was back at her post.

"Er, it's all right. I've sorted out what I came here for," Celine sounded composed as she walked to the lift, thankful that the doors opened as soon as she pressed the button.

Once home Celine looked at the photos, this time checking every detail. She studied the one taken outside the bar. The girl was wearing a tight fitting black top and short skirt and was smiling into the camera. Celine could just decipher the name of the bar – Virgo. The irony did not escape her as she wracked her brain trying to remember where she had seen the sign before. Then, before hiding the evidence, she carefully lifted the long black hair from the dressing table and placed it in an envelope with the pictures.

For some reason that was beyond her she cooked a chicken casserole for him and put a bottle of white wine to chill in the fridge. Self pity was beginning to engulf her like a choking smog, replacing the fury and disappointment that had at first bombarded her. She had always trusted her husband and thought that they had a good, solid marriage. They didn't even argue very much as she let James get his own way. He was a bit of a sulker and Celine hated the heavy atmosphere and silence that a row produced. Perhaps she wanted to prove to him what a stupid move he'd made cheating on such a devoted wife who looked after her appearance, was affectionate, kept an organised home and prepared delicious meals. Why else would she go to all this trouble cooking for him?

6 o'clock. No sign of him. 7 o'clock. She tried calling him at the office but he wasn't there. Maybe he'd noticed that the photos had been taken from his filing cabinet. Maybe one of his colleagues had reported to him that his wife had visited the office. Maybe he was with her. The thought of him making love to someone else was unbearable. She wanted to scream, to smash their belongings on the floor and throw his clothes out of the window but the rational part of her won over and she restrained herself. What good would a tantrum do? He would despise her even more.

At 8 o'clock she opened the wine and took a large slug before turning off the oven. Taking the drink with her, she wandered into the bedroom and took the envelope back into the sitting room. Slumping into James's leather armchair, she retrieved the photos and stared at them again before throwing them on the floor in disgust. She went to the kitchen and poured herself another large glass of wine. Never a heavy drinker, she felt dizzy as she made her way back to the armchair. Then it hit her.

Of course - The Virgo Bar. She had seen it on a night cruise that she and James had taken with their new friends Wendy and Duncan. The canal cruise had taken them through Amsterdam whilst a guide pointed out various landmarks. Celine remembered Duncan joking with James as they passed the red light district and Wendy had made a cheap jibe about the name of the bar. "No virgins here I'm afraid." And they'd all laughed. It was no longer funny.

"What sort of men go to places like that?" Celine had whispered to Wendy as the men wandered off to the bar to get some more drinks.

"You'd be surprised," Wendy said in her matter of fact way. "Often, respectable married men like to give it a try. I wouldn't put it past Duncan not to have been at some time." She chuckled and Celine thought that she could not be serious.

Mental pictures, like a cinema screen played across her imagination. She saw him holding the woman in his arms, laughing with her, making love to her. Sickened by the images, she forced them from her mind; she needed to concentrate.

At 9 o'clock she ate some lukewarm casserole and, feeling drained, bundled up the photos once more and hid them in her underwear drawer. James would never look there. By 11 o'clock she decided to go to bed after carefully hanging up her trouser suit and taking off her makeup. She lay awake for several hours, waiting to hear his key in the door but fell into a restless sleep before he eventually came home, waking her with a start as daylight was just breaking. He tripped over something in the hall and she heard him swearing. Jumping out of bed she ran at him shouting like a virago.

"Where have you been? What is going on?"

"I had an important business meeting. Stop over reacting," he slurred as he staggered into the bedroom.

He was too drunk to make any sense and so she left him to sleep, knowing that it was impossible to reason with him when under the influence. She'd seen it all before. One of her late uncles had been an alcoholic and she wondered if James was becoming one. Maybe he had always been one and just covered it up. She wondered how on earth he would be able to make it to the office and do a day's work. Somehow she no longer cared about his future and hoped he'd get the sack.

Wandering into the kitchen, she was disgusted by the mess and proceeded to tidy up, putting the rest of the casserole and the wine into the fridge.

'Let the bastard get his own breakfast,' she thought as she got into the shower, the red-hot needles easing the tension in the back of her neck. Turning the thermostat to cool, she lifted her face to the water and tried to clear her head.

Wrapping herself in a large white towel, she decided to confront him with the pictures but when she entered the bedroom he was gone.

"James." She called at first softly, but then, as she wandered from room to room found herself shouting.

He had gone.

By now she was feeling frantic. There was no way that she could make a scene at his office. She made a pot of tea and gathered her thoughts.

The Virgo Bar. The Virgo Bar.

She relived everything that Wendy had said about the red light district in Amsterdam. The day passed in a sort of dream. She paced about and went through James's clothes again looking for evidence. That evening she didn't bother to cook a meal but decided to do something to bring about a resolution.

Hurrying into the bedroom, she put on some lipstick, brushed her shoulder length hair and decided to look for him – or at least find this girl with the long dark hair. Outside the sky looked threatening, so she grabbed her raincoat together with her car keys.

~ ~ ~ ~ ~ ~

WARNING LIGHTS

The car seemed to take her of its own accord into an area that she had never ventured into before. She parked with difficulty and decided to enter the first bar that she came to and ask some questions. The district was seedy and the lights of the girly bars flashed red, like warning danger signals. What she found most distasteful was the way girls sat in their windows in provocative poses, goods for sale, some wearing cheap revealing underwear and lit up like live mannequins in a shop window. It was as if they were a picture, the window frame and glass a part of the whole. She watched in morbid fascination as a girl opened the window to chat to a customer and then, their terms agreed, she opened a door for him to enter her world – a part of the picture. The curtains were drawn and in less than ten minutes he left, unashamedly and the girl returned to the window, her hair and lipstick unmolested.

The place was called Diamonds and holding her head high, she approached a girl who stood, topless, behind the bar. Celine reached into her bag and pulled out the photos.

"Do you know this girl?" she asked in English, wishing that she'd tried to master the difficult Dutch language.

The girl sneered at her, shook her head and walked away.

Celine was aware that the men in the bar were staring at her as she walked out. Somehow she didn't care; she was determined to find her husband's tart. 'How long has he been seeing her? Does he love her? Were they lovers before her father died? Does this mean that he no longer loves me? Does he have some secret perversion that I can't fulfil?' The questions buzzed around in her head like agitated wasps.

Before she reached the second bar, she was approached by a young police officer who spoke to her with earnest intensity.

"I'm sorry, I don't speak Dutch." Celine's upbringing had taught her to be respectful to the police.

"What are you doing in an area like this? It's clear that you are not a prostitute. This district can be dangerous." He looked as puzzled as she felt suddenly vulnerable.

"I'm looking for this girl? Can you help me find her?" She was working on instinct. After all, the girl could be a respectable secretary for all Celine knew.

"I will take you to her if you promise not to cause a fuss. This girl is not a common prostitute but works as a call girl in a club close by." He replied, not needing to question her motives. Perhaps he'd seen it all before.

Feeling her heart pounding in her head, she allowed this news to register. She did not want to hear it but realised that her instinct was correct. She followed him up a series of narrow streets, past a coffee shop that sold marijuana, the unfamiliar smell wafting out of its doors making her nauseous. Past a couple high on dope, holding onto each other and giggling uncontrollably. Past bicycles chained

15

together forlornly waiting to be released and put to some use again. Past a girl in a miniskirt smoking as she leant against a lamp post, her eyes blank and unseeing. This was an alien world to Celine and she tried to imagine James frequenting such a place. She must have made a mistake – she always did have a vivid imagination. They weaved their way up a narrow alley that smelled of urine and vice until the policeman arrived at a nightclub. Loud rock music played and Celine wanted to run. But before she could escape the policeman pointed in the direction of a girl with long, dark curly hair wearing a close fitting red evening dress and too much cheap dress jewellery. She was just on her way out and brushed past Celine, a hard glint in her dark, almond shaped eyes. She was the girl in the photos. She was her husband's lover. Celine was afraid of the white-hot hatred that she felt for this unknown person. Never before had this emotion engulfed her so strongly and for a moment she felt herself energised by the rage inside her. It was only the presence of the police officer that restrained her from attacking this girl who had been inside her apartment, held her cat, laid in her bed and been intimate with her husband.

Following her into the street she tapped her on the shoulder. The girl's perfume was sweet and heady.

"I need to talk to you. I'm James's wife."

The girl swung round, stared at Celine and, for a brief moment, a look of recognition came into her eyes. Her red painted lips parted in a short gasp. The stranger must have recognised Celine from the photo that stood on the sideboard in the sitting room.

"You leave my husband alone or..." Celine's words trailed off – or what. What could she do? She felt as helpless as a drowning kitten.

"I not speak ze English," the girl had a thick, guttural accent. With that she disappeared back into the sanctuary of the club and, as if on cue, the policeman came out, blocking the doorway so that Celine could not follow her rival any further.

"Come on. I'll walk you back to your car." His eyes were grey and kind, his voice quiet. It had started to rain, at first a soft drizzle but soon a torrent. They walked in silence to her car where he said a formal "Goodbye," and disappeared into a small alleyway.

She stalled the engine and then composed herself and tried again. Feeling numb, Celine drove the car as if on automatic pilot in the direction of home and wondered what to do next. Would James be home by now?

The road ahead looked long and dark.

Home alone, Celine pulled a book out of her bedside cabinet. It had been a birthday present from her parents, had a blue tartan cover and a metal clasp that could be locked with a miniature key. She opened it to the first blank page and made an entry as follows:

This, the year that my dear father died, I realise that the two men that I loved and trusted have disappeared from my life – one suddenly, the other gradually. My heart is broken and I don't know what to do about it. All I can think is - why?

2

CIRCUMSTANTIAL EVIDENCE

Summer arrived early the year that Celine discovered that James had a mistress. It was little consolation and the sun did not melt the barrier that now stood between them like an immovable glacier.

Returning home after her encounter with the girl in the red light district, the place felt eerily quiet and Celine knew instinctively that James was out. The adrenaline that her anger had produced had fired her up for a row - she wanted an explanation, and fast. She relived every moment of her eventful day and night and wondered if James had missed the stolen photos.

In frustration she paced the floor until exhaustion made her drop into bed where she tossed and turned until she fell into a desperate sleep.

She was driving her car when she came upon the girl standing against a wall. Feeling burning hatred, Celine put her foot on the accelerator and knew that the speed would kill her. Without fear she watched as the girl screamed when the car smashed into her – blood mingling with the scarlet material of her dress.

Celine woke up with a start; the dream had been so real. Too real. For the first time in her life she realised that she was capable of murder. She glanced at the clock. 7am. There was no sign of James and for a moment she wondered if he had spent the night with his mistress, as she had not heard him come home. Then she heard the radio and movement in the kitchen. She had planned her strategy and, after splashing her face with cold water, she retrieved the carefully concealed evidence.

Having had time to assimilate all that she had discovered, she was ready to confront him. He was making coffee in the kitchen while the radio played some classical music in the background. Celine recognised the soothing tones as the Pastoral Symphony. She was still startled by James's new, youthful appearance as she stared at him pouring coffee. An insane image of her pouring scalding liquid over his head as the music played on frightened her. This is the man that she had loved since she was twenty years old but whom she now hated enough to inflict pain and scarring. Perhaps death.

Behind her back she grasped the photos that she had found in his filing cabinet as if they were dangerous ammunition. Feeling light headed with apprehension; she looked him directly in the eye and said, "James, I know what's been going on. I have proof that you have a mistress."

Without flinching he took a sip of his coffee and protested, "I don't know what you are talking about."

"This is what I'm talking about," she heard herself screeching as she threw the evidence onto the kitchen table.

He stared at the pictures for a few seconds but said nothing. Instead he pushed past her, rushed into the hall, grabbed his car keys and was gone.

Gone.

She had lost him. She paced the floor, sobbing and abandoned. His silence was an admission of guilt. He had not tried to explain or apologise. Anything would be better than being pushed aside like a sack of refuse. She had longed for a plausible explanation so that they could laugh at the stupid mistake and then everything would be back to normal again. Celine wondered if anything would feel normal again.

"Two can play this game," she thought to herself as she dried her tears.

After a long soak in the bath she decided that if he could experience how she was feeling right now then perhaps their marriage could be saved. Feeling better after applying a generous amount of body lotion and a splash of matching perfume, she dressed quickly in some comfortable jeans and a tee shirt and phoned Wendy, her English friend who, with Duncan, her husband, had been with Celine and James on the river cruise.

"Hi Wendy, this is Celine. How are you?" She tried to sound cheerful but knew her voice was brittle.

"Bit tired but fine. I was out late last night. Duncan's in Belgium on business again and Tom took me out for dinner."

This didn't surprise Celine as Wendy had a string of men who were more than happy to escort her out to dinner when Duncan was away on business, which was frequent. It seemed that her husband did not have a problem with this arrangement. This led neatly to her next question.

19

"I don't want to go into details but could you arrange a date for me with Marcus Jackson?"

"Sure. Marcus will be surprised but will jump at it. Is everything all right?"

She had not meant to, but hearing a familiar English voice at the end of the phone had brought on more tears and she found herself recounting the events of the past few days. Feeling a mixture of guilt at the irrevocable slurring of James's character and relief that she had shared her problems, she hung up and wondered if she had lost her mind. Respectable, married Celine going out on a date with a notorious American womaniser.

Trying to pass the time, Celine decided to try and do something routine, so she gave herself a manicure, painting her nails pale pink and was about to do the same with her toe nails when the phone interrupted her. She noticed her hand was trembling as she lifted the receiver.

"Celine. Marcus says he'll meet you tonight at eight in the Captain's Bar in the Hilton and then he'll take you for dinner. Okay?"

"Yes. Fine. Thanks Wendy – you don't waste time do you?" She felt a hollow laugh emanating from deep within which betrayed her true feelings.

As she pondered what to wear on her date, she remembered that she had left her suitcase in the spare room. So preoccupied had she been that she had not bothered to unpack after her trip back from England. Methodically she put her clothes away and felt a pang of homesickness as she hung up the black dress that she had worn at her father's funeral. Eventually, her mother would find out about James, the man that she had always approved of as a good catch. Celine was grateful that her father would never know the shocking truth.

James didn't come home for dinner, which did not surprise her, but this gave her the opportunity to get ready for her first illicit date. As she was carefully applying some concealer under her eyes she heard some plaintive crying outside the bedroom door.

"Sasha. I'm sorry I forgot to feed you." She picked up her cat and felt its familiar soft fur against her cheek. 'My loyal cat still loves and needs me,' she thought. As she opened a tin of food the cat weaved in and out of her ankles mewing and looking up at her. Tears pricked her eyes again but this time she held them back and made for the bedroom. Its ultra modern furniture was stark and she longed to be in England in her parents' house with its antiques and Persian rugs. In a matter of weeks she had lost the two most important men in her life - her husband as well as her beloved father. The abstract paintings on the wall of the rented apartment looked grotesque, their screaming colours jarring her frayed nerves.

Celine glanced in the mirror and decided that she looked all right considering she felt so battered. She had taken a grey silk dress from the wardrobe which flattered her curves, slipped on some high heeled strappy shoes and completed the look with some turquoise and silver beads. She was determined to make James jealous but he was not there to see her. Instinctively Celine knew that he was with the woman with the dark curly hair. Perhaps they were having dinner together somewhere. In an act of gratifying defiance she took off her wedding ring and threw it on the dressing table before leaving the apartment. She had decided to leave the antique ring with the row of five diamonds on the third finger of her right hand - it felt comfortable and familiar.

Marcus was waiting for her in the Captain's Bar as arranged. He looked debonair in his expensively cut suit, white shirt and silk tie. As soon as he saw her he walked across the crowded room to greet her.

"Celine, you look lovely, as usual. Would you like a drink or shall we go straight to the restaurant?" His voice was deep, his accent a lazy drawl. Gazing into her eyes, he took her hand and brushed it with a kiss where her wedding ring should have been. It was a practised procedure that worked well for him.

Realising that she hadn't eaten all day and was feeling faint, she opted for the restaurant. Marcus seemed to be well known there and the headwaiter escorted them to a table in the window. Celine followed him as if in a dream; everything seemed unreal. She took the large, leather bound menu from the maitre d' and decided to order something light, as she was still not hungry.

She and Marcus made small talk even though she was sure that Wendy had told him about James's misdemeanours. For this she was grateful and she tried to enjoy the evening. Her fish was cooked to perfection but it seemed to stick in her throat. As she sipped her wine she suddenly felt weary and wished that she was home in bed - but not with Marcus.

Marcus, the enigma who was always at every social function. People joked that he was a spy or an arms dealer. He was wealthy but when asked what he did for a living would say, "Oh, this and that."

He took her home in a taxi and, as they turned into her avenue, he leant over and kissed her gently on the mouth. He tasted of breath mints and Celine was glad when it was over.

"Can I see you again beautiful lady?" he whispered.

It sounded so alien. James was a man of few words and fewer compliments.

"I'll be in touch. Thank you for a wonderful evening. No, I'll see myself to my door. Bye."

"Don't leave it too long. I've enjoyed your company – it makes a change chatting to such an intelligent woman. Bye." He sounded disappointed but she knew that he was never short of female company.

Putting her key in the door, she held her breath. Would he be in? Would he confront her with rabid jealousy, take her in his arms and swear never to see the other woman again?

Silence filled the darkened flat like a deadly vacuum. "The bastard's out again," she thought as more rage began to simmer inside her.

She flicked the bedroom light on. He was asleep.

Oblivious.

Celine's fury erupted like a boiling volcano as she looked at her husband lying in their bed in a peaceful slumber. She began to understand why otherwise normal, rational people committed crimes of passion.

Feeling as if she was drowning but that if she reached out a hand no one would be there to grab it, she ran over and shook him out of his sleep and yelled, "Wake up you bastard. How dare you sleep as if nothing's happening? If you don't do something about giving up this woman I'm getting a divorce. You don't even speak to me – how on earth do you expect us to do anything about our marriage if you don't communicate. What is wrong with you?"

Getting slowly out of bed, James said groggily, "There's nothing wrong with me."

That did it. So he was trying to imply that all this was her fault. Quiet, gentle Celine found herself on the point of hysteria as, sobbing, she slapped James sharply across the face. His eyes darkened and he retaliated with a blow across Celine's cheek that was already marred with mascara running down her face like muddy rivulets.

In that moment the pedestal on which she had placed him crumbled in a heap of dust.

Before she could do anything he disappeared into the spare room, locked the door and refused to open it.

After ten minutes of banging the door in futile frustration, Celine finally gave in to her exhaustion and fell into their large bed where she tried to grab some elusive sleep. Self-doubt was starting to gnaw at her and she began to wonder if indeed there was something wrong with her. Was she boring? Did she lack sparkle and wit? Was she not good enough in bed? Was she unattractive? Going into the bathroom with the marble tiles she stared at her reflection in the mirror for a few moments. Her eyes were puffy and she looked as if she hadn't slept for weeks. Bile rose in bitter waves and she brought up her expensive meal that Marcus had bought her. Feeling slightly better after being sick, she waited until she heard James leave for the office. She had made a decision that would bring matters to a head. Then, having brewed some strong coffee, she phoned Wendy.

"Hi, how did your date with Marcus go?" Her friend sounded cheerful.

"Oh, he treated me like I was the only woman in his world but I didn't really enjoy it. Sorry to sound so ungrateful. I do appreciate you contacting him for me." Celine took a sip of her bitter brew and momentarily enjoyed the rush of caffeine. Taking a calming breath, she put her plan to her friend.

"Wendy, I've decided to give James an ultimatum and I wonder if you could put me up for about three nights. I'll leave a note for him telling him where I'm staying but if he doesn't contact me I'll go back to England and get a divorce." Her voice sounded efficient as if she was dictating a letter to a secretary. She felt eerily calm and detached.

"Of course you can. The place is like a morgue with Duncan away on business, so I'd be glad of some company. Stay as long as you like."

"Thanks a million but it will only be for a few days. That's all it will take for me to know where I stand. I'll just pack a few things and be round if that's okay."

"Sure, come on over. I'm in all day."

Celine hung the phone up and looked around her flat as if for the last time, before grabbing a notepad and pen.

'James,' she wrote, 'I am staying with Wendy for three days. If you want to talk and try to save our marriage contact me there. You have her number. If I don't hear anything I will return to England and get a divorce.' As she wrote the word divorce she paused as if the impact of her actions had just registered but she finished the note. For a crazy moment she wondered if she should sign it: 'Your soon to be ex-wife, Celine' or 'Your enraged partner, Celine.' She decided to leave it unsigned.

Packing her belongings into a suitcase, she realised that she need not have gone to the trouble to unpack. The emptiness inside her was growing stronger by the moment and the nausea that she felt did not help. She kissed her beloved cat goodbye, somehow knowing that she would not be returning to the apartment. Then, propping the note on the dining room table, she picked up her case and drove round to Wendy's place.

After the third day at Wendy's apartment it was clear that James was not interested in a reconciliation and so she booked a flight back to England after phoning her mother to explain the whole sordid scenario.

"Well! I just can't believe that James could do this to you. You both seemed so well suited to each other. And he's from such a respectable family and has good prospects. I'll arrange for someone to meet you at the airport tomorrow." Her mother's sympathetic tone wrapped around Celine like a warm blanket and she was grateful that she had somewhere to go upon her return to England.

Wendy drove Celine to the airport the following day and pecked her on the cheek before watching her disappear into the departure lounge. She was relieved when Celine had gone as she was entertaining a new gentleman friend that night and needed the apartment to herself. Wendy secretly thought that Celine had over reacted and that she should just find herself a lover and have a little fling, but did not voice this to her friend. So James had a bit on the side – it would blow over in time. In Wendy's experience these things usually did. Celine just needed to toughen up and not take life so seriously in her opinion.

Celine had an hour to kill before her flight and treated herself to some expensive perfume and a bracelet. She had always been rather frugal but imagined James buying his mistress such luxuries and so the act brought her momentary revenge. As she was stuffing her purchases in her hand luggage, she heard her BOAC flight being announced and got into the long queue. She found it strange to be travelling alone again so soon.

"Will Mrs Celine Smedley please make her way to the information desk? I repeat, Mrs Celine Smedley to the information desk."

Celine jumped as she heard her name being paged over the loud speaker and rushed over to the desk, wondering what had gone wrong. Her ticket seemed to be in order.

"Mrs Smedley. A phone call has come through for you." A polite receptionist wearing a scarlet jacket, matching lipstick and an efficient manner handed her the phone.

"Celine. I'm so sorry." James voice was choking with emotion. "Please don't go. Come home, we can work this out. I'm so - "

"James, they are boarding my flight. I'm going back to England. Look, if you want to talk - phone me at Mum's."

"All right, but promise me one thing?" He sounded calmer.

"What? Look I have to go."

"Go and see my mother. Promise?" James pleaded.

"Goodbye, James." Celine, feeling a mixture of relief and suspicion, hung up the phone before he could reply.

She was the last to board the plane and wondered if she should have just gone back home to the apartment - she had so many questions that she needed to ask him. What had made him change his mind? Why hadn't he phoned her at Wendy's place? Why leave it until the last minute to apologise? And if he thought for one minute that she'd visit his mother - he could think again. The woman was a monster and hated Celine.

Picking at her tasteless food on the flight she wondered what the future held. To make matters more complicated she had missed her period.

What a time to be pregnant!

Later, she was disappointed that her old, familiar bedroom did not feel the same as when she was a young girl and offered little comfort. Celine wrote in her journal as she sat up in the single bed that she had slept in as a teenager.

The last few days have been a roller coaster of betrayal and confusion. I feel so lonely. Part of me wants to have James back but, the more rational part, is telling me to run and keep running. I will make an appointment to see the doctor tomorrow, as I feel sure that I am carrying his child. If it wasn't for this baby I don't think that I could face seeing James again.

3

MOTHER-IN-LAW

Although her mother-in-law, Jennifer, insisted that she was a delicate and rather sensitive creature, Celine had found her to be a tough, bitter woman. Yes, she doted on her only son, James, but any other woman in his life needed to have nerves of steel to endure any relationship with her. Celine's father-in-law seemed to be overshadowed by his wife and rarely spoke. James was not as close to his father as he was to his beloved mother.

Jennifer had been polite and almost friendly with Celine – until the day of the wedding. From then on she became a nightmare.

Their wedding had been a small, family affair. This was what James wanted and Celine was happy to go along with his ideas. She was so in awe of him that she would have jumped off a building if James had suggested it. The ceremony went smoothly and without fanfare. There were no bridesmaids and Celine looked elegant in a pale blue silk dress and jacket. It was as they were signing the register in the vestry of the old parish church that Jennifer spoke out, loudly and clearly for all to hear.

"No girl would be good enough for my son. Still, he's had a good run I suppose." Her unholy words shattered the peace and Celine glanced up at James for a reaction. Her groom looked blankly back at her as if there was nothing unusual about what had just been uttered. The vicar blushed and looked sympathetically at Celine.

It was like an omen of things to come.

The honeymoon was short – just a few days in London, as James could not afford the time off work. He was an efficient, if cold lover and Celine did not experience the closeness that she had been longing for as a married woman. Always dress conscious, she had spent a lot of time planning her wardrobe. Although she was naturally drawn to slightly artistic colourful fabrics and embroidery, she knew that James did not approve, so bought some traditional tailored clothes.

"How do I look?" She asked him on their first morning as a married couple.

"Smart. But don't wear beige – it drains you. You know I like to see you in tweeds. And stop backcombing your hair. It looks like a bird's nest at the back."

"Tweeds! I don't want to look like your mother." She bit her tongue, knowing that the slightest criticism would be abhorrent to her new husband.

Celine found herself to be a natural homemaker and enjoyed furnishing their first house; a small semi that they rented on the outskirts of Taunton. She had left her job and moved with James as he had a new office to run and knew it was only a matter of time before they would be sent abroad. As she had always liked cooking, she enjoyed experimenting with new and exciting dishes that James devoured each evening after coming home from work. He was too busy with his career to help around the house and limited his tasks to cleaning the car from time to time.

Then she had a brainwave. She decided to invite Jennifer for afternoon tea and impress her with her home baking skills. A batch of scones lay cooling on the worktop, some homemade shortbread had been sprinkled with castor sugar and a magnificent coffee and walnut cake stood on one of her best plates. The house shone, smelled of polish and fresh flowers and Celine was pleased with her efforts.

At 3 o'clock sharp the doorbell chimed and Jennifer stood on the step looking smart if somewhat severe in a brown suit with a fur collar, a matching hat, court shoes, bag and gloves. She did not smile when Celine greeted her.

"Come in – how was your bus trip?" Celine could not quite bring herself to kiss her mother-in-law so just stood to one side to let her in.

Jennifer swept past her regally and walked straight into the living room.

"The kettle's boiled. Shall we have some tea now?" Celine realised that she was jabbering with nerves and took a deep breath.

"Yes thank you. I'll make myself comfortable on the sofa. Put your feet up is what I always say. Don't stand if you can sit and don't sit if you can lie down – that's my motto. Your brasses look shiny – who cleans them for you?" Did Celine detect a slight smirk on her mother-in-law's face?

"I do of course – why?" She replied.

"James used to do mine for me when he was a boy. He'd do anything I asked. He was such a good boy." She announced with an air of triumph.

Celine wheeled a trolley in with gritted teeth. It was burgeoning with goodies plus her best china cups and saucers, which were a wedding present from her parents.

"What would you like to try first? A scone maybe."

"Nothing for me. I can't eat anything freshly made - it gives me indigestion. I might like it, but it doesn't like me." Jennifer barked from her reclining position.

With a fixed grin Celine cut herself a large slice of cake and poured the tea.

"Not enough milk." Jennifer handed her the cup back.

Knowing that whatever she did it would not be right, she topped up Jennifer's tea with a fixed smile.

Later that evening as James was devouring some of the same coffee cake, Celine recounted the afternoon events.

"Mummy has to be careful – she has a delicate stomach." He responded with a rather full mouth.

As the years went by, Celine learned never to criticise Jennifer as this could bring on a full-blown rage from her husband. She also learned never to disagree with her in James's presence as he always sided with his dear, delicate mother who had the constitution of an ox. Celine was beginning to hate her.

It was with trepidation that Celine moved in with her in-laws for two weeks before the move to Holland. Their lease was up on the rented house and they were prepared for a life of travel.

"I want thirteen pounds a week for your keep. The sheets are in the airing cupboard and I think it best that you do the cooking." Outside was as frosty as indoors and a leaden sky scattered a light smattering of snow on the ground.

'Welcome to our home,' Celine thought to herself as she smiled wanly at the tyrant who had borne her husband.

The first few days went fairly smoothly and, as Jennifer took herself off to bed at 7 o'clock each night, the evenings were relatively relaxing. Celine cooked Christmas dinner, which was eaten in formal silence, and Jennifer took herself off to bed at her usual time. It was not a cheery Christmas and Celine was surprised to get a jar of facemask from Jennifer. Underneath the label proclaimed, Sample, not for re-sale.

New Year's Eve was bleak.

"I'm off to bed – must have my ten hour's sleep or I won't be able to manage."

"Goodnight, Mummy. Happy New Year." James kissed his mother on the cheek.

"Goodnight dear." She responded in a baby voice that she reserved just for him.

At 10 o'clock his father wandered off to bed, leaving James and Celine alone with a glass of sherry and the television. They saw the New Year in quietly before creeping up to bed.

Celine came to slowly the following morning and wandered downstairs to put the kettle on while James slept peacefully. It was late for her – 9 o'clock.

"What sort of time do you call this?" Jennifer barked.

"Oh, it's a bit late I suppose. We saw the New Year in." Celine wondered what she had done wrong.

"It's disgraceful – a married woman coming down at this sort of time."

For the first time Celine decided that she would confront her mother-in-law or this sort of behaviour would go on for the rest of her married life. She was fed up with being criticised and picked on.

"For goodness sake – don't be so petty." Celine said as calmly as she could under the circumstances.

"Well – watch your manners young lady!" And with that Jennifer stormed out of the kitchen and into her bedroom where she stayed for two days. James's father, Ronald, took trays of food in to her and both men acted as if nothing had happened. The atmosphere was chilly and Celine began to think that it was a good idea to move away and start a new life abroad, away from the fearsome clutches of her mother-in-law.

It was with relief and anticipation that she boarded the KLM flight to Amsterdam to start a new phase of her married life. She was sure that life in a different country away from the clutches of Jennifer would improve their marriage.

But since that time Celine's resentment towards her mother-in-law had developed into hatred. Surely, if James adored his mother so much, he could at least respect her, Celine. She was tempted to phone Jennifer and tell her about James's adultery with a call girl but decided against it. Jennifer would only say that it was all Celine's fault - of that she was sure. No, she would not contact her as James had asked when he had phoned her at the airport. It would only add to her misery. If she was pregnant, James could tell his mother.

4

SAMANTHA

Cheltenham in 1968 was swinging. Samantha and her best friend, Christine, never missed the Saturday night dance at the Town Hall. It was here that the talent was to be found - both in boys and in the top rock groups. It was here that they twisted, did the hippy, hippy shake and any other dance that happened to be all the rage at the time.

They were also dedicated followers of fashion. The Town Hall was buzzing that Saturday evening in the early summer as Christine and Samantha checked their all-important appearance in the ladies' room. Mascara thick and black, lipstick pale to the point of insipid, skirts short and earrings huge. Christine's dark hair was backcombed to the limit and so stiff with lacquer that a force ten gale would not have moved it. She wore a pink and white paisley dress that just covered her panties and kitten heel shoes, while Samantha had on a black and white diamond patterned dress and white shiny boots. The only thing that did not fit the mould of the times was that her long hair was tied in a haphazard ponytail with a large black velvet ribbon. Thus armed, they approached the dance floor with confidence.

Samantha had just broken up with a smooth character called Terry and was disappointed that he didn't seem to be at the dance. She was secretly hoping that he would have her back if he spotted her. After all, they had only dated four times and he had hardly had time to get to know her. Still, there were plenty more fish in the sea, she reasoned. As she scanned the large balconies looking for Terry, her eyes stopped for a moment on a guy who she had never seen before. He was not as tall or good looking as Terry but had an enigmatic look that she found attractive. She wondered if he had noticed her. It appeared that he had not.

"There is a house in New Orleans," the group belted out from the stage, "they call the Rising Sun."

She was dancing aimlessly with an insignificant youth, disappointed because Terry was not there, when she looked over and spotted him again. He had come downstairs and was looking straight at her. Samantha decided that she liked the look of him, in spite of the fact that he was not dressed like a Mod. In fact he looked rather un-cool in a sports jacket and cravat. His brown hair was speckled with a light dash of grey at the temples, which Samantha thought made him look debonair. He did not wear it in the latest style, layered on top and long at the sides, but in a traditional style with a side parting. Glancing at her watch she noted that it was almost 10.30pm and that Christine's strict and rather fearsome father would be waiting outside to take the girls home. She had to act quickly. Strolling over to the stranger, she looked up into his green flecked hazel eyes and, without flinching, asked him the first thing that came into her head.

"Didn't I see you at a party in Swindon Village last Saturday?"

He looked puzzled and replied in a cultured voice that he hadn't seen her. Just as they were starting to chat she was thwarted. Christine joined them, her eyes bright with curiosity.

"Sam, Dad's waiting outside to take us home. Come on."

Samantha could have happily throttled her.

With that, and trying to maintain some dignity, she left. He hadn't even asked her for a date.

At work the next day she couldn't get him off her mind. She wasn't interested in serving customers their morning coffees, was distracted and uncharacteristically kept getting the orders wrong. Thoughts of Terry were being replaced with thoughts of this reticent stranger.

At about 11 o'clock the restaurant manageress called her over to her desk. Samantha was concerned that a customer may have complained about her indifferent service. How she longed for a more challenging job.

"You have a call," the manageress snapped in her cool Scottish accent.

The staff was not allowed to make or take personal calls at work, except in an emergency. Wondering who it could be, Samantha took the receiver from the manicured hand of her lofty manageress.

"Hello, it's Paul. We met last night at the dance."

She caught her breath, her stomach fluttering. It was Paul, the quietly spoken one with a gentle manner and who dressed so immaculately. As she gathered her thoughts he broke in.

"Would you like to come to the cinema tonight to see West Side Story?" He asked the silence.

"How did you get this number?" was all she said.

"You told me where you worked."

"Oh, of course," she blustered, "and yes, I'd love to see West Side Story."

She had a date.

Samantha's courtship with Paul was sudden and she felt as if she was floating in a bubble, as his attention to her was more than anything she could have hoped for. Being that bit older than her, she admired his experience with the ways of the world and loved it when they discussed politics and world events. He was no callow youth but a mature, thoughtful man. After their sixth date he surprised her. They had returned from a drink in the popular Cellar Bar in the Montpellier district of Cheltenham and, as he parked his grey Austin A70 outside her home, he kissed her tenderly until she was breathless.

"What are you doing next month?" He asked with intensity.

"Nothing special, why?" She laughed, not having a clue what was to follow.

"How about taking time out to marry me?"

Without hesitation she responded, "Oh Paul, yes, I'd love to marry you."

Samantha had met her future husband at the ripe old age of eighteen.

~ ~ ~ ~ ~ ~

They had started as little ripples but with each passing day the feelings of panic had become swelling waves. In just under a month Samantha was to be married and it was not going to be the sort of wedding that she had imagined as a young girl. It was all so sudden. Paul told her that he wanted them to be married this month, June 1968, and to top it all, in Mauritius. Why Mauritius? Because he'd been offered a posting as a surveyor on the tropical island. It was not difficult to persuade her that this would be an idyllic place to start married life, living in paradise. The problem was that she just did not have enough time to plan properly. Nor did she have a wedding dress.

It was no good asking her mother, Betty, for advice in choosing the all-important gown – she was pretty clueless when it came to fashion. Justine, Samantha's cousin, was to have helped her look for a dress the previous week but had called it off due to illness. Then she remembered Paul's sister, Jenny, a real trendsetter with snappy dress sense. Samantha dialled her number.

"Hi Jenny, it's Sam here. I still haven't got around to buying a wedding dress. Are you free tomorrow to come into town? I've looked in the wedding dress section of Cavendish House and been to a few bridal wear shops but all the dresses are too big to fit into my suitcase. I know that it's short notice but..."

"Of course. What time shall we meet?" The voice at the other end of the phone reassured her.

It was all arranged. They were to meet in Samantha's lunch hour on the pavement outside the cosmetics department at Cavendish House the next day. What if she couldn't find anything that would fit into a suitcase? It was all such short notice. The whirlwind romance had taken her by surprise and now marriage was a certainty. There was no time to lose as Paul had signed a contract to work in Mauritius for two years – starting in two weeks. His prospective boss had agreed to give Paul a few days' leave for the honeymoon. Paul was insistent that a wedding in Mauritius would be so much more romantic than a hurried affair in England and they didn't have to worry about which friends and relatives to invite. It would be just the two of them and totally hassle free. Samantha had to agree with him on that score.

On the whole, Samantha and her mother got on agreeably and enjoyed each other's company. They would always take breakfast together in the small kitchen, seated at a foldaway pine table, which just housed two matching utilitarian chairs. The meal started with cereal, followed by either a boiled or fried egg or grilled bacon and tomatoes, toast and marmalade and all washed down with several cups of strong tea. That morning Samantha was not hungry. She only managed to force down a piece of toast and several cups of tea much to her mother's concern. Samantha felt as if she was letting her down – getting married so far away. She had always been close to her mother, Betty, and sometimes took a parental role, comforting her when life seemed hard. Samantha's father was a distant memory, lost in the mists of time, as he had died when she was five years old. It had been necessary for Betty to work as a shop assistant in a local grocery store since his death. The place had changed hands recently and been transformed into a new type of shop; the supermarket had been born and Betty no longer served customers but worked at a till instead, something she found impersonal and rather trying.

Betty was wearing an unconvincing brave face about the wedding of her only daughter. "You go – Paul seems a nice enough man and he can offer you a future. Decent men are hard to come by. I'll be all right." She pushed her tea absentmindedly to the centre of the kitchen table and then moved it back again before getting up to tackle a mound of washing up. Samantha automatically got up from the table and reached for a rather faded tea towel with a picture of Blackpool Tower on it and proceeded to dry the dishes.

"We'll save up and pay for you to come out for a visit, Mum. It's supposed to be very beautiful there and Paul tells me he'll find us a big enough house to rent with at least one spare room."

Betty sniffed as she reached for a frying pan before plunging it into the sink of soapy water and scrubbing it with vigour. "You know I can't stand the heat. Two years will pass quick enough. Just promise to write to me every week on that thin paper."

"Of course, Mum. I'll send you photos as well. We'll have someone take wedding pictures." Her voice was gentle and Betty knew that her daughter meant every word she said.

Samantha found the routine of the walk from home to Cavendish House along familiar streets comforting. She endured working in the smart departmental store situated on the leafy boulevard called, rather grandly, The Promenade, but always felt that the job was second best. She had wanted to be an artist but money was short and, after leaving school at sixteen, she took the first job available – as a waitress.

Part of her didn't want to get married in Mauritius. She'd had a sheltered life and was as green as a lettuce. Her family would not be there. Justine would not be there to do her hair. Jenny would not be there to do her makeup. Mum would not be there for moral support, or her uncle to give her away. She had never travelled abroad before and was not looking forward to the long journey alone.

It was a busy morning serving coffee and cakes to plump matrons in the restaurant it was soon 1 o'clock and her lunch break. Samantha hurried downstairs, through the fragrant cosmetics department where girls looking like clones wearing a little too much makeup stood behind glistening glass counters. Out in the fresh air, she looked around for Jenny. She wasn't there. Samantha felt the unwelcome waves of panic return.

"Get a grip," she said to herself.

She need not have worried. Within minutes Jenny was rushing along The Promenade to greet her looking just like a fuller version of Twiggy in her mini skirt, boots and multi coloured crochet top.

"Hi, Sam. Let's find this dress for you. How long have you got?" Jenny enthused.

"Fifty minutes," she replied, glancing at her watch, "At this rate I'll be getting married in a swimming costume."

Jenny giggled. "We'll find something - you're in excellent hands. Just follow me." She tried to hide her doubts with a grin as she strode purposefully into the department store. A practical shopper, she avoided the bridal gown section with its opulent display of full skirted gowns and headed straight to the evening dress rails to rummage. She needed to find something that would fit into a suitcase without crushing and, it had to be white or cream.

There it was.

A long, white, silky dress. It looked perfect.

"Surely it can't be my size," said Samantha as Jenny grabbed it to look at the label.

"Size ten. C'mon," she commanded as she steered Samantha to the fitting room, bearing her trophy, a determined glint in her eye.

It looked as if it had been made for her. It was stylish and figure hugging, plain at the front and with thin shoulder straps. Samantha turned around to examine the back, hardly believing her good fortune.

"Do you think the back's a bit daring?" she asked.

"It looks groovy, Paul will love it. You've probably noticed he appreciates good clothes. He's always taken an interest in my fashion fads even though he's never been one to wear trendy clothes himself." Jenny remarked as she adjusted the open lacing at the back whilst openly envying Samantha's willowy figure. The shop was unusually quiet and soon the dress was in a voluminous bag, wrapped in crisp tissue paper. Next, the accessory department to find a headdress as a veil would be too bulky to pack. A delicate tiara, matching necklace and earrings were soon purchased and, energised by the success of the hunt, Jenny then guided Samantha to the shoe section of the store where a pair of silver sandals were acquired at lightening speed. Jenny reminded her that the sand might burn her feet during the wedding ceremony. Samantha hadn't thought of that, her only seaside holiday being a trip to Blackpool before her father had died. All she could remember of that was sitting on his shoulders as he pointed to lights strung across the sky. He had told her she was in fairyland and she had believed him. She glanced at her watch as she fumbled for her wallet. Her hands shook slightly with excitement and relief. The whole lot had been purchased in fifty minutes. At this rate she would not be late back in the restaurant and her boss would not give her a hard time. Lunch times were always busy and standards were high.

"Someone must have been smiling on you today," Jenny laughed, "the staff discount was better than a kick in the teeth too."

"Thanks, Jenny," Samantha breathed, giving her a hug before scurrying back to the restaurant, munching on a chocolate bar to alleviate her sudden hunger.

Samantha's future in-laws, Jessica and Thomas, called to see her at Paul's small but immaculately clean and tidy bedsit that evening with a card and a couple of wedding presents. Although always pleasant, Samantha found them slightly intimidating with their plummy accents and confidence that was just short of arrogance. Paul's mother was always groomed to perfection, moving in a cloud of Rive Gauche - her clothes looking quietly expensive. Jessica had a habit of lifting her right eyebrow when listening to Samantha that she found unnerving. Paul's father, with his ramrod back and grey, slicked back hair, wore similar clothes to his son – conservative and impeccable taste. Samantha's mum looked very much the poor relative in their company with her homemade dresses, worn at heel shoes and hair that she permed herself in the kitchen, leaving a wild halo of frizz which took at least a month to subside.

"Open the small present now." Jessica handed Samantha a parcel neatly wrapped in pink with a matching bow.

Inside was a very old looking box containing a small diamante brooch shaped like a bow. The dainty antique piece of jewellery nestled on a bed of faded cream silk.

"Oh, thank you, thank you – it's beautiful." Samantha pecked Jessica on the cheek.

"It belonged to my Grandmother - I thought you might like something old." She smiled at her future daughter-in-law, glad to be giving a token heirloom to such an appreciative girl. She was also secretly pleased that her quiet son had at last found a soul mate. It had been good to have her son back in Cheltenham as he had hardly kept in touch when he was living and working in Edinburgh. Paul was never one to mix easily and she had sometimes wondered if he was destined to live alone. Jessica did not quite approve of Samantha's bohemian style of dress or unusual jewellery, and thought that Paul could have chosen someone more middleclass, but she seemed to be a kind girl and liked to cook, so her son would not go hungry. But why did she insist on wearing her long hair in that ridiculous pony tail with all those strands of hair falling about her face and neck – she never would understand this younger generation with their mini-skirts and Beatle mania. Samantha was a pretty name, so why did the girl like it when people called her Sam?

"I have something blue and something new so this is just right. May I borrow your son – then I have all I need?" Samantha looked beautiful when she smiled, her expressive eyes warm and thoughtful.

"Keep him as long as you like – we don't want him back." Paul's father jibed, his head to one side. Thomas roared with laughter at his own joke before coughing and lighting up a cigarette that he took from a silver case.

Paul looked on proudly at his fiancée. He'd travelled a lot as a child as Thomas had been an army officer with many overseas postings, so he was not nervous about going to live in Mauritius, seeing it more of an adventure than a challenge. He wanted to try some scuba diving when they were out there and was looking forward to being enriched by a new culture and enjoying the local food.

"We're passing your mother's house on the way home so we'll give you a lift if you like." The question was more a command than a request and Samantha, who would have liked to have spent longer with Paul, found herself blushing.

"Thank you. That's very kind." She needed an early night she reasoned looking longingly at Paul who just winked at her.

Jessica looked triumphant but was not fooled by the quiet acceptance in Samantha's tone. She had noted that underneath the gentle exterior that this girl possessed was the embryo of determination and strength that had not fully developed. Perhaps it was her steady gaze or the set of her jaw that gave this away.

The ride in the Bentley was rather splendid even if the car did look incongruous as it pulled into Samantha's housing estate. Samantha stifled a giggle as she noticed net curtains twitching at the rare sight of such a grand car in the neighbourhood.

All was quiet in the house and so she crept upstairs, not wishing to wake Betty who had obviously already gone to bed.

The dress was hanging up in her bedroom. She had done a trial pack and it fitted into her case perfectly. Soon she would be on the plane heading for the sun. Taking the brooch out of its box Samantha pinned it carefully to the front of the bodice and stood back to admire the effect. Perfect. There was just one more thing to do before Paul left.

Write their wedding vows.

It proved to be more emotional than they had thought as they wrote down their promises to each other. The next day would be the first step in their transition to a new life. Paul would be leaving alone to find them a place to live in Mauritius.

~ ~ ~ ~ ~ ~

As soon as Paul was offered the job abroad life became exciting, as if she was awaiting the promise of a surprise present. He would take his final surveying exams there and so his career would not be held up by their time abroad. His boss had advised that Paul travel at least a week before his fiancée so that he could find suitable living quarters. Samantha was disappointed to hear this news but decided to use the time to pack and say farewell to friends and family. She had already handed in her notice at Cavendish House and wondered if she would be able to find work in such a far-flung place as Mauritius. Paul assured her that he would be earning enough for both of them but Samantha had never been one to sit around and the thought of not having a job was as alien to her as the thought of living abroad.

Then came the jabs. Typhoid, yellow fever, tetanus and cholera. They felt queasy and had sore arms for several days. And, all too soon, it was time for Paul to leave. He was almost nonchalant about their new life that was to be spent on this dot in the vast Indian Ocean.

"Sweetheart, the time will fly by and I'll be there waiting for you at the airport. You have nothing to worry about except buying a beautiful dress. Now shall we have a wee coffee?"

"That would be nice. You know you have the strangest accent."

"I'm an international citizen, my love, and having lived in Scotland, I'm bound to have picked up a few wee sayings."

"Did you like living there?"

"Let's just say that I'm glad to be further south or I might never have met you."

He gave her an eloquent gaze and she was assured of his deep love for her. She would follow him to the ends of the earth if necessary.

Paul was right, the time hurried by and soon it was time to bid a tearful farewell to her mother and set off with her uncle to the airport, her nervousness now replaced with anticipation. She was missing Paul and longed to be in his arms once more.

It was heart rending saying goodbye to Betty and mother and daughter hugged in the kitchen for a long time as Samantha's uncle stood at a distance shuffling from one foot to the other. He would take her to the airport and Betty would go to work as usual. Not wanting to let her only daughter go, Betty sniffed as she went to the fridge for a plastic container.

"Here, I've made you some ham sandwiches. Get your uncle to pull into a layabout for something to eat on the way. Can't have you going all that way on an empty stomach."

Samantha laughed, "Oh Mum thanks. They're lay-byes, not layabouts. I'll miss you so much. Look after yourself and I'll be back before you can say - "

"John Robinson!" Betty gave Samantha one last hug and then watched the car disappear around the corner. Her heart breaking, she went to Samantha's room, lay on her bed and breathed in her lingering perfume. Then she allowed the tears to stream down her face until she could cry no more. She wept for her daughter, her late husband, the dog that died two years previously and then moved on to weep for the state of the world, starving children in Africa, the loss of her brother in World War Two and all the heroes who had died defending freedom. When she could weep no more, she made some tea and wandered around the empty house as memories invaded her every thought. Samantha as a newborn, so dependent on her for everything. Samantha as a toddler, energetic and questioning. Samantha asking where her Daddy had gone when he died, her eyes full of confusion. Samantha's first day at school, clinging onto her mother's hand and begging her to take her home. Samantha on Christmas Eve, pretending to be asleep as she waited for Santa to call. Samantha having her eighth birthday party and shrieking with excitement when she got her first bicycle. Samantha at Grammar School, working hard but disappointed that she had to leave and get a job. Samantha's first date, looking so beautiful that Betty's heart ached. Lastly she remembered the day that she had told her that she was to marry Paul and the tears fell again. Each day for a month after that Betty played Samantha's records and pretended that she was home until eventually she became used to the space that had been left behind. It was time to finally say goodbye.

Samantha was hardly a seasoned traveller when she boarded the BOAC VC10 at Heathrow Airport in the summer of 1968. The only childhood holidays that she had experienced, apart from the trip to Blackpool, had been the weeks in the school holidays that she spent in a hamlet in Gloucestershire with an aunt and uncle. These were blissful days, spent in a cottage on the edge of a farm where she played outside on endless summer days with the local children. She vowed one day to have her own country cottage looking out across the Cotswolds.

Vulnerable and inexperienced, Samantha found her way to her seat on the plane, praying that her wedding dress would arrive intact. She greeted a jewellery laden matron wearing heavy makeup and a grim expression who was to be her aloof travelling companion for the entire trip and she just knew that they would have little in common. Samantha's heart pounded with unexpected fear as the plane left the familiar British soil and soared through the clouds. Feeling as if her stomach had been left at the airport she closed her eyes and prayed that the feeling would stop soon. "What have I done?" she thought. "No turning back now."

Soon they were up in the clouds, the strange feeling had left and she opened her eyes to glance out of the window. To her surprise she began to enjoy the exhilaration of being in the skies. She had many hours to wonder what lay ahead and tried to concentrate on a novel. Her travel companion had spent the first hour of the flight knocking back whiskey and was soon snoring, leaving Samantha with her own thoughts. There was to be an eighteen hour flight to endure, stopping in the Middle East, Africa and India to refuel.

A stewardess with a brittle smile and big hair awakened her from her reverie.

"Are you disembarking at Entebbe?"

Samantha was so naïve that she thought that the stewardess meant was she getting off the aircraft, so, she told her haltingly that she was.

"Fill this in please," the efficient one commanded as she handed her a form before moving quickly on.

This she did dutifully before experiencing a bumpy landing in Africa. It was good to stretch her legs as she left the confines of the plane and wandered into a scruffy airport. Her senses were on

PORT OF THE DAY

ve Premier League Football
xy Sports 1, 7.30pm

Queens Park Rangers are to make good their escape
n relegation danger, they might have to win games
st mid-table clubs with little left to play for, such
ansea City, whom they held 1-1 away, thanks to a
om Jamie Mackie (right). But actually, Rangers'
cent form has been against sides challenging at
of the table, so can they turn that around tonight
e to the Swans (kick-off 8pm)? Plus, **Live Spanish**
(k.o. 9pm) is the capital derby, Atletico Madrid v
adrid, whose coach Jose Mourinho is edging closer
cord of winning a fourth of Europe's major leagues.

M OF THE DAY

Little Dieter Needs To Fly
BBC2, 11.20pm

Having seen his native Germany
bombed as a child, Dieter Dengler
grew up to serve as a pilot with US
forces in Vietnam, but then became
a prisoner of war. As he relives his
captivity and escape, this
documentary directed by Werner

Ivory Wars: Out Of Africa, 9pm

Rageh Omaar views the illegal ivory
seized by the Kenyan Wildlife Service

White Heat, 9p

The friends are re
it's the final epis

BBC one

6.0 Breakfast 41168522 **9.15 Animal
24:7** 4190744 **10.0 Homes Under The
Hammer** 75928 **11.0 Don't Get Done,
Get Dom** 7103676 **11.45 Cash In The
Attic** 356096 **12.15 Bargain Hunt**
1923541 **1.0 BBC News; Weather**
59980 **1.30 Regional News** 34068676
1.45 Doctors Freya goes beyond the
call of duty to help a drug addict.
627096 **2.15 Escape To The Country**
Thatched properties featured in the
series. 8085270 **3.0 BBC News;
Regional News** 6814299 **3.05
CBBC: Horrible Histories** 1922034
3.35 Lockie Leonard 4232676 **4.0
All Over The Place** 218 **4.30 Young
Dracula** 102 **5.0 Newsround**
2409763 **5.15 Pointless** 95913

BB

6.0 CBeebies
8.30 CBeebie
Dan's Story T
Chuggington:
9.35 Small Po
The Koala Br
Mr Bloom's N
Baby Jake 31
Zingbop 9424
4625657 **10.4**
11.05 Night G
FILM: Tycoon
drama.
Aintree
on the
Nati
Pe

overdrive as she put her feet on foreign soil for the first time. Searing heat, choking dust, peeling paint and unfamiliar spicy smells enveloped her. She wandered around the tiny airport for a while and then into the loo and, glancing at her watch, realised that it was time to get on board the aircraft again.

Relieved, she got back on the plane feeling tired and thirsty. The brittle stewardess asked her what she was doing back on board so Samantha told her that she was going to Mauritius. With a school marm gesture she took the form that she had just filled in and ripped it up in disdain. That would teach Samantha to waste her time.

At last, the plane landed in Mauritius. As she walked down the steps of the aircraft, the blazing heat assaulted her. She scanned a sea of black faces as she looked for her fiancée and spotted Paul waiting for her in the tiny shoe box of an airport, his head higher and paler than any other on the balcony. Neatly dressed as usual, he looked happy, his fair complexion slightly tanned.

Paul embraced her warmly, "Welcome to Mauritius. Il fait chaud ici?" he grinned.

She nodded before kissing him, oblivious to the stares of passers by.

Their new life had begun.

Suddenly her jet lag disappeared as she gazed out of the car window. Paul drove in the newly acquired, if slightly used Ford Corsair along dirt tracks. They passed mud huts with thatch roofs and she hoped that their housing would be a little more substantial. Chickens and pigs tried to commit hara-kiri in front of their wheels and Creole and Indian women, babies tucked into their hips stared at them as they drove through several villages. The poverty was shocking to Samantha's pampered Western eyes.

An odour of wood smoke mingled with coconut oil and sweet fragrant tropical flowers hung in the moist air and Samantha felt as if she could have been on another planet. Flowers with strange exotic blooms cascaded in the most unlikely places. Red and purple bougainvillaea was rampant and colours seemed brighter and more intense than she had ever seen before - as if she was part of a Gauguin painting.

Soon they arrived at the Grand Baie Hotel where they were to be married the following day. Paul had found a temporary flat for them to live in after the short honeymoon. It was small, simply furnished and had an unusual odour. Garlic and chillies soaked the atmosphere in Mauritius but then she could not recognise the smell, as she had not yet been introduced to such delights.

The hotel was perched right on the beach. Palm trees swayed and flowers danced in the gentle tropical breeze as if in celebration of the marriage between Samantha and Paul.

"Can I stay the night with you. No-one will know." Paul whispered after kissing her at first tenderly but soon with passion.

"No, darling. We've waited this long so one more night won't make any difference." Samantha believed that she should wait until after the wedding before sleeping with Paul. Her strict convent schooling had made an impression on her and, so far, he had been understanding.

"Are you sure you'll be all right here in the hotel on your own?" He looked concerned.

"Yes, I'm so worn out that I'll be asleep before my head touches the pillow. You go back to the flat and I'll be waiting for you tomorrow." She held him close, not really wanting him to go.

"Goodnight darling. I love you so much. I can't wait to see you in your dress. You will be a picture, I just know it." And with one last kiss he left.

The dress was lifted out of the case and hung up. The moist tropical air soon erased the few creases that the trip had inflicted.

"I'll be a married woman tomorrow and I won't be in this bed alone," she thought as she drifted off to sleep, under the shrouds of a mosquito net.

The next day she was woken by a loud thunderclap. She jumped out of bed, dreading what she might see when she opened the curtains. Gone was the tropical paradise as rain lashed viciously against the windowpane. It seemed to taunt her, "You won't get married on the beach. You won't get married on the beach."

The hotel staff was used to unexpected downpours and assured the anxious bride that a conference room was provided in case of such eventualities. Disappointed, Samantha went through the routine of having her hair done professionally by the resident hairdresser. She was just admiring what the hairdresser had done with her long fair locks when a knock at the door made her jump.

"Who is it?" she called out, suddenly superstitious and hoping Paul was not there.

"Your bouquet Madam," was the cheerful response.

Samantha wasn't used to all this luxury. For a moment she wondered who "Madam" could be. Composing herself, she opened the door.

The bouquet was stunning. Red and white anthuriums, which looked as if they had been made into appropriate heart shapes of wax, had been arranged professionally. So exotic. Paul had thought of every last detail and it was perfect.

Except the weather.

They were to be married in an hour and it was still pouring with rain. The threatening sky was like lead.

Grabbing her rosary she prayed, "Please God, let it stop raining so that we can get married on the beach." She kissed the familiar rosary and felt a few tears pricking her eyes. Deep down she wanted to be married in a Catholic church but Paul had his own belief system that did not include church.

She slipped into the dress, being careful not to get make-up on it. As she put her sandals and jewellery on she glanced out of the window for the hundredth time that morning. She was greeted by a break in the clouds and then, miraculously the rain stopped.

By the time she met Paul in the foyer the sun was streaming down and a rainbow decorated the sky like a celestial wedding bower.

"You look beautiful. What a gorgeous dress!" Paul admired his bride to be as he stroked the soft fabric in appreciation. He was such a loving man, so unlike other boys she had known and always so interested in her clothes. Paul took an interest in his appearance too and she had never seen him looking scruffy. Kissing him on his clean shaven cheek she breathed in the familiar scent of aftershave and toothpaste.

She was so happy she could have danced out of the hotel and on to the beach. Paul looked handsome in his cream linen suit, an anthurium in his buttonhole that matched her bouquet perfectly.

They said their vows solemnly, holding a bible and looking into each other's eyes.

"On this special day, in the presence of God and our witnesses, I give you my sacred vow that, as your husband, I will always be with you and support you. To console and comfort you in difficult times, to respect you, protect you and to love you for ever." Paul's voice sounded strong and she wondered if perhaps living in the midst of the beauty of creation would help him to stretch his mind and heart to accept a belief in God.

Birds sang an enthusiastic anthem in the background as if to encourage the newlyweds.

"I give you my sacred vow, as your wife, that I will always be with you and support you. In times of sickness and in times of health, in times of joy and in times of sorrow, I promise to love you forever. I promise that I will laugh with you and to grieve with you, to be truthful and honest with you and to cherish you for as long as we both shall live," Samantha responded with conviction.

At times, it was so emotional that they could hardly speak. The Creole pastor, hired for the occasion, seemed moved and wiped a tear from his eye, "I pronounce you man and wife," he boomed.

A bottle of champagne was chilling in an ice bucket nearby. Soon they were toasting each other - laughing and crying at the same time.

"Here's to us," Paul said, shaking a box of confetti over them both.

After the photographer had taken endless pictures they wandered down to the water's edge where they finished their champagne, and gazed out to sea. They stood mesmerised for about ten minutes before Paul returned to the hotel to get some sun tan lotion. Carefully lifting the hem of her gown and kicking off her sandals, she paddled into the warm sea, grateful that she would be living in such a perfect location for the next few years. The whispering sea caressed her feet and ankles and Samantha wondered what the future would hold in this new land that was to be their home. They both wanted children and she hoped that one day they would have a boy and a girl to seal their union.

5

MAURITIUS

After the wedding ceremony Samantha and Paul wandered up to the pool area where other guests bought them some drinks. Samantha had not eaten any breakfast that morning - she was too nervous. Elated and tipsy, she scanned the gardens looking for her husband. There he was, a crazy grin on his face, jumping into the pool - fully clothed. Sometimes his behaviour was a bit bizarre. Samantha decided it was about time she was a little less straight laced and, without thinking, she too jumped into the pool.

A suffocating fear enveloped her. What had she done? The weight of the dress started to pull her under the water. She tried to swim but the more she moved, the more the dress tangled around her thrashing limbs like a phantom octopus. Samantha could hear her heart pounding in her head as she touched the bottom of the pool. Her limbs felt heavy and her lungs about to explode.

'I'm going to die on my wedding day,' she thought as she struggled to breathe, 'swim, swim. You'll be fine. Don't panic. You can swim. No, hold your breath, no, you can do this - swim, swim - my God help me please - my legs are trapped. Paul, Paul - where is he - rescue me. Mum, we swam in the sea in Blackpool. Little legs moving now they can't move. My wedding dress, beautiful dress - heavy - full of stones - pulling me down, down, down. Death? No. No. No. Buzzing, loud in my ears. Death, where is thy sting? Forgive me Father for I have sinned. No more swimming. All is black. Our Father in heaven. Black. Buzzing, buzzing, now quiet. Oh, the light - wonderful, peace, love, thank you for the love. Love holding - enveloping. No fear. Whoosh, spinning fast to the light - glorious roller coaster. In a new place now. Music. Pushing on my lungs 1,2,3. School swimming class - chlorine burning my eyes. Why am I up here looking at myself? Is that me lying by the pool? Stop pushing so hard - bitter, bitter taste. Leave me alone - I'm happy here. Don't want to come back. The ground feels cold. Where is the light? Voices far, far away - getting louder. His voice is near now. Why so much panic? Let me go back. It's okay. His lips on my forehead. I love you.'

She came to lying on her stomach, bitter water gushing from her mouth. Someone was pushing hard on her lungs. The ground beneath her felt hard and cold and, in her disorientated state, she thought that she was with her class at the local swimming pool.

Paul rolled her over onto her back and gently pulled the hair from her face.

"You'll be all right. Don't worry."

"What, what happened? Where -?"

"I think you almost drowned." His voice was gentle.

Then it all flooded back to her as he helped her to her feet.

Everything seemed very dark. Then Samantha noticed that black clouds had suddenly blotted out the sun as fat raindrops descended onto her already wet face.

"My dress will be ruined," was all she could mutter as she was helped to the comfort of their hotel room.

After a hot meal in their room, Paul carried his bride to the bed that had been waiting for them. He was a gentle lover and afterwards he held her in his arms with tenderness.

"I'm sorry it hurt my darling. Next time it will be better."

And it was.

To make up for the unfortunate start to married life, the couple had two blissful days on honeymoon. Making love, sunbathing, swimming in the shallow, tepid sea without fear and enjoying the new found intimacy of their relationship before moving into their new home.

The excitement of the wedding over, Samantha made a firm decision to avoid alcohol. It reminded her too much of drowning and it took a long time before she could venture into a swimming pool again.

After settling into their new apartment in Curepipe, Paul's boss' wife, Shirley Watson, came to teach Samantha the rules of how to become an acceptable expatriate wife. Shirley was deeply tanned, had short brown hair and wore the compulsory mini skirt of the sixties. To Samantha she seemed almost middle aged but, in retrospect, she realised that she was probably only about thirty five. Looking at Samantha with a keen eye, she announced with a slightly bored drawl, "You look so young - you must have been a child bride."

For the first time she felt like one.

They sauntered to the local shop, a wooden shack that sold basic groceries, and Shirley taught her how to barter in French. Street vendors were frying unusual looking delicacies which she later discovered were chilli cakes, a delicious mixture of ground lentils and hot green chillies.

"Gateau piment," they called out with gravelly voices as they passed.

"Don't eat those - the stalls are filthy." Shirley commanded.

Having lived in Africa before Mauritius, Shirley was a typical colonial wife. She explained the necessity of getting a servant as soon as possible and said that she would arrange it.

Feeling slightly dazed, Samantha greeted Paul when he got back from his day at the office in the capital, Port Louis.

"Hop in the car. We'll drive to the beach," he said after changing into some shorts.

They revisited the place of their marriage for a stroll along the beach. Grand Baie was heaven. Turquoise sea ebbed gently onto white sands. Apart from a few fishermen, there was not a person in sight. Only palm trees swayed in the tropical breeze like graceful dancers.

"It's the most beautiful place I've ever seen." Samantha was once more enchanted by the vision in front of her.

"I thought you'd like it here," he said, his eyes sparkling like the sea.

Holding hands they strolled bare foot in the sand and Samantha felt a deep contentment as a sudden sunset hit the sky, followed by a silky darkness.

Shirley had informed Samantha that her social life would revolve around the Gymkhana Club where the young couple would meet up with other ex-pats over gin and tonics.

The Watsons were hospitable and the newlyweds attended a Sunday curry lunch at their beach house that weekend. This was served African, rather than Indian style, with side dishes of peanuts, sultanas, grated coconut and sliced banana. Pudding was slices of garden fresh papaya onto which lime juice was squeezed. Samantha relished her first taste of the sweet creamy fruit that melted like ice cream in her mouth.

After the meal, a quiet Creole maid removed the dishes and started the mammoth task of washing up. There were several small children present who were beginning to get noisy. This would not do. Shirley called for her maid to come to the rescue. Forgetting her

French for a moment, Shirley gesticulated to her servant with an impatient wave of the hand, "Oh, faire chose!"

"Do thing!" Samantha translated silently in her schoolgirl French, wondering what she meant.

As if by sixth sense, the long suffering maid rounded up the children and took them out of the adults' way.

They sat riveted as Alison, another lunch guest who'd lived in Mauritius most of her life, told them all about a pregnancy test that had failed.

"I pee peed into a hot potty," she explained loudly for all to hear, "and it didn't work."

"Well, you were expecting old girl." Her husband slapped her on the back, winking to his audience.

Everyone found this hilarious and it didn't take Samantha long to get used to the more exuberant way that expats spoke of life. This was all so different from the usual Sunday roast that she shared each week at home with her mother as they chatted about their uncomplicated lives. Somehow Samantha knew that life would never be quite the same again.

~ ~ ~ ~ ~ ~

THE GYMKHANA CLUB

Scratching an angry mosquito bite on her ankle, Samantha was cross with herself for feeling so homesick. She was missing her mother, her friend, Christine, and even her work colleagues. Everyone in the clubhouse seemed to be so ancient compared with her.

"Boy," he barked as he clapped his hands.

Samantha looked up from her drink to see an old colonial with a handlebar moustache ordering a gin and tonic. Obediently a barefooted bar man dressed in white trousers and a gold buttoned tunic responded, his face expressionless. The 'boy' was Gobin, a man in his late forties and used to being addressed in such a disrespectful manner. Lal was the other bar man who was rumoured to be a Communist. Not that this bothered anyone just so long as their gin and tonics were served promptly, with plenty of ice and due reverence.

Several months had passed since arriving in Mauritius and Paul and Samantha were relaxing on wicker chairs in the Gymkhana Club lounge, which looked out onto a small golf course. The club house was like something from a Somerset Maugham novel, constructed out of timber and with wind battered shutters at the windows. Everyone present was white except for the staff. Only whites could apply for membership. This included the Franco Mauritians, who originally hailed from France. They could be quite snooty in a Gallic sort of way and spoke good French as opposed to the local patois.

"You Engleesh wiz your geen and toneecs," the chic Bernadine shrugged, "I only dreenk champagne and only at Christmas."

Ceiling fans moved the warm air in a desultory manner and the smell of curry, old polished wood and insect repellent pervaded the atmosphere. Paul and Samantha were part of colonial life in Mauritius at the Gymkhana Club. They were now members, accepted after an interview that posed as a formal cocktail party, which she found rather intimidating. Now that she had been labelled a child bride, she had hoped that the committee would approve of her, as she knew that Paul had no problem and chatted away easily, answering their probing questions with his charming smile.

"Welcome to Mauritius and to the Club, Old Boy," a retired army general slapped Paul on the back.

Samantha felt increasingly out of place and knew that Mauritius had more to offer than this and wondered if her youth was being taken from her with each passing day. Her new lifestyle was a far cry from the dances at Cheltenham Town Hall and she missed the music, the fashion and the fun. The swinging sixties had not reached these shores, nor were they likely to. Perhaps she was too young to marry and should have waited until Paul returned from Mauritius. Then she would have had time to mature a little and catch up with him. She had been told that it was not acceptable, nor indeed practical, for colonial wives to work so she decided to learn French and, hopefully, have her first child.

Paul worked with a young British bachelor called Alan Duval. His mother was English and his father a typical mix of Creole and French. Alan used to joke about his heritage, singing, "My Old Man's a Creole," to the well known tune of "My Old Man's a Dustman." He had some local Mauritian friends who he introduced to Samantha and Paul soon after their arrival on the island and their stuffy social life changed overnight. All his friends were of Creole or Chinese origin and were young and more easy-going than the old colonials. Most didn't speak much English and so before long Paul and Samantha were communicating in a sort of French. When they got stuck Alan would happily translate.

They were all at Flic en Flac beach one sultry day, watching a group of three Indian women taking a dip in the sea fully clad in their jewel coloured saris when Alan announced to Paul and Samantha, "You know that I've got a six month contract in Australia coming up soon. Well, I'd like to keep my house on and so I wondered if you'd housesit while I'm away. You must be finding it a bit claustrophobic in a flat in this heat."

This was good news. Samantha had visited Alan's house several times and found it enchanting, unlike the stark, utilitarian apartment that she and Paul shared. Within a month they had moved in.

Maison de Poupée, The Doll's House, seemed an apt name. It was in this slightly faded home that the newly weds lived for a short while during their time in Mauritius. Bijou would be another way to describe this tiny wooden house that was built in the colonial style. The garden was burgeoning with purple and red bougainvillea. A cloud of creamy white frangipani contrasted with the scarlet hibiscus and a giant guava tree sprawled rampantly in front of the house, dwarfing anything else that vied for space. At night the air was filled with a heavy tropical scent of flowers. Wood smoke also hung in the night air as many Mauritians cooked over an open fire. Crickets and cicadas serenaded each other tirelessly as night fell in this Garden of Eden.

Geckoes made their gloomy homes behind the pictures and were welcome guests as they gobbled up the irritating mosquitoes when they felt brave enough to venture out. Mauritian mosquitoes always seem to be ravenous and had a liking for Samantha's English flesh. Cockroaches were another menace and every home, however clean, was infested with them. She got to be an expert at crushing them with a sandal and soon got used to the crunchy sound that they made as they were hit. One rainy day a snake decided to pay a visit to the kitchen through an open window. Heart pounding, she sprayed it with Shelox, a powerful insecticide, and ran out, closing the door behind her. It must have had the desired effect, as she never saw this writhing reptile again.

Maison de Poupée was cosy and, like Latimee, rather ancient.

Latimee, an old retainer, lived in the grounds in the dépendance that was not much better than a shack with no electricity or running water. It was the custom for a lot of servants to live in this manner and was often the only housing that they would ever have. She crossed the garden every day to sweep the floor of Maison de Poupée and polish it with a bross coco, the husk of a coconut, which was widely used for that purpose. Latimee did a sort of hypnotic dance as she placed one foot on the bross coco as the other was used to guide her around the rooms, bringing the floor to a brilliant shine. Latimee was diminutive in build, heavily etched with wrinkles and plaited her thinning grey hair into a long, straggly plait. She always wore an immaculate cotton sari draped around her slight figure and, like most Mauritians, moved slowly in the tropical heat. Her languages were Patois and Hindi but the young couple managed to communicate with her somehow.

It was on a particularly sultry day that Samantha was sitting in the tiny lounge reading - it was far too hot to be outside, when suddenly the sky became ominous as if in preparation for a tropical storm. Stretching out to switch on a table lamp, she was immediately thrown across the room by the force of the electric current that ran through her. She lay there terrified and numb for several minutes until she managed to regain her senses and realise what had happened; she had been a human "earth" for the powerful electric current.

Shaken up and, with trembling legs, she ran into the yard to the nearest human contact calling, "Latimee, Latimee!"

Realising something was wrong, Latimee, with set jaw, rushed out of the dépendance brandishing a hefty stick. All four feet ten inches of her was ready to tackle any intruder who dared to break into Maison de Poupée. Fearless, she ran into the house to confront this imaginary thief.

Samantha followed her and after some sign language and much pointing to the lamp it was understood what had happened. Breaking into a toothless grin, Latimee realised that all was well now, relaxed her warrior grip on the stick and retired in thoughtful silence to her quarters.

When Paul returned home that evening it was decided that they should look for a more modern dwelling. Having had two near death experiences within six months, Samantha didn't want to take any chances.

"This place was only on loan while Alan's in Australia working on that contract. I've heard that there's a much bigger place to rent in Quatre Bornes and you can still find a maid out there to help. Leave it with me sweetie." He held her close and she was so grateful to have a husband who considered her feelings before his own.

Just to be sure that all was well Samantha decided to pay a visit to the doctor. Dr Chung was a neat Chinaman with delicate hands and an ageless face.

Waiting in his clinic, Samantha felt a mixture of excitement and apprehension. If her instincts were correct she hoped that no harm had been done after receiving such a strong electric shock.

"Come in," Dr Chung bowed slightly as he ushered her into his cramped consulting room that smelled of antiseptic and camphor wood.

"Good morning doctor." Samantha found the room oppressive and wished that she was back in England at a time like this.

The doctor, a neat man, sat behind his important desk and seemed to grow in stature as if grateful for the barrier that it produced.

"Yes, what can I do for you?" He was shuffling some papers and had not yet made eye contact.

Samantha explained rather breathlessly, her pretty head tilted to one side, the details of her ordeal with the electric current and then, regaining her composure, told him her real concerns.

"I think I might be pregnant and I'm worried that, if I am, the baby might have been killed." She felt her throat contract and fought back the tears.

After asking her some questions he told her to get on the couch. The examination was brief and his touch reassuringly gentle.

"You are about three months pregnant I'd say." He told her in a matter of fact tone as he washed his hands.

"Oh, is the baby going to be all right?" Fear and apprehension was fast replacing the joy that she had felt upon his announcement.

Reaching for a metal instrument that resembled a small trumpet he placed it on her slightly swollen belly and placed his ear on the end. The wait was interminable.

"Heartbeat sounds strong. Come back and see me in a month." Dr Chung smiled and Samantha felt reassured that all would be well.

That night she told Paul her news.

"Oh, darling, this is wonderful. Do you feel all right? Oh, I hope we have a girl. We could dress her up like a little doll." Paul was effusive.

"Yes, it's great. But you won't be disappointed if we have a boy, will you?" Samantha thought his reaction a little strange.

Paul cleared his throat and blushed slightly, running his hand over his immaculate hair. "Of course not, a boy will be great. Just so long as the baby's healthy. That's all that matters."

He embraced his wife, kissing her gently on the lips.

Paul was attentive to his young wife, bringing her tea in bed before he went to work, making sure that she rested enough and assuring her that he would help as much as possible once the baby was born. Samantha had a healthy pregnancy that was just as well as the medical facilities were basic on the island. Neither did a clothes shop exist, so Samantha tracked down a sewing girl who whipped up some maternity creations that Samantha and Paul had sketched. He enjoyed shopping with her in the only material shop for miles around, offering his advice on materials and colour combinations.

"You should have been a fashion designer - you're really good at this. We both should have gone to Art College. It would have been more interesting than waitressing and surveying." She remarked as she marvelled at his talent for dress design.

"I know but it might not have provided us with such a good income my love. Now what colour do you think - navy blue with a red trim would look lovely." He had designed a maternity dress that would be cool in the heat but stylish and still in fashion.

Kim was born one week late in a private nursing home. After six hours of labour Samantha screamed at Paul who was rubbing her back and sympathising.

"That's it. Never again. Oh my God. I can't stand it. No more children. You can sleep in the spare room."

"Can't you do anything to lessen the pain, doctor?" Paul was pale with concern.

"Yes, just a little injection. It won't be long now. Push mother. Push again." The Indian doctor encouraged.

"I can't." Samantha flopped back on the pillows, her hair wet with perspiration, her eyes wild.

"Come on Sam, one more push." Paul was holding her hand now, pleading with her.

She gave a gargantuan push and the baby's head appeared.

"Well done mother. Baby will soon be here." The doctor and Creole midwife worked as a practised team.

Five minutes later Samantha was cradling the baby as if the trauma had not happened, a look of wonder on her tired face.

Paul was ecstatic. Their son had survived his electric shock and was blissfully ignorant of the creepy crawlies that Samantha loathed.

In a mysterious way motherhood had made Samantha deeply religious. She would gaze at her son and her gratitude that he was born healthy had strengthened her faith. The miracle of motherhood had brought with it a spirituality that brought comfort and peace. Each morning she would say her rosary and every Sunday would take Kim with her to mass. However, Paul, kind, good Paul, would become stony if she tried to persuade him to see a priest. He had an aversion to religion and Samantha, not wanting to spoil an almost perfect marriage, decided to leave the matter and continue her faith journey alone. Only occasionally, tired after being woken by the baby, as she sat suckling him in the secret hours of the night, did she entertain the thoughts that she should have married someone of the same faith. But she knew that marriage was a compromise and was grateful that she and Paul were in love and such good friends. Although they had made friends with many young Mauritians, they were a self-contained couple and, once they had become parents, the constant partying stopped. But they were content in each other's company. In fact, Samantha felt that, apart from her irrational fear of some reptiles and insects, her life was almost perfect. As promised, she wrote to her mother each week. Betty was thrilled to be a grandmother but declined the offer of a visit. She would wait until Samantha's return to England before seeing her grandson. They would have Kim christened upon their return to England - something that Betty was looking forward to with anticipation.

However, Samantha now had an English friend some fifteen years her senior who was unlike the crowd that frequented the Gymkhana Club. Louise was a gifted musician and artist who was not interested in cocktail parties at the Gymkhana Club. It was Louise who introduced Samantha to a passion that would eventually change her life forever.

~ ~ ~ ~ ~ ~

Samantha decided that she could take or leave spiders, unless they were the variety with particularly hairy legs and fat bodies. Rats, cockroaches and lizards, with their vile bodies, she had never had an affinity with.

It didn't matter how clean she tried to keep each place where she lived in Mauritius; she always shared her home with an abundance of cockroaches. Sneaky creatures, they like to forage at night.

Breast feeding Kim made Samantha ravenous, particularly in the middle of the night, and her favourite snack was a bowl of corn flakes. One night, as she sang gently to her new baby as he suckled noisily, she promised herself a treat before grabbing some much needed sleep. Grateful that, at last, Kim was almost asleep she carried him to his cot whilst gently patting him on the back to bring up any wind. After an enormous burp, he sighed before falling asleep.

Gingerly putting Kim into his mosquito net covered cot, she entered the tiny kitchen, hungry and bleary eyed. As she switched the light on there was a noisy rustling sound. Immediately she was wide awake, knowing instinctively that it had something to do with creepy crawlies. To her horror the sound was coming from within the corn flakes packet, so she tentatively opened it and eight enormous cockroaches scurried out, having feasted on her expensive, imported cereal. She let out an involuntary scream that woke Kim so that he too joined in the racket.

"What's up? What happened?" Paul stood in the doorway of the kitchen, groggy from sleep and with his normally sleek hair standing on end.

"Cockroaches in my corn flakes. Paul, I - "

"Come back to bed. I'll chuck the stuff out and we'll get some more. You look whacked and so am I."

"Sorry - I don't think I'll ever get used to these wretched creepy crawlies. Kim's in a state now and - "

"Leave him to me. I'll change his nappy and rock him back to sleep. Now just go back to bed - that's an order." He kissed her on the cheek.

So she munched on a banana before creeping back to bed and falling into a dreamless sleep.

Although not an avid shopper, Samantha was disappointed with the quality of Mauritian shops. There were a few tiny grocery stores run by Chinese immigrants and her local comprador was Fuk Chong, an ancient wizened man whose store never seemed to close. He stocked up his tiny shop from floor to ceiling with everything from candles to imported Botswana beef, which was as tough as its native country.

The first Christmas was spent in Samantha and Paul's third and final dwelling in this Indian Ocean paradise. Paul had indeed found them a beautiful house to begin parenthood. It was a flat roofed solid, whitewashed home with three bedrooms, a bathroom with noisy plumbing, an elegant living room furnished with antiques, a basic kitchen and a separate laundry area where a dhobi arrived each day to beat the living daylights out of the washing before draping it on the bushes outside to dry. Sloping gardens surrounded the house where tall palms reached to the clear blue skies. Luscious papayas, mangoes, bananas, lychees and pineapples flourished in the fertile land and Samantha was pleased to give away most of the produce as the small family could only eat so much fruit. She relished all the extra space after living in the Doll's House and the electric wiring was reliable much to her relief. Although it was too hot to feel like Christmas, the season was almost upon them, so she decided to try and get enough ingredients together to make a Christmas cake. She had always loved baking and had received her first cookery book as a present from her mother on her twelfth birthday.

She put her order in with Mr Chong, to the fascination of Nancy, her new Creole maid who had never seen such ingredients before. Samantha sweated over the concoction, beating the ingredients with a wooden spoon in the suffocating heat. After an hour baking in an ancient, unreliable oven a passable fruitcake was produced. Feeling proud of her minor accomplishment, she decided to let it stand overnight to cool before storing it in a cake tin. Not wishing any flies to contaminate this culinary achievement, she placed a large plastic colander over it for protection.

The next morning she wandered into the kitchen to make some tea and was startled by a rustling sound coming from the top of the store cupboard. Horrors! A large black gecko with a distended stomach was underneath the colander, having feasted on the cake during the night. Lured by the cake, he had somehow managed to get under the colander but the bloated creature could not find his way out. Holding her breath, Samantha gingerly lifted up the colander and the greedy gecko darted out to the nearest hideaway. She stared at the cake and felt slightly sick.

When Nancy came into work later she explained to her in faltering French about the lizard. Samantha told her that she no longer wanted the cake and would throw it away as it had been nibbled by an unwelcome guest. Nancy looked horrified and said that she and her family would love to have the cake and that they would eat it with fresh green chillies. This sounded a bit different to the usual marzipan and icing. Samantha was assured the following day that the cake was indeed delicious, no doubt aided by a certain piquancy.

The two years sped by as the couple enjoyed parenthood, excursions to the beach and exploring the beauty of Mauritius. Soon Paul's contract would come to an end and they would need to return to the Cotswolds. As they packed their crates to be shipped back to England, Samantha felt weak and dizzy and she wondered if, perhaps, she could be pregnant again. She hoped so, but did not mention how she felt to Paul as she thought she would have a check up at the doctor's when they returned to Cheltenham.

Apart from her forays with the insect and reptile population, these were happy times for Samantha. Happy also because she had not yet discovered Paul's secret.

6

PARK LIFE

It was a balmy day in Cheltenham and Pittville Park's familiar scenery brought a measure of comfort to Celine as she sat on a bench in the sun and watched the children play. She tried to imagine sitting in this same spot with a pram but somehow could not put herself in that position. Although she had at one time taken it for granted that she would have a family, because James was adamant that he never wanted children, Celine had come to terms with the fact that they would be a childless couple. But now it was as if fate had stepped in and she and James were to be parents. She hoped for a true reconciliation, as all she had ever yearned for was a happy family life. She wondered if, perhaps, she had been hasty leaving him in Amsterdam to go and stay with her mother. He had assured her that he was no longer seeing the girl with the long curly hair, but she was not convinced. The thought of being a single mother filled her with dread. As she contemplated the state of pregnancy she remembered with a wry smile the way that her mother, Veronica, had presented her with some of the facts of life.

Veronica made an embarrassing attempt to explain periods to Celine when she was twelve years old. She had taken her younger daughter into the bedroom and shut the door as if about to reveal an international secret to MI5. The conversation proceeded in hushed tones.

"I have something to tell you."

Celine was all ears.

"When you get older you'll bleed." This sounded alarming and Celine wondered from where she would bleed. The naive girl was too scared to ask. She wondered if her older sister, Janet, bled in such a way.

"You will have to wear a towel," she proceeded whilst examining the pattern on the carpet intently.

For some reason Celine figured that this flow of blood would be emitted from her belly button and had visions of wrapping a large towel around her midriff.

"When this happens you must not tell your father but Janet or myself will give you a towel."

Celine was none the wiser and wondered why her father was not allowed to hear about this momentous event.

"Even the Queen has it!" she announced. And with that she left the room leaving Celine in bewilderment. She wondered how the Queen managed to look so slim with a bath towel wrapped around her tummy.

Two years later the awaited event occurred but Celine was not alarmed as she had learned the facts of life in the school playground from more enlightened friends.

A child crying brought her back to the present. Looking over to the toddler who had fallen over, Celine wished that she had discovered her pregnancy in happier circumstances. Her recent visit to the family doctor was fraught with embarrassment and she cringed when asking him to run a test for venereal disease. He was unfazed by the request and she was relieved when the results came back negative. However, the pregnancy test had shown positive.

She told her mother that she was pregnant after the results came through and, to her surprise, the shock did not bring on a migraine. When Celine was going out with Nick as a teenager and talking of going to Art College, Veronica had suffered many migraines. It was interesting that they stopped when she got a job as a trainee fashion buyer and stopped seeing Nick. Celine's mother never approved of Nick, as he was too much of a free spirit and, therefore, did not meet her preconceived requirements for a future son-in-law. James, on the other hand, was a different story. He was a Chartered Accountant with prospects, came from a respectable middle class family, and was well spoken and dressed conservatively. The pressure to get engaged to him was constant until Celine acquiesced and Nick became a sweet memory. James was always charming to Celine's mother and complimented her frequently on her cooking. The atmosphere at home became more tranquil and Celine believed that she loved James, found his brooding intensity beguiling and convinced herself that Nick had just been a teenage crush. She longed for a steady, reliable boyfriend whom she could trust after being led to believe that Nick had changed irrevocably since going to art college. Sometimes, Celine wondered if Nick had become rebellious because his parents had died when he was a young child and an aunt had brought him up. Perhaps she would never know.

She decided that it was time to put Nick behind her now that she had met the more mature and sensible James.

After much thought, Celine decided to postpone telling James that he was to be a father; there was no hurry and she was unsure what his response would be. She was longing to tell him but would bide her time.

"I've only got a short time left on my contract here in Holland, darling." James sounded enthusiastic when he phoned her from Amsterdam. "The company want me to go to Hong Kong to familiarise myself with the job there and to check out some accommodation. I've been offered a good posting and I want you to come with me. I miss you. The cat misses you. Promise me you'll have me back," he cajoled. Celine had never known James so emotional but she still needed time to think. However, the more she considered her options the more confused she had become.

"You go to Hong Kong. I'll give you my answer soon. I'm getting used to flying on my own, so the trip won't be a problem." She had told him.

She wondered if a baby would pull them together or drive them even further apart. Feeling that she needed to get away from her mother's constant chatting had driven her to take a walk in the park to clear her mind. She would stop vacillating and give James her answer the following day.

Strolling over to the cages that held the wildlife, she gazed at some chipmunks racing around their prison of a home. One of them was expending a great deal of energy on a treadmill and Celine couldn't help but compare it to her wasted years with James. She had even given up her career to follow him to Holland so that he could further his job prospects. A baby would put paid to her returning to her old career as a fashion buyer.

The sun was getting stronger and she enjoyed its gentle caress on her bare arms. Wandering to the next cage, she gazed at a pair of doves, kissing in domestic bliss in their prison. A pair of peacocks inhabited the adjoining cage where the male strutted and displayed his jewel coloured feathers to his dowdy mate and an ironic smile played briefly across Celine's lips as she thought of how James had started to use aftershave and bought himself a new wardrobe to impress the foreign girl with the dark curly hair. The sound of children playing was so normal, so every day, that for a moment she forgot her worries and returned to the bench once more to watch the scene that was being acted out before her eyes. It was good to be alone, away from her mother's constant fussing and righteous indignation. She had looked forward to having some time with her but was finding it claustrophobic, especially as her mother still treated her like a teenager.

Celine watched some mothers spreading out blankets on the fresh, cool grass where picnics were taken out of bags and displayed under ancient trees. A football rolled down a gentle slope and a lithe mother wearing bellbottom trousers and a top displaying a bare midriff rushed after it. She juggled a large beach towel and drink with one hand and pushed a pram with her other, motherhood making her ambidextrous out of necessity. Children noisily played on swings, climbing frames and slides and boarded a static train, their imagination taking them who knows where.

The leaves whispered as a brisk breeze stirred them and toddlers ran on uncertain legs. Like her future - everything seemed so uncertain.

In the distance, she spotted a lone father who seemed preoccupied with steering a pushchair. She stared at him, the only man in the play area, and was startled when two pigeons took off in flight just inches away from her head. Free.

The young father had found a spreading tree to sit under and seemed to glance over at Celine from time to time while his toddler played contentedly at his feet. He seemed to be writing something in a notepad.

'Is he writing a note to his wife?' Celine thought. 'Is he happily married or does he feel trapped like those chipmunks in their cage?' She sighed and looked up to the cornflower sky with its fluffy clouds floating by.

A little girl, with loose curls kissing an innocent neck, ran towards her with wide eyes and a large smile. Celine wanted to pick the child up and hug it to her but she just returned the smile.

"Come and see the squirrels," her mother called out. The child rushed off and the brief encounter was over.

'My goodness, maternal instinct must be kicking in,' Celine thought as she placed a hand on her still flat stomach.

Outside the play area, beyond the railings, dogs ran in abandon, free of the shackles of their leads. One carried a stick in its mouth, challenging its owner to take it from him. And the parrots squawked in their prisons. Have they ever known freedom? Do they dream of jungles and rain forests when darkness falls? She closed her eyes and remembered happier times when she and James used to walk hand in hand through this park after going out on a date. Slowly she drifted into a half sleep.

Celine's reverie was broken with a tap on her shoulder as a note was dropped into her lap from behind. Automatically, she read it:

Hello stranger. How's life? What are you doing in the park? Nick.

Nick. Celine's mind went blank as she turned around to see who on earth would write her such a note. Nick! He was the father who had been playing with the toddler under the large chestnut tree in the distance. Jumping up she hugged him, at the same time wishing that she'd put on some make-up before going out.

"Nick, what a surprise!"

"It's good to see you after all this time. Meet Jeremy – my son." His warm brown eyes looked down at the toddler who gazed intently at Celine the way small children do, candidly and without guile.

They had a lot of catching up to do. Nick had been Celine's only serious boyfriend during her teenage years and everyone thought that they would marry – until she met James that is. James, six years her senior, had seemed so deep and sophisticated. Then, after Celine's marriage, Nick had married Eloise, a girl that he'd met at Art College who had a penchant for bizarre clothing and vivid hair tints.

"How's Eloise? Do you have any more children?" Celine was curious to know all about Nick's life. If anything the extra years had made him even more attractive, his once long hair was now short and his tanned face made him look slightly Latino. The beatnik beard had been erased, revealing a strong jaw line. She couldn't help but wonder if life would have worked out better if she had married him instead of James.

"No, just Jeremy. Eloise left me six months ago. Boy, was she a manipulator, but I just didn't see it at the time. She said family life was not for her, that she felt trapped and so she ran off to Greece and left me holding the baby. Not that I mind. Jeremy is my whole world. What about you? Do you and James have a family?"

"No, no family. To be honest I'm not sure what the future holds. We are going through a bad patch at the moment and I've left him." Why was she telling him this? She certainly wasn't looking for sympathy.

"I'm sorry. I hope it works out for you. Look, I have to get back and give Jeremy his tea. We only live around the corner – why not join us? I make a fairly decent cheese on toast." His eyes twinkled and she remembered how kind and unselfish Nick had always been. That was until he went to Art College.

Celine did not hesitate.

"I'd love to," she replied. They escaped the play area through a yellow gate and strolled towards the town.

Nick's flat consisted of a few rooms in an elegant, if slightly faded Regency building, in what used to be a smart part of Cheltenham. The once grand houses had all been converted to flats. Inside, the hallway felt chilly and had the desolate air of a shared house with unwanted mail piled up on a dusty shelf and a rusty bicycle discarded haphazardly against a grubby wall.

"Not much to look at but it gets better," Nick said without apology as he mounted the stairs, Jeremy in one arm and the pushchair in the other. Unlike James, Nick had never been materialistic.

Celine was ushered into a colourful living room with huge sash windows overlooking a green. Each wall was painted a different colour and was used as a foil for Nick's work. Ethnic rugs were scattered on the floor and batiks were thrown haphazardly across the sofa and armchair. Toys were also strewn across the floor and on the coffee table but the flat looked clean and homely and had a comforting smell of toast and ground coffee.

"Wow Nick, these paintings are amazing, your style is so bold and I love your use of colour." Celine was drawn to one particular picture in oil of a waif like girl sitting on a bench reading, the sunlight bouncing off her hair like a halo.

"That's Eloise reading in the park. I sketched her in happier times and then did the painting." Nick was busying himself in the small kitchen that was attached to the open plan living room.

Eloise. Celine blamed the girl in the picture for her break up with Nick.

She remembered the first and only time she met her. Celine was working in a fashion shop on The Promenade in Cheltenham and was down hearted as Nick had left to study graphic design in London. They had been dating for over a year, had talked of eventual marriage and agreed to having four children. Two boys and two girls. It would be perfect.

63

"As long as they're not both sets of twins." They laughed a lot together when they were each seventeen and the cares of the world had not eroded their dreams.

She first saw Nick standing chatting with some friends at a youth club. It was her first visit and she was feeling nervous. He had glanced over to her while Buddy Holly sang out from the record player, 'Little Sister Don't You Cry.'

"Want to jive?" He extended his hand to her as a fait accompli.

They danced and chatted and drank orange squash and then it was time to go home.

"I have to be in by 10 o'clock."

"Can I walk you home?" His eyes sparkled and she loved the way that they crinkled at the sides when he smiled.

"I only live three doors away." Celine wished it was much further.

"Then we can walk round the block a few times."

He reached for her hand as they turned the corner and that was how it all started.

Then Nick moved away but he wrote each week telling her about college, and, more importantly, about their future together. He told her that he loved her and could not imagine a future without her.

Eloise had spotted Nick at college and wondered why he didn't have a girl friend - he was gorgeous. She had flirted with him and even tried asking him out but he said that he was unofficially engaged to a girl called Celine who worked in Cheltenham at an up market shop called Laisters as a trainee fashion buyer. Trying to look innocent, Eloise had asked casually if she could see a picture of his fiancée. Without hesitation Nick took a photo out of his wallet.

"Attractive girl. Hope you'll be happy," she remarked after memorising every feature.

Eloise plotted and planned and made a trip to Cheltenham. It was a grey, drizzly Saturday afternoon when she got off the train and she knew that town would be busy.

It was not difficult finding the shop where Celine worked and, holding her head high, Eloise looked around for the tall, slim girl with shoulder length chestnut hair that she had seen in the picture and soon spotted her tidying a rail of clothes. Yes, the girl wearing a navy suit and matching high heels was definitely her. She knew exactly what she would say. Looking every inch the art student with her crochet rainbow waistcoat and long skirt, she sauntered over to her rival.

Smiling sweetly she asked, "I'm looking for a special blouse for my mother – can you help?"

"I'll get one of the girls to help you." Celine smiled at this rather bizarre looking customer.

"You look familiar. Do you know someone at Chelsea Art College called Nick? I think I've seen your photo in his room?" Eloise's silky voice belied her mocking gaze.

Looking startled, Celine responded, "Yes, I know Nick. He's my boyfriend. Are you at the same art college?"

"Yeah. It's good that you and Nick have an arrangement and that you're not the jealous type. Boy, does he play the field. Mind you, with his looks it's hardly surprising that he uses them to get the birds." She laughed and enjoyed the wide-eyed look of horror on Celine's face. Seeing that her strategy was working well she elaborated as she could tell this girl was innocent and perhaps a little gullible. Like a cat playing with its victim, she revelled in her game.

"We all come to him when we want a joint. Fab isn't it. He's always the one with the dope when we need a smoke. Doesn't even charge me for it. Yeah, great guy Nick. Anyway, nice to meet you. Celine is it? Yeah. I think I'll go somewhere else for the blouse. Bit dear in here for a poor art student. Bye."

And with that she left, leaving a lingering smell of patchouli behind, before Celine could challenge her.

That evening, still reeling from Eloise's news, she met James and her life took a different course. She had been invited to a party and, even though stunned to hear how much Nick had changed, decided to go anyway. As she took her last sip of Babycham he had approached her.

"Can I get you another of those?"

She nodded as she looked up at the stranger with the cultured voice. His dark hair was combed neatly to one side and his blue eyes were like liquid crystal. Unlike Nick he was conservatively dressed and had a serious manner. This boded well as Celine had already convinced herself that Nick had fooled her into a commitment that was one sided. James drove her home to her parents' house in his sports car and kissed her slowly and firmly before asking to see her the following evening. Celine ran in to tell her parents about her new boyfriend, James.

Nick's usual letter arrived the morning after meeting James. She ripped it up, scalding tears running down her face and replied.

Dear Nick,

It was wonderful while it lasted but we both seem to have moved on. You with your new life at Art College and me in the business world. I think ours was just puppy love and I can't see it working. I'm sorry. I have met a man called James who I think is serious about his feelings for me. So it is with a sad heart that I feel it right to say goodbye to you, Nick. I will always remember you and there will always be a place in my heart for you. Please don't reply to this letter.

Love and many happy memories, Celine

He did not reply to her letter and within six months James and Celine were married.

She looked up again at the painting of Eloise and wondered how it was that their marriage had failed. Just as she was poised to enquire, the toddler climbed onto her lap.

"Mamma." Jeremy looked up at the painting, pointing with a chubby finger, his bottom lip beginning to tremble.

Celine felt sorry for the toddler and wondered how a woman could just walk out on her child. To distract him, Celine picked up a wooden toy train that was lying on the floor and began pushing it towards him, making unselfconscious puffing sounds through pouting lips. The child grabbed the toy, forgetting his absent mother as he became lost in his own world of play. Celine watched the toddler and tried to imagine how she would cope, living in a flat and bringing up a child alone. The thought filled her with dread and, for the first time since discovering she was pregnant, considered an abortion. A new bill had been passed in parliament and this once illegal act was now available on the National Health Service, eliminating the risk of infection – or worse. Grief and disappointment had obliterated what she thought were her strict moral codes. And now she was considering the murder of her unborn baby.

"Come and wash your hands, Jemms, your tea's ready." Nick swept a now whinging Jeremy into his arms and took him to the bathroom.

Celine was filled with admiration for Nick. It would have been unheard of for a single father to bring up a child even ten years ago. She also felt guilt and remorse that she could even consider killing the young life within her and her throat started to contract. Sitting down heavily on the sofa, she hugged a large teddy bear to her chest

- drawing comfort from the soft innocuous fur. Choices, choices – the choices of the modern woman. So freeing and yet so condemning. Her thoughts were racing in confused turmoil.

"I'm going to break all the rules and plonk Jeremy in front of the T.V. so we can eat in peace and catch up on our news." Nick switched on the small television and then, without ceremony, placed a mug of strong tea and a plate of cheese on toast on the coffee table in front of Celine.

In spite of knowing about his past it felt strangely comfortable as they chatted, munched, laughed and reminisced. Avoiding the subject of Eloise's visit to the shop, Celine talked of happier times when they danced at their youth club.

'No wonder he went off the rails when he went away to college - he must have found his time with me pretty tame. Probably why he slept around and smoked dope. Just as well Eloise warned me of his behaviour.' She thought to herself.

But she still felt a certain serenity in his company and couldn't help but think how different his home felt compared with the cold, affluent elegance of the rented apartment in Amsterdam. Nick explained to her that he had given up painting to make a living in freelance advertising, working from home.

"I've promised myself that when Jeremy starts school I'll get the old easel out again and just hope that any dormant inspiration will spring to life again."

Jeremy decided that he preferred to sit next to Nick and so he eased his way between them still munching and clasping the toy train with sticky fingers. He gave a deep sigh of contentment as he slouched quietly, his gaze drawn to the television.

Celine found herself talking to Nick about a new life in Hong Kong as if it was a forgone conclusion. Her mind suddenly felt clear as if a fog had been swept away by the comforting atmosphere of Nick's company. His deep brown eyes never left her face as she told him about how she wanted to try and make a go of her marriage. Her words sounded strong, but inside her resolve was tenuous and she knew that if she didn't leave quickly her old feelings for Nick would resurface. She resisted the impulse to stroke his face, to hold his once familiar hands in hers. Besides he had betrayed her at college and was not to be trusted any more than James. She decided to let go of any residue of sentimentality and be realistic.

"I must get back. Mum will be expecting me; she's still fragile since Dad died. I'm glad you spotted me in the park. It's been great."

"You've got my number. Give me a ring if you have time before venturing out to the Far East." Nick kissed her on the cheek in a brotherly way before walking her to the door. "Wave bye bye to Celine, Jemms." But he was too engrossed in the cartoons to register.

Impulsively Celine kissed the toddler on top of his head and realised in that moment that an abortion was out of the question.

Back at her mother's house she penned a few lines in her journal, as was now her custom. The act was somehow cathartic and helped her to bring her unruly thoughts to order.

I am still attracted to Nick but I don't think he feels the same about me. To tell him my feelings would only make life even more complicated than it is already. But I am beginning to be pleased that I am pregnant and think I will be a good mother. James has left for Hong Kong and I have decided to join him. I must try to forgive him for the sake of our baby.

7

PAUL'S SECRET

A tingle of excitement made Paul shudder slightly as he turned the corner of the suburban cul de sac in a quiet part of Cheltenham. He and Samantha had taken a bungalow on a six month lease and were using the time to look for a home of their own. It was old fashioned and needed decorating but it was a reasonable rent and would do until they bought their own place. Samantha was hankering after a cottage in the country, thinking it would be a good place to bring up their young son, Kim, but Paul wasn't sure. He would prefer to live in a flat in the centre of town so that he could be near the shops. Putting these thoughts to the back of his mind he concentrated on his plans. Tomorrow was Saturday and Samantha would be out all day. He had every moment planned down to the last detail. The anticipation was almost unbearable.

He couldn't wait to get home and change out of his everyday business suit that he had to wear each day with a white shirt and subdued tie. Being a surveyor in a well established firm in the town demanded it.

"Hello sweetie, I'm home," he called out when he entered the hall with its worn carpet and faded beige patterned wallpaper.

"Hi, I'm in the kitchen," she came into the hall wearing a large apron and drying her hands.

All was quiet as Kim was staying with Paul's parents for the weekend. Normally, he would have missed the shrieks of excitement from his young son on hearing the sounds of his homecoming but this time it was different. Paul was glad of the quiet as he had his own thoughts to relish.

"Your dinner's almost ready," Samantha pecked him on the cheek before returning to the kitchen.

She looked even paler than usual, her skin almost transparent, accentuated by the dark circles under her eyes. Poor Samantha had never been the same since contracting that dreadful illness in the tropics. The fever had started within a day of them returning to England and, at first, Samantha thought that she had caught the flu.

But it turned out to be more serious than that and Samantha had spent two desolate weeks in the tropical unit of a hospital in London where she had to undergo a series of tests to eliminate typhoid, cholera, malaria and other more obscure maladies until, eventually, it was decided that she had a rare illness called Sprue. The doctors had said that now she was in a more temperate climate her health would improve but she still had little stamina. How she missed Nancy and the dhobi who had been such a support when Kim was a baby. Now she had to contend with cleaning, cooking and laundry. Paul did what he could to help and never complained but he too was adjusting to life back in England and, at times, seemed preoccupied.

Going into the bedroom, Paul opened the wardrobe they shared and scanned the contents. He knew exactly what to do tomorrow. He took off his jacket and tie, flung them with disdain onto the bed and wandered into the bathroom to wash his hands. Paul washed his hands a lot. Glancing into the mirror he noticed that his hair was starting to look thin on top.

"Still tomorrow is another day." He felt optimistic as he massaged some of Samantha's hand cream into his dry skin.

The radio was playing an old Doris Day song. He found himself humming along. 'Que sera, sera whatever will be will be, the future's not ours to see. Que sera, sera. What will be, will be.'

As he entered the dining room he was greeted with the delicious aroma of curry. He and Samantha had acquired a taste for spicy food since living abroad and she was an inspired cook in spite of her low energy levels. A large bowl of steaming Basmati rice stood in the centre of the table surrounded by a pile of fragile pappadams, a fragrant chicken curry and a lentil dhal. In spite of her weight loss she still looked beautiful and Paul pushed down any feelings of guilt as she smiled at him.

"Just some chutney to get. Sit down – it's ready."

"Looks wonderful. Thanks. I'm starving." He smoothed his napkin over his lap, ever fastidious.

"You know I'll be out all day tomorrow, so I've left you some ham and salad for your lunch." Samantha reminded him as she sat down at the table and started to dish up mounds of rice.

"Mm, that's fine." Paul murmured his response a little distractedly.

That night he slept restlessly. He couldn't wait for morning when he'd have the place to himself. In the end he got up at six and made himself a cup of tea, avoiding the eyes of the man on the crucifix that hung on the wall. Samantha's devout Catholicism was starting to irritate him although he never divulged the fact that he was an atheist to her – it would break her heart. He had become expert at side stepping any probing questions about faith, or lack of it, with obscure comments such as, "Well, just look at the beauty of nature – it makes you think." These platitudes would keep her off his back until the topic would raise itself again.

As he sipped his tea from a hideous mustard coloured cup that the landlord had provided he planned his day once more. He would take the 10 o'clock bus into town, have a coffee in Cavendish House department store, wander round the shops then have a light lunch in The Black Tulip. He'd make himself a ham and salad sandwich before Samantha got home so that she wouldn't be suspicious. Paul figured on catching the 3 o'clock bus home that would give him at least an hour to spare before Samantha returned. If she ever found out what he got up to it would probably kill her.

Breakfast was eaten in silence. Samantha left the house for her day at the church promptly. Paul sighed with relief as she picked up her bag and kissed him goodbye - he was dreading some sort of a hitch.

The same frisson of excitement went through his body when he heard the door slam. Walking purposefully into the garage, he retrieved a ladder and then scurried with it into the hallway where he climbed into the loft. Taking care, he brought the cardboard box down and placed it on the bedroom floor. Breathless, he took each item out, stroked them and laid them lovingly on the bed.

Savouring each moment he slipped on a fine woollen jacket, all the while checking his reflection in the mirror. He viewed himself from every angle and was delighted with the result of his labours. Not that it was hard work. He'd cherished every delicious moment of it.

"You look marvellous," he told himself.

Grabbing his keys off the hall table and holding his head high he set off along the empty cul de sac to catch his bus. He felt alive and exhilarated as he drank in the sharp spring air.

He liked the looks that he was getting in Cavendish House. Perhaps some of the customers were attracted to him. He ordered a coffee and chocolate éclair and then, fortified, checked out the clothing department. All this was done slowly and in a measured way as if each moment was to be cherished like a precious jewel.

On his way to the bus stop he spotted Nigel Harrison, a colleague from work. He was plodding along in his boring work suit, his wife by his side, clutching a British Home Stores carrier bag.

'BHS not a patch on Cavendish House,' Paul thought.

Nigel was almost up to him now. Paul's heart began to beat faster. Then they passed, Nigel giving him a sideways glance and, looking slightly puzzled, carried on walking. Paul was pleased with himself.

It had been a wonderful day. Paul's feet were aching as he reached the front door but he felt elated. He fumbled for his front door keys, sad that the day was drawing to an end but promised himself a repeat as soon as possible.

~ ~ ~ ~ ~ ~

SAMANTHA'S SHOCK

Teresa Brown was always on time and was waiting outside, as promised, at 9.15am. Samantha had said her rosary as she did every morning in front of the crucifix in the bedroom. She was looking forward to a day at the church hall. She was beginning to wish that she had become a nun and wondered, if this was her calling, why God had not told her before she had met Paul. They had given her the job of sitting at the door to take the money as experience had taught her recently that she could not stand for too long.

"Hello Teresa, how are you today?"

"Just fine, thanks. How are you and Paul?"

"Oh, we're all right thank you." Samantha was a little concerned about Paul; he was very jumpy at breakfast. She was not going to confide in Teresa, who was known to have a wagging tongue; she didn't want the whole church to know about her recently strained relationship with Paul.

The bazaar was a success. They managed to raise £100 for the new church roof and Father O'Connor was delighted.

"Come and have a cup of tea Sam, you must be on your knees." The thin priest with the soft Irish brogue had missed the pun. Stifling a giggle, she pushed her long, fair hair behind her ears and grabbed her purple fringed handbag. He had closed the doors on the last customer and was eager to get home to add the finishing touches to the following day's sermon.

Samantha's avante guard dress and skinny, model like figure made her stand out amongst the rather staid ladies at the church bazaar. She knew she was a curiosity to them, having lived in the tropics and still being so young but she kept herself to herself, only sharing with her priest the inner turmoil she was feeling since returning to the UK.

There was at least another hour's work to do clearing up before Teresa would run her home.

As Samantha got up she felt very peculiar. Her legs gave way and she held onto the back of the chair for support. Father O'Connor sat her down and called Teresa over.

"I think Samantha may have overdone it a bit. Would you take her home, Teresa? We have plenty of volunteers so don't worry about coming back to clear up."

"Of course, Father. Come on Samantha, I'll take you home now. You need to put your feet up with a strong cup of sweet tea."

Teresa helped Samantha into the bungalow, stepping over a ladder that had been left in the hallway, made her some tea with an extra spoonful of sugar and sat with her until she felt better.

"Now are you sure you'll be all right. I can wait with you until Paul gets home," Teresa comforted.

"No, I'll be fine, thank you." A little colour had returned to Samantha's parchment cheeks.

As she heard Teresa drive off she picked up her rosary beads and clutched them to her thin chest. She wondered where Paul could be. He had told her that he was going to spend the day at home, pottering with his beloved model railway that he'd retrieved from his parents' home. They had virtually no friends. Paul had become such a loner since they had returned from Mauritius. Still, he was a good, respectable man and she was grateful for that. She went to the fridge to get some milk to pour herself another cup of tea.

"That's funny. The ham's still there," she thought, "I hope Paul's all right. I hope that Kim's okay and..."

Just at that moment she heard the key in the lock and breathed a sigh of relief. Always the dutiful wife, she went into the hall to greet her husband.

Who was this strange woman with the thick red hair standing in the hallway? She looked as shocked to see Samantha as Samantha was to see her

'Where's Paul?' she thought in panic.

The woman looked vaguely familiar. Then it hit her with the force of a steamroller.

It was Paul.

Samantha felt dizzy. She screamed involuntarily as the grotesque woman wearing a wig and women's clothes that looked like those of her late aunt just stared at her like a stranger. The cup of tea crashed to the floor. Her marriage was shattered along with the shards of china.

Paul's secret was out.

8

A FRESH START

Amsterdam was in the past and now Celine was ready for a new life. The flight to Hong Kong was long and tedious but Celine felt optimistic that a different country in which to live would herald in the restoration of her fractured marriage. As the plane was freed from the confines of earth so she started to look forward to the challenge of making her marriage work.

Her travelling companion was a Chinese lady of about fifty who presumed that Celine understood Cantonese as she kept up a constant flow of chatter – undeterred by any lack of response. At meal times she would gaze at her food in disbelief and, having retrieved a pair of chopsticks from her bag, would proceed to place anything that did not take her fancy onto Celine's plate. After much protesting Celine finally gave up, deciding that it must be a custom and something she would have to get used to. In her commodious bag the Chinese woman had some strange, odiferous dried objects wrapped in newspaper which she inspected from time to time before wrapping them up again and placing them reverentially back in the bag. It all helped to pass the time. Much later Celine was to learn that the objects were traditional Chinese medicine.

The landing at Kai Tak Airport was rather alarming as the plane descended between banks of skyscrapers before landing on the runway that jutted out into the harbour. So close were the passengers to the buildings that it was possible to see people hanging out laundry on poles as they leant precariously out of windows. Wanting to close her eyes from sheer terror but mesmerised by the view, Celine gazed upon the scene as the plane landed bumpily. Suddenly excitement replaced her lethargy. Would James be pleased to see her? Would life here live up to all that he had promised her? In his letters he had explained that Hong Kong was an exciting place with many restaurants offering delicious cuisine and with a culture that was just waiting to be explored. But all this was secondary to Celine's expectations. Would he be pleased to hear that he was to be a father?

As she trundled along to collect her luggage, a flashback of the time when James collected her from the airport in Amsterdam hit her. 'That was then, this is now,' she thought as she wheeled her burdensome trolley through the arrivals lounge. She had freshened up with the complimentary toiletries and cologne that BOAC had provided for their passengers and put on a little make-up. The pregnancy was not obvious and, although she was still throwing up most mornings, the doctor had assured her that this would soon pass.

She had not seen James since that fateful day when he stormed out of their apartment. All their communication since then had been by letter or telephone. He had flown straight from Amsterdam to Hong Kong and now she was joining him to hopefully reignite the dying embers of love. She felt her heart lurch as she caught sight of him towering above the multitude of raven haired Chinese crowding the terminal. The noise level was high, as everyone seemed to be yelling and jostling, as if no one knew about personal boundaries. Celine pressed through the melee towards her husband.

"Darling, I've been waiting here for over two hours. Your flight must have been delayed." He greeted her with a kiss on the cheek.

"Sorry. Yes, we were a bit held up at Heathrow. It's good to see you again." She heard herself say rather unconvincingly. She noted that James was not wearing aftershave and was dressed in his usual traditional manner, which reassured her. He had a light tan and looked relaxed, as if nothing had happened between them. This irritated Celine as she was hoping that their split up would have had a degree of wear on him and would have displayed itself on his face. Part of her wanted him to suffer as she had suffered.

They pushed their way through the crowds and out into the car park. The heat and humidity assaulted Celine with a severity that took her breath away. Everywhere was crowded and noisy. Noisy traffic, noisy pedestrians, noisy hawkers selling their wares on the crowded pavements. Rickshaws weaved in and out of the dense traffic, their drivers like stick men with dark leathery skin dressed in singlets and shorts. Celine wondered how the slight figures could pull the weight of fat cats with such speed. She found it distasteful and exploitative but listened as James explained that these people would be grateful for the work. A fish in a foreign pool, she felt disorientated as the culture shock hit her.

A quick crossing on the car ferry took them from Kowloon to Hong Kong Island. Low clouds sat atop the mountains, which were cluttered with skyscrapers. Dusk fell quickly on this journey in her new homeland and Celine gazed at the neon lights that flashed on, illuminating the landscape. James drove into their apartment block in the quieter mid-levels. There was no grass to be seen anywhere – just concrete – soaring, stark concrete.

"Here we are. Jardine Buildings. We're on the twenty first floor." James pressed the button in the lift. He barely made eye contact with Celine and she wondered when it would be the right time to tell him of the pregnancy. Jet lagged and exhausted, she knew it would not be tonight.

The apartment was similar to the one in Amsterdam - characterless and spacious but with one difference; the stunning view of Hong Kong harbour which spread out before her eyes like a feast. She stood on the large balcony for what seemed an eternity, just staring, into the distance. The lights in the harbour caused a blue haze to penetrate the balcony giving it an unreal air. Large ships, like floating towns loomed above the small junks where whole families lived and everywhere lights twinkled along the coastline like some oriental fairy land.

"Wow, what a view!" Celine was transfixed and drank in the panorama. "I see why this place is called the city that never sleeps."

"Yes, it's an exciting city. Want one of these?" James called out as he poured himself a gin and tonic.

"Oh, no thanks but I could do with a cup of tea. I'm going to hop into the shower in a minute but first I must have a quick tour of the flat. Which way to the kitchen?"

James wandered into the kitchen to get some ice for his drink, forgetting to put the kettle on. Celine followed him, curious to see her new accommodation. Off the spacious kitchen was a tiny room, rather like a prison cell, which was furnished with a metal framed bed, a hardback chair and a cupboard. Next to that was a white tiled room with a sink, small shower with a rusty rail around it but no shower curtain and a hole in the floor that served as a toilet.

"Good grief – the bathroom is terrible. How on earth am I supposed to squat down to use that toilet?" Celine was alarmed by the lack of facilities that an executive apartment supplied in an alien land.

"That's the amah's quarters." James remarked dryly.

"Oh, of course, but we don't have an amah do we? You never mentioned - "

"You never asked. Actually we do but ours won't be living in. She's part time and comes in Monday to Friday. You'll meet her tomorrow." James busied himself putting ice into a tall glass.

Celine wandered around the soulless luxury that was her new home, pondering the thought of having an amah, and was relieved to find two bathrooms, each with Western style toilets. She knew that living in such a home was important to James, a sign that he was a success. Looking gratefully at the double bed she turned it down and, in this simple action, remembered the long, curly hair that she'd found on the pillow in Holland. The memory admonished her; made her feel insecure and she wondered if she would ever be able to trust her straying husband again or if their relationship was blighted forever.

Peeling off her clothes she flopped into bed promising herself a shower after her drink but fell into a deep sleep as soon as her head touched the pillow. She awoke nine hours later feeling muzzy and, for a brief moment, wondered where she was. That same familiar dream had haunted her slumbers.

Her hand was pushing the call girl's face into the jagged broken glass on the pavement. Harder, harder – let her feel the pain. She didn't care that the girl was bleeding. Rivulets of blood mingled with her black curly hair causing it to matt with the dust on the pavement, forming a hideous paste on the ground. And still she kept pushing. Unrelenting and without compassion.

Rubbing her eyes as if somehow this would erase the hatred that she feared was causing her heart to become bitter, she reached across the unfamiliar bed for her husband but he was not there. Panic filled her for a moment. Had he abandoned her in this strange land across endless oceans?

"Cup of tea. I made a fresh pot as the other had become rather stewed." A slight grin flicked across his handsome face as he carried in a tray. He had lost weight since she last saw him and his flat belly and slim waist made her wonder if he was working too hard.

'My husband. The man I love. The father of my child,' she thought.

"Sorry, darling – I didn't mean to fall asleep on you like that." She smiled in spite of the ravages of the dream that still seemed so potent.

"I let you sleep as long as I could but I've got to be at work in fifteen minutes and the traffic here is thick. Don't forget that the amah will let herself in at about 10 o'clock. She'll do all the cleaning and so on. There's food in the fridge – see you at about six." His tone was brisk, his sky blue eyes difficult to read.

"Okay. Er, what's the amah called?"

"Ah Foo. Oh and don't drink the water from the tap. There's some boiled water in the fridge." He kissed her swiftly on the forehead and was gone before she could ask him any of the questions that were buzzing in her mind.

Celine sipped her tea and tried to figure out if James had any feelings for her at all. And, if he didn't, why on earth had he tried so hard to persuade her to join him at the other end of the earth? A familiar wave of nausea swept over her as she rushed to the bathroom.

Before taking a shower she penned a few lines in her now familiar journal.

So, here I am in the Far East! James has not offered any apologies for his affair in Amsterdam, or shown any emotion at seeing me, so what was all that pleading with me to stay with him about on the phone? None of this makes sense but I am determined to like it here and can't wait to tell James about the baby. But I keep asking myself if I can make him love me.

~ ~ ~ ~ ~ ~

THE COFFEE MORNING

Celine could see why the notice in the bathroom warned her to open the window before running the hot water as a geyser on the wall belched out noxious fumes. She opened the window to an eerie sight; blackness and a huge drop to the ground as the next block of flats was just inches from theirs. Trying not to look into the abyss she slipped into the shower and stood under its refreshing stream for a long time until she felt that the grime of the flight had at last been erased.

Ah Foo arrived punctually at 10 o'clock. Not having experienced the luxury of a servant before, Celine had needlessly tidied the flat and wondered what sort of person this amah would be. Having done this she felt foolish, realised that she was apprehensive and hoped that they would get on well. It was important to Celine that her home would be harmonious. Would she feel as if the stranger was an intruder in her new home or would the domestic help be a God send?

It certainly felt too hot to be doing housework and cooking. The air was sodden with the high humidity so that the slightest movement induced a sweat that did not seem to evaporate.

The amah was dressed in traditional black baggy trousers and a white cotton Mandarin collared top. It was hard to identify her age as, apart from a cobweb of fine lines around her eyes, she seemed wrinkle free but her long hair, which was worn in a pigtail, was turning grey and thin on top. She was small and slightly built.

"Morning Missie. I Ah Foo. I cook flied lice and pork for you and Master tonight. Been market –got good choi sum." She proceeded to produce some fresh greens from a roll of newspaper written in busy Chinese characters that she had been carrying in a fluorescent pink plastic string bag.

Celine must have looked suitably impressed as this was followed by a large, grin highlighted by two flashing gold teeth.

"Thank you Ah Foo. Er, what time does Mr., I mean Master, normally have his supper?" The word master seemed to stick in her throat like a loathsome object.

This question was followed by a rapid explanation which Celine found difficult to understand as words like chicky liver and no likey were interspersed with cackling laughter. Celine just nodded her head, hoped that she smiled at the appropriate time and decided to take things as they came along. She was sure that she was going to like Ah Foo, even if communication might prove to be a challenge.

Disappearing into the kitchen, the amah proceeded to wash the floor with gusto leaving Celine standing there wondering how on earth she was going to spend her time in this new place. Feeling disorientated, she made for the bedroom and unpacked her two suitcases methodically, hanging her clothes in colour order in the much appreciated, large walk in closet. Colour coding her clothes was automatic since working in the fashion business. That done, she wondered how she would manage to fill her days until motherhood would keep her busy. A wave of loneliness engulfed her; she had no friends to phone. No one to visit in this vast, unfamiliar city.

Before she had time to feel sorry for herself or regret flying across the world to join James, the phone by the bedside rang.

"Hello. You must be Celine - hope you had a good trip. I expect you're jet lagged. I'm Octavia, the wife of James's boss. I've got a few of the girls coming round this morning. How about I pick you up in about an hour and you can get to know some of us?" The voice was confident, plummy but not unfriendly.

"Oh, that would be lovely. Do you know where we live?"

"Of course. I'll come up and just check that your amah is up to scratch."

Having found a navy dress that looked cool enough for the stifling heat, she dressed hurriedly before throwing a few things in a matching blue handbag. She was looking forward to meeting some new faces – all part of the fresh start. Here nobody knew about her past. She could be whoever she wanted to be.

Octavia floated into the apartment carrying a bouquet of waxy pink flowers and reeking of Miss Dior. She was slim, lightly tanned and attractive in a horsey sort of way.

"Welcome to Hong Kong. These are for you." She smiled at Celine with her mouth but not quite her eyes.

"Put these in water for Missy." She commanded, looking the servant up and down with an experienced eye at the same time inspecting the flat, no doubt looking for any tell tale signs of dust.

"You back lunchy Missy?" The amah, nursing the flowers like a wedding bouquet, enquired of her new boss.

"No, she'll be having lunch with me." There was no arguing with Octavia.

As they made their way across the car parking area, a driver wearing a grey uniform, his face expressionless, jumped out of the car and opened the passenger doors for Octavia and Celine who, by now was feeling slightly intimidated by this colonial wife.

"Back to Chater Mansion, Wong Lee, but go past So Kee Store on the way."

"Yes Missy." And with that they swept out of the drive and into the soup of traffic that was part of life in Hong Kong.

So Kee Store was a small shop situated in a busy area and seemed to sell everything from matches to sacks of rice. Shelves were piled precariously with groceries and youths wearing vests, shorts and flip flops scurried about filling cardboard boxes while a Chinese matron with a severe haircut barked orders at them in rapid Cantonese.

Upon seeing Octavia enter she smiled in recognition.

"You want take order away now?" she asked her at the same time as writing on a note pad and answering the phone.

"No, this is Mrs Smedley. Her husband has opened an account with you and now Mrs Smedley will be placing telephone orders with you." Octavia announced this with an air of boredom and Celine wondered how many other naive wives she'd introduced to this new way of life.

"This my phone number. You phone – we deliver within one hour. Close 10 o'clock night time. Only shut three days each year - Chinese New Year." These sound bites were delivered like machine gun fire before Mrs So Kee returned to her relentlessly ringing phone.

The business connection complete, Celine was whisked back to the car which was parked illegally on the pavement and causing a traffic jam which prompted much honking of horns. Wong Lee seemed to be oblivious to the disruption that was being caused and was dozing behind the wheel, his peaked cap falling over one eye.

Unperturbed, Octavia smoothed out her dress as she sat next to Celine in the back of the Mercedes and regaled her with the pitfalls of life in Hong Kong.

"Always look through the peep hole before opening the door of your flat. You can't trust anyone these days. Hong Kong isn't what it used to be." Celine listened intently as she gazed at the crowds scurrying about like ants on a mission.

At last they arrived at a mansion in its own gardens in the affluent Peak District. It felt slightly cooler if rather damp and a gentle mist enveloped the top of the mountain. As they got out of the car and entered a spacious hall way Celine was enthralled by the antique black lacquer furniture which stood formally against the walls. Chinese silk rugs were scattered on highly polished floors and exquisite porcelain graced tables and display cabinets. A medicinal smell of camphor wood permeated the air.

"Sit down Celine - you must be exhausted." Octavia waved a manicured hand at a rather formal sofa carved out of rose wood and upholstered in red silk.

The door bell rang and within minutes a young amah, dressed in the same type of uniform as Ah Foo but looking like a China doll ushered four ladies into the drawing room – three English who were in their late thirties and one Chinese of indeterminate age. All were wives of James's work colleagues.

Introductions followed and, after a few formalities, each one, with the exception of Sandra, the Chinese girl, chatted with some animation about the difficulties of finding good servants. Celine felt as out of place as if she'd just arrived from the planet Zog and listened in amazement. She noticed that Sandra did not speak much but would smile knowingly at Celine from time to time as if in sympathy.

"Jolly good. Refreshments. Hand them round Ah Ping," Octavia commanded. She looked as cool in her immaculate cream linen dress and pearls as Celine felt hot and crumpled.

Instead of coffee, tall glasses were offered, each containing ice and a slice of lemon. Celine was looking forward to a cool glass of lemonade on such a hot day.

"Now, Celine, you must join the Ladies' Recreation Club. You'll find it an absolute necessity, as you don't have a garden. There's a good restaurant there as well as a pool and some tennis courts. We go there all the time. Tell you what, I'll get Ah Wong to take you past on the way home so that you can put your name down. Welcome to Hong Kong!" Octavia raised her glass and everyone took a grateful sip of the nectar.

Taking an unladylike swig, it was only after she'd swallowed it that Celine realised that coffee mornings in Hong Kong were going to be rather different to those in the West.

Her glass contained a hefty gin and tonic.

She slept for two hours that afternoon then, still feeling groggy, pulled her journal out of her handbag. Her pen seemed to write of its own accord.

It's early days but I'm not sure that I'm going to like being an expat. I need some direction and so called coffee mornings are definitely not for me. And why did James get me to come all this way to Hong Kong only to be so distant with me? I hope that when I tell him about our baby that he will change. And I can't leave it too long because he will notice the swelling in my belly! Also, my bust has gone up a size and that can't be a bad thing. Maybe I can find a job or I'll go crazy.

CHOPSTICKS

Sandra phoned Celine the following day, speaking in the clipped Cantonese accent that Celine was already becoming accustomed to.

"Hi there. It was good to meet you at Octavia's. I wondered if you would like to come out for lunch tomorrow. No point trying to park so we'll get taxi into town and I'll take you to good restaurant. Okay."

"That would be great. What sort of time?" Celine found herself smiling at the thought of having a Chinese meal with someone who knew about the local food.

"I'll come tomorrow at half twelve. The food is excellent there and I'll show you how to use chopsticks unless you know already."

Sandra was on time and had a taxi waiting outside for them. It was not far to the Central District but took a while to get to their restaurant because the traffic was chaotic as usual. Although Sandra had a strong accent she spoke English well and told Celine that she was married to a Scot who worked in James's department. She was attractive and had pulled her long shiny black hair into a ponytail. Her creamy skin was devoid of makeup but she wore expensive jewellery.

Celine watched Sandra elbowing her way through the crowds and decided to follow suit, as nobody seemed to mind. They entered an enormous restaurant that was already heaving with customers. It was so noisy that Sandra shouted, "We'll sit here."

Immediately a waitress arrived at their table bearing a huge teapot and filled a couple of glasses with fragrant jasmine tea.

"Mm goi," Sandra responded.

Then to Celine she said, "First word you must learn. Say it after me – it means thank you."

"Mm goi," Celine mimicked feeling pleased that she was part of the scene if only in a small way.

"Very good. Now say 'Nei ho ma?' – that means, 'How are you?'" Sandra encouraged her.

Celine repeated the phrase and wondered if she would ever learn this strange sounding language.

"You want me to order – do you like chicken?" Sandra asked pulling her short skirt down without success over her slim knees.

"Yes, that's fine. I like everything. Well, except tripe - I can tell I'm in expert hands."

"No food here not tripe, very good quality." Sandra looked shocked.

Celine wondered if she had insulted her new friend, "Er, no, that's not what I mean. Tripe is cow's stomach lining, I think. It used to be popular in England at one time. Sorry I should..."

"No problem. I not heard of this cow stomach but we Chinese eat all bits of animal."

The waitress was called over and took an order that was barked at her in rapid Cantonese. She wrote on a small pad of paper, her face completely blank. Within minutes a round bamboo container appeared on the white starched table cloth and Sandra removed the lid. Soon a fragrant steam greeted their nostrils.

"This is dim sum. Many sorts - this one's steamed dumplings with pork and it's very tasty. Now this is how you must hold your chopsticks." Sandra proceeded to coach Celine in the art of using chopsticks that was not as simple as it looked.

Clumsily Celine practised until she actually managed to get a dumpling from the basket into her bowl without dropping it. She was having fun.

Dish after dish followed. Fish steamed in ginger, sticky rice, crispy lemon chicken and all the while the jasmine tea was topped up and drunk. Sandra chatted easily as she ate, at times holding the bowl just under her chin as she shovelled rice into her mouth with her chopsticks. The last dish was a clear soup that tasted slightly fishy. Sandra's slight frame belied her gargantuan appetite as she ate frantically. Looking around, Celine noticed that all the other customers were eating as if it was to be their last meal. The only Westerner there, she felt as if she was watching a play from the audience as the scene played out before her foreign eyes. She noticed that as soon as people had finished eating they left – another custom that she would eventually take for granted.

A waiter scooped a large fish from a tank at the far end of the restaurant with a practised flourish of his net.

"What is that waiter doing?" Celine asked.

"Customers choose fish from tank and now waiter will take it into kitchen to be cooked. Really fresh so it's best way."

As Celine pondered this she realised that it was an understatement. She was also aware that she had a lot to learn about this fascinatingly foreign place. It made Holland seem like an English county.

The girls got on well and Celine was surprised at how open and easy to talk to Sandra was.

"How long have you been married to Angus?" She ventured.

"We've been married for six years but I'm not happy. Angus drinks too much and doesn't come home until late at night. Hong Kong is a bad place for British men. They do what they want." Sandra looked downcast.

Celine's heart sank and she wondered if this was the right place for them to make a fresh start. Suddenly the heat, the smell of food and the noise enveloped her and she wanted to get out. Trying to remain calm she looked over to her new friend, "I'm sorry to hear that. I hope you can work it out. Look, I ought to be getting back. Shall we get the bill, and then perhaps you could show me where to find a taxi rank. Thank you so much for bringing me here." She fumbled in her bag for her purse.

"Already paid for. No problem. I'll take you to find taxi but be prepared to wait, as it is always busy. You're a nice person so we can be friends. Okay?"

"Okay!" Celine responded with a smile. "I must go to the loo after all that tea though."

Sandra took her through the throng to a small toilet at the back of the restaurant. As she sat gratefully on the Western style toilet she heard the most appalling sounds coming from the washing area. It was a cross between a freight train and strangling.

As she came out she saw an elderly Chinese lady clearing her lungs and spitting unselfconsciously into the basin before leaving. This was another custom that she would have to get used to. Sandra explained that it was normal to clear the lungs in such a way and not considered rude. However, she warned, "Never use a tooth pick without covering your mouth with your hand. This is considered very bad manners."

However much Celine tried to go Dutch on the meal she could not persuade Sandra to take any money but was soon to find out that this was typical Oriental hospitality. The custom was that next time Celine would pay.

The two young women made their way through the frenetic activity of Central district to join a long queue for a taxi. The meal sat heavily in Celine's stomach and her friend's words weighed even more on her mind. "Hong Kong is a bad place for British men." She wondered if James would be an exception and wished that her trust in him could be as strong as it was before they had moved to Holland.

That night she demonstrated her chopstick skills to James but it seemed that he already was accomplished in the art and was not that impressed.

"How long have you been using them?" She asked her husband.

"Ever since I got here. I've even managed to eat snake with them. Quite tasty really – it was a bit like chicken."

James never ceased to surprise her.

She now made jottings in her journal most days.

TEA AT SAM'S

Sandra is a likeable person and not like the other wives that I met at Octavia's who all seemed rather competitive and snobbish. Maybe I can take a Chinese cookery class or something to make myself useful. James loves it here and I hope that I will too.

9

R AND R

All that Celine had gleaned from the so called coffee morning at Octavia's Hong Kong mansion was that there was no way that she was going to fit into the role of a colonial wife, and so she decided to look for a job as Ah Foo had relieved her of any domestic responsibility. She was grateful that the morning sickness had disappeared, although James had never noticed her suffering, but she was used to that. Her old zest for life was returning and she felt healthy and optimistic.

Scanning the pages of the South China Morning Post she came across an advert.

"Models Required for Wig Showroom."

As she thought about it, the position seemed increasingly suitable. The hours were short and so she felt she could cope with the job during her pregnancy and if she was to model wigs, for photographs perhaps, then her bump would not be an issue. There was no mention of pay or details about the job, but she thought she would give them a ring before she lost her nerve.

Celine gripped the telephone in anticipation, deciding that if nobody answered then she would not bother phoning again. Part of her hoped that there would be no one there but after only three rings a cheery voice with a thick New York accent answered the phone.

"The Wigasun, how may I help you?"

An interview was arranged the next day, which gave her time to do something with her hair and nails. She had never modelled before and thought she was being rather presumptuous in applying for the job. Remembering an advert that she had seen in the South China Morning Post for Jane's Home Beauty Service, she cut it out and put it in a drawer, promising herself a treatment when she had time.

The next day dawned hot and humid - a typical Hong Kong sultry day. Usually brisk in her movements, she was learning to move slowly in the heat and so gave herself plenty of time to get to the interview. Sitting on the Star Ferry, which went to and fro between Hong Kong Island and Kowloon that was joined to mainland China, she gazed at the splendid harbour before queuing for disembarkation. Standing at least six inches taller than the average Chinese, she felt every inch the foreigner as she was swept along on the bustling Nathan Road. The crowds were so thick that it was impossible to walk at any other speed than the one set by the teeming mass.

The showroom was in the busy main shopping area of Kowloon and was situated in one of the many high rise buildings, on the first floor up above a shop. Pop music was blaring out, the walls had been decorated with silver foil and, to add to the funky look, psychedelic posters covered the walls. A flamboyantly dressed, extrovert American couple, Buffy and Simon, greeted her. As she became accustomed to their accents she realised that the place was not called the Wigasun but The Wiggy Scene. They didn't want to know about her previous work experience and enthusiastically asked if she could start work the following day when all would be revealed. Maybe she was mesmerised by the décor and the hypnotic music, but she agreed.

Full of enthusiasm, Celine arrived punctually the next day. She had shared her news with James the night before but he seemed more interested in reading the paper and so she gave up. The Wiggy Scene was electric with activity as pop music thumped away in the background as twelve European girls chattered excitedly. Buffy, wearing a long blonde wig and a pink cat suit called them to order and explained the format for the day.

The job entailed modelling different types of expensive wigs, which were all the rage at the time. As the wigs were not made from natural hair, they had an unreal sheen as if they'd been dipped in metallic paint. The girls spent an hilarious half hour trying on the merchandise and joking with each other. So far, it all sounded very easy and too good to be true.

It was.

Next came the crunch. The girls were told to go out onto the streets in pairs while two of them stayed in the showroom. Those on the streets were instructed to stop any G.I.s and persuade them to come up to the Wiggy Scene for a free drink. There the two remaining models would meet them. Effortlessly, they would sell them wigs. Of United States military men there was no shortage roaming the streets of downtown Kowloon. The controversial Vietnam War was still raging and Hong Kong was a popular destination for the battle weary and often disillusioned soldiers to have R and R. This stood for rest and recreation. There was not much rest involved but a lot of recreation - most of it spent in the local bars and brothels.

Realising the implications and the memory of the Red Light District of Amsterdam still raw, Celine was the first to speak up.

"Surely we can't stop soldiers on the streets - they'll think we are escorts, or worse. They won't want to buy wigs." The others were unanimous in their agreement.

They were assured that everything was above board and that all they had to do was offer the soldiers a drink and they would be putty in their hands. They would be begging the girls to sell them wigs for their women folk back home. Not wishing to be a spoilsport, Celine thought she'd at least give it a try but insisted that she would not go on the streets but would stay behind in the relatively safe territory of the showroom. Those who were game were sent out like lambs to the slaughter. And so it was that she remained in the showroom with Melissa, another English girl, a professional model who had appeared in British magazines. Celine had made another friend, as there was plenty of time to chat while they waited for the unsuspecting customers to arrive. She learned that Melissa was married to a ship's engineer called Simon and had been living in Bombay. It was there that she had been involved in the film industry and had played the role of the gin swigging memsahib in many a Bollywood movie. She was confident, outgoing and chatty and Celine was sure that she could sell ice cream to Eskimos. Wigs to servicemen would be a doddle for her.

After about an hour of listening to tales of India, her attention was broken by footsteps and loud banter as six G.I.s sauntered into the show room chewing gum and looking expectant.

"Is this the Wigasun?" one of them asked.

"Yes, this is the Wiggy Scene – come in!" They greeted their first potential customers with enthusiasm and offered them a seat. A soldier, who looked as if he should still have been in high school, gazed at Celine like a hungry puppy.

"I haven't spoken to a round eyed girl for over a year." He was almost drooling.

The look in his eyes was telling her that wigs were the last thing on his mind. Feeling embarrassed and rather sorry for him, she offered him and his fellow soldiers a free drink, which they readily accepted. They had been used to paying inflated prices for drinks in the girlie bars. The battle weary soldiers sat down to relax and wait for what was on offer. Melissa appeared from behind a screen wearing a blonde wig and started to present her audience with her well rehearsed sales patter, while Celine disappeared behind the screen to sport a short black wig. As she was tucking her thick hair into the constraining hairpiece she could hear loud groans and complaints coming from the showroom. Oh dear, it was as she expected. Their bitter disappointment had not made them desperate to buy wigs but rather to leave the premises in search of some fun elsewhere.

At home that night Celine was keen to share the day's events with James. She recounted every detail over dinner and waited for his response; half hoping that he would be shocked and forbid her to go back again.

"What do you want me to say?" He drawled.

"Well, do you approve of me working there?"

"Do what you want. You keep saying that you haven't got enough to do here. Subject closed, all right?" He got up from the table and switched on the television, putting an end to any further discussion.

All right, so she would go back and make the most of her dubious employment.

The same pattern repeated itself at the Wiggy Scene over a number of days. On the third day only half of the team turned up for work and, at the end of the week, they had stopped serving whiskey and soda but orange juice and lemonade was offered instead. Buffy and Simon were looking worried. It seemed that their business strategy had failed dismally.

Payday arrived and still not a single sale had been made. The remaining models, or rather sales girls, asked about their wages - a subject that their bosses had been carefully avoiding.

"I'm really sorry gals but we haven't made any money so we can't pay you. However, you can each have three wigs if you like - just take your pick. There's a really big selection."

Each of the models noisily selected their 'payment' and left, never more to return to The Wigasun, otherwise known as the Wiggy Scene.

But Celine was philosophical about the experience. She had forged new friendships, some which were to continue for the duration of her time in Hong Kong. Later this would be something that Celine would regret.

What a week, she wrote in her journal, *it's a whole new world out there and rather exciting. I enjoy the company of my new model friends and haven't laughed so much since I was at school. These girls are more fun than the colonial wives and are not interested in the quality of servants or who they met at the club. The colonials speak a language that I cannot share. Pity I never got paid, but the wigs are better than nothing and already we've agreed to wear them at a party that Melissa is planning. James thinks I've been taken for a ride, which is probably true - but I don't care. I'm beginning to like my life here.*

~ ~ ~ ~ ~ ~

WENDY

James was always such a killjoy at these parties. With frequent regularity someone from the Wiggy Scene would throw an informal, fun and often impromptu bash. As they were getting ready to go to one such event at Melissa and Simon's place, Celine pleaded with James,

"Please stay until the end. You miss all the fun."

"The last do was so boring and you know I hate dancing so what's the point in my staying. You stay as long as you like. I can't bear it when someone gets a guitar out and you all start singing - I've got better things to do," he protested.

As they arrived the music was already belting out a Beatles' number and Melissa looking stunning in a white, backless dress that showed off her deep tan greeted them warmly. A rich aroma of heady spices filled the air, mingled with perfume and aftershave.

"Hi, great to see you. Gin and tonic, James and the usual orange juice for you?" Melissa was the perfect hostess.

"Yes, please. Celine used to drink the odd glass of wine but lately she's gone completely tee total for some reason." James sounded irritated and Celine detected a note of scorn in his voice. She realised that she'd have to break her news to him soon to explain why she was not drinking alcohol. Besides, she was excited now and wanted to share her circumstances with all her friends. Her husband should be the first to hear of the pregnancy.

"There's a curry buffet on the table. Help yourselves." Melissa indicated the food. "The curries have turned out well, but the chapattis

are a bit on the tough side - just dip them in the sauce, Indian style."
She announced this without apology.

Melissa's curries were delicious, made from authentic recipes taken from her sojourn in Bombay.

"Thanks Melissa, I'll just wash my hands if I may." Sighing, Celine went to the bathroom just off the large living room, retouched her lipstick and adjusted the blonde wig that was her payment for working at the Wiggy Scene and which was feeling rather tight. She wondered if she looked pregnant and if anyone had guessed her secret.

It was as they were balancing their plates on their laps and savouring the spicy food that Celine got a surprise that would change her life forever.

Melissa, always the extrovert, was wearing a blue and pink Afro style wig the night that Billy turned up with his date at her party.

He was a tall, good looking Scot who was rather fond of the whiskey. He never seemed to have a regular girl friend - probably because he was too fond of the whiskey. Billy worked for a large banking organisation and was introduced to Celine by Melissa and Simon. The three friends had been based in Bombay in the late sixties and continued their friendship in Hong Kong. Whenever there was a party, Billy was there. Usually, at around one in the morning Billy would sit, nursing his Scotch in a world of his own. He seemed a sad, lonely figure amidst the merry making.

But tonight was different. He arrived with a glamorous date.

At first, Celine did not realise who he was accompanying until a familiar voice called out, "Hey, you two what have I done to you for you to ignore me?" She laughed as she greeted them both with her slight North Country accent.

"Wendy – what on earth are you doing here? I haven't seen you since Amsterdam." Celine was the first to speak up.

"Duncan's company has posted him here but, as usual, he's away. Taiwan this time and so Billy told me about a curry party and I couldn't resist. What are you doing here? And what's this with all the strange wigs?" Her eyes twinkled with mischief like a fifteen year old who had been let out for the night.

"Celine worked for about a week for a ridiculous wig company. I've got a posting here. Great, isn't it?" James's eyes seemed fixed on Wendy's cleavage.

That night James stayed until the end of the party and didn't leave Celine to find her own way home, something that she had done several times, rather than miss the fun. But tonight, after midnight, when the lights were dimmed, they had a slow dance, much to her delight. She melted in his arms, the tiny unborn baby between them and she wondered if she should tell him the news when they got home.

By one in the morning Billy had disappeared. No one had seen him for over an hour and the party was definitely over.

People had started to wend their way home; the music had been turned low. Apart from Wendy and Celine the only remaining guest was James who by then, was a little drunk and uncharacteristically chatty.

"Stay the night. We've plenty of room and it would be fun for us to go to the Hilton for a slap up breakfast in the morning," Melissa offered with enthusiasm. "Some of us are going to the beach tomorrow so we can all meet up at Repulse Bay in the afternoon."

"No, I'll get a taxi thanks. Duncan's on an early flight back tomorrow and I really should be there to greet him. Don't know what's happened to Billy. He was completely pissed, so probably just wandered off home. Thanks for a great party. Good to see you two again looking so well. Small world." And with that Wendy left after blowing a kiss to them all, leaving a waft of perfume behind her.

Melissa insisted that Celine and James stay and so they made their way to a spare room with its heavy rosewood furniture.

"The bed's made up and you have an en-suite bathroom. Use any toiletries you need. Sleep tight."

James took Celine in his arms and, for the first time since her arrival in Hong Kong, made passionate love to her. They fell asleep in each other's arms and Celine felt content and confident that their marriage would work out. Their baby would have a happy home after all.

In the morning Celine woke at about eight and, not wishing to wake James, didn't use the en-suite bathroom but decided to take a shower in the main bathroom off the living room. As she wandered in she yelped in surprise.

There he was. Billy.

He was fast asleep sitting on the lavatory. He must have been there all night.

She recalled that she had not said goodbye to him when the party was over. Unfazed by all this she walked over to Billy and shook him awake. This took a while, as he was quite hung over. Then she left him to have a shower and find his way to the kitchen for some strong coffee.

Half an hour later Billy joined them all for a caffeine laden drink, red eyed and disorientated.

"Aren't you working this morning?" Simon asked him.

"Yes," he replied thickly, looking worried.

He had the befuddled air of someone who had mislaid a valuable item.

"I have the branch keys in my pocket but I can't remember which bank I have to open up."

He left them none the wiser in search of a bank with a queue of staff and customers trying in vain to get in.

It was a rather subdued group of four that made its way to the hotel for a hearty American breakfast.

When she got home later on that afternoon James went for a rest and she sat in the shade on the balcony and wrote in her journal:

I am so thrilled that James was attentive last night and feel sure that he really loves me. Any day now I'll tell him about our baby. It was weird seeing Wendy again - small world. I hope she doesn't tell James about my date with Marcus. I must have a word with her soon about that, although I did nothing wrong, especially compared with what James got up to.

10

BREAKING NEWS

It was during a typhoon that Celine broke the news to James about the pregnancy.

The first storm warning had been issued on the radio and she felt a mixture of frightened anticipation and dread. When the third warning was announced she phoned So Kee store to stock up on provisions, not forgetting candles, matches and thick sticky tape. After each item was ordered the same question was asked by the shopkeeper, "And then....?"

The only time an order had been incorrect was when she ordered Brasso to polish the metal legs on a campaign table. A brush used for cleaning a baby's feeding bottle arrived in its place. Celine supposed "Brasso" sounded the same as "Brusho" to Chinese ears. The item was changed within an hour; such is the efficiency of the Oriental entrepreneur. As usual, the delivery was brought to the door in lightening time by a Chinese youth wearing the customary shorts, vest and flip-flops. He never wore a smile and was always expressionless. After a while she gave up trying to get any response. Smiling was not part of the service. Celine checked the order carefully to see that the all-important sticky tape had been delivered. It had.

When the fifth warning came it was clear that Ah Foo was not coming to work and James thought it wise to stay at home. Celine had a feeling that the enforced time that they would have alone together would be a good opportunity to break the news to him.

But first she had to carefully apply the sticky tape to the windows.

"Stick each piece diagonally to prevent the windows blowing in," Octavia had instructed her.

The heat and humidity had become even more oppressive than usual as the pressure built up. Gentle zephyrs had changed to obstreperous winds within a matter of hours.

Then the rain started.

It descended from furious clouds in great sheets causing flooding and havoc. A mauve mist hung over the harbour as boats made their way to the refuge of the typhoon shelters.

'Hong Kong. Fragrant Harbour in Chinese. Where commerce rules; where work is god.' Celine mused as she finished applying the last piece of tape. She had learned a lot about this new, alien culture and was beginning to admire the industrious nature of the local people who only stopped work at Chinese New Year and during typhoons - playing mahjong and eating, both favourite pastimes. By the time the seventh storm warning was issued, anyone foolhardy enough to be outside would be risking their life. All boats would be safely moored in the specially constructed typhoon shelters but anyone unlucky enough to live in a shanty on a rooftop could say goodbye to their flimsy home. Refugees from China would swim in shark infested waters with nothing except the shorts and tee shirts that they escaped in and would sometimes live in cardboard shelters until they had earned enough to rent a bed space. Such was the cost of freedom. Many lost their lives in those dark waters. The ex pats were the lucky ones, safe in their tower blocks. Celine was still shocked by the contrasts of wealth and poverty. But, she had heard stories of refugees becoming wealthy, influential business people and admired their courage.

Celine and James stood mesmerised looking out of their sitting room window and down into the large communal car park as small, uprooted trees and wayward garbage blew about in the screaming gale. It was good to be in a building that was substantial even though it was thirty storeys high.

"Want a cup of tea?" She asked him with a gentle smile.

"Yes, that would be nice. Thanks."

He followed her into the kitchen and on impulse Celine put her arms around his neck. Now was the time.

"Darling, I have some wonderful news."

"Oh, did you get another job?" he ventured.

"No, better than that. I'm pregnant." The wind outside shrieked as she waited for his response.

After a weighty silence he responded. "Are you sure? I thought you were using birth control." He looked at her in disbelief, his body suddenly tense.

"Well it obviously didn't work. I'm three months pregnant and all is well." She felt him unwrap her arms from around his neck, the first sign of rejection. Instinctively, she knew that there would be more to follow.

"Why didn't you tell me before – we could have got rid of it. Can't you have a hot bath and a gin or something?" His eyes were cold with latent anger.

"I don't want to get rid of it. What are you trying to do to us? A child will be wonderful James." She grabbed his hands as if willing him to understand and wished that she sounded more convincing. He just shook his head from side to side, his face dark with fury. She dropped her hands to her sides, her body slumping in a gesture of hopeless resignation.

"God – I don't believe this." And with that he stormed into the sitting room and poured himself a stiff whiskey, which he downed in one gulp before pouring himself another. Celine went into the bedroom, lay on the lonely bed and cried bitter tears of disappointment. He did not follow her. She knew from experience that tears did not affect him. He had never offered her comfort or consolation, even when her father had died. She wondered if he ever felt any emotions or, if they had been buried so deep that he didn't know how to find them.

And still the typhoon raged outside as they spent the remaining hours of the storm in the prison of their marriage. They skirted around each other like caged animals waiting to be released into who knows what.

Evil black clouds obliterated the harbour view and the rain fell as thick as fingers leaving devastation in its wake.

The worst of the typhoon's frantic activity only lasted a day but the ensuing rain and wind continued for longer. Then came an eerie stillness as if nature had exhausted itself. They were both relieved when James returned to work. The silence between them had been deafening.

When life returned to a semblance of normality, the radio brought stories of casualties and death - mainly of poor fishermen or those living in shacks in this millionaire's paradise. James was now speaking to Celine but only in monosyllables, his mouth in a permanent sulk. He did not mention the baby and acted as if their conversation had not happened.

They decided to venture out into the now soundless air. As they drove over potholes, James avoided fallen trees, mud slides and debris. But this was nothing compared to the apocalyptic sight that assaulted them as they turned into a nearby residential area.

"My God, where's the hillside? Where're the flats?" Celine shrieked. She felt sick as she looked up to see that the familiar mountainside had disappeared.

James swung the car round as a roadblock prevented them going any further.

He looked ashen with shock. "Landslide. It's taken another block with it."

"Oh, James. Who could survive that? Please, let's just go home. This is terrible." Involuntarily, she placed her hands over her belly as if to protect her baby from what could have been.

James called into So Kee Store on the way home to buy a South China Morning Post. Breaking news - the front page screamed out. A whole section of mountainside had collapsed, taking with it a sky scraper block of inhabited apartments. As this horror went tumbling down the mountain like an unruly domino, it took with it another block of apartments in the road below, killing hundreds of people.

Celine cried as she tried to imagine what panic, shock and suffering must have taken place that fateful day when the typhoon struck. Eventually, the debris and bodies were cleared and the mountainside concreted over like some macabre icing over a ruined cake.

It was just after these events that James was offered another promotion and an even larger apartment. The concreted mountainside was right next door, a constant reminder of what had happened during that terrible typhoon.

As a matter of courtesy Celine showed the apartment to Ah Foo, who now worked full time and lived in.

"No missy, me no live here. If move here, I go." Ah Foo was uncharacteristically insistent.

"Why not? You'll have better quarters and it's a much more modern apartment," Celine was curious to know what the problem was.

"Lot dead people nearby. Me no likey. Bad fung shui."

Not wishing to lose Ah Foo, Celine persuaded James to stay put. At least they could agree on something.

Celine hoped that as James became accustomed to the idea of fatherhood that he would soften and at least become resigned to the fact. This was not the case and Celine's desperation increased.

It was time to tell Ah Foo her news of the pregnancy and she hoped that the amah would not object to the extra work that a baby would bring.

"Velly good have baby Missy. I help you look after him. You have number one son – velly lucky."

Very lucky – somehow Celine doubted it but she knew she would love her baby whether it was a number one son or a daughter.

She pondered a little before writing in her journal that evening:

Well, it seems that James is not going to take to fatherhood after all and I just know that he will not like to be seen out with me looking fat. I wonder what I am doing in this marriage, but feel stuck again. All I can hope is that when he holds his baby his heart will melt. I think he has a heart, but sometimes I wonder!

11

KRISTIN

"Mum, Ricki's pushing me." Four year old Nina ran into her mother's bedroom, followed by her six year old brother.

Kristin was carefully applying eyeliner and continued, unperturbed, by her noisy offspring.

"I'm going to count to ten," she placed the top on her eyeliner, "and I want you both to be ready at the door. One, two , thr - "

Both children ran to the front door and waited for their mother to take them to school. Nina's trip only took a few minutes as she attended a play group in the same block of spacious apartments in the Peak District of Hong Kong.

"Just cos you go to big school you think you're it." She told her brother before flouncing off to join her friends, glad to have the last word for a change. Ricki looked at his shoes, too embarrassed to reply in front of Nina's play group leader, a solid Irish woman with a soft heart. The following year Nina would join her brother at Kennedy Road Junior School and have a uniform. In the meantime, he made the most of having the upper hand.

"I've just got to go back to the flat for my work box, Ricki. Hurry up or we'll be late." Kristin chivvied her son to the lift to take them from the fifteenth floor down to their ground floor apartment.

Ricki was used to his mother working and didn't mind, as she was always there to collect him from school in the afternoon. Following Kristin into the bedroom, he watched her go through the large, white plastic box with a handle that contained the tools of her trade. Kristin smoothed down her uniform, had a quick check in the mirror, then picked up her work box and handbag before hurrying out to the car parking area in front of the apartment block - Ricki running behind her to keep up. The VW Beetle that Harry had bought when they had first arrived in the colony eighteen months previously stood in the large car parking area in front of a small lawn where other expatriate children from neighbouring apartments played in safety.

As usual, the traffic was chaotic but at least summer had not descended. The soupy heat and humidity had the effect of draining Kristin's usual abundant energy if not her enthusiasm.

"Bye sweetheart - have a lovely day." She said loudly before kissing Ricki on the cheek.

"Bye, Mum. And please don't call me that name or kiss me in front of everyone," he whispered before joining the throng of school children making their way up the steps to school.

She smiled, knowing that secretly Ricki loved a kiss and cuddle but she would remember not to show him up in front of his friends again.

Switching from mother to businesswoman was a simple metamorphosis and she was looking forward to another full day of treatments. Before driving off to her first client of the day, she checked the name, address and treatment in her appointment book. Mrs Smedley, leg wax, Conduit Road. Her whole day was carefully mapped out in her mind; the amah would arrive at eleven to clean the flat and collect Nina from nursery school at 1 o'clock. Knowing that one day she'd have her own business, she put all this frenetic activity down to experience. Meanwhile, Kristin was content to beetle around the city meeting old and new clients before collecting Ricki from school and later Harry from work.

Harry enjoyed his walk to the secondary school where he worked as a teacher, but was ready for a lift home at the end of a busy day. It was his first posting abroad and he, his wife and two children had settled in well but he sometimes worried that Kristin was taking on too much with her work schedule. He didn't mind helping with any domestic duties and spent a good amount of time with their children but sometimes Kristin seemed driven by an unexplained ambition. Secretly he was proud of her, but at times he found it hard to keep up with her constant dashing about. Out of all the friends and colleagues that he knew, she was the only wife with a family who worked. But he knew that she would hate the round of coffee mornings and flower arranging classes that most expatriate wives became involved in to fill their long days. No, Kristin was a career woman with vision and had landed a job within weeks of arriving in the colony, working as a mobile beauty therapist for a small outfit called Jane's Beauty Service as part of a team of six therapists.

Harry waited patiently outside the Island School where he worked and wondered what stories would greet him when she picked him up. A considerate man, he was a good listener. At last she arrived, full of apologies and smiles.

"Sorry darling, got held up with a facial lady. She wanted her eyebrows trimming and they were like caterpillars." She continued a stream of chatter all the way home but he didn't mind. He adored her.

They arrived home just as the amah was ready to leave.

"I peel potatoes Missy. Licky playing with friend outside. I go now."

Kristin thanked her amah and fetched a grubby looking Ricki from outside before putting the potatoes on to boil. Sometimes she felt as if one pair of hands was just not enough. She was running a bath for the children and changing out of her uniform at the same time when the phone rang.

It was Jane, asking her to go to the Mandarin Hotel, one of the best of its kind, to give a certain Mrs Jenkins a facial the following day.

"I think this lady is rather important and so I told her that I'd contact my best therapist."

"Well, I'm glad you think so highly of me. Excuse me a minute, Jane. Harry, could you turn off the taps. Sorry about that - it's hectic here as usual. Yes, I'll be there. No problem." Kristin told her boss.

She was looking forward to her visit to the Mandarin Hotel but was still haunted by thoughts of the young woman who had just had her first leg wax earlier that day. As she left Harry to clear up the dinner plates and the children were tucked up in bed, she luxuriated in the shower. The hot needles of water soothed her aching back as she recalled her visit to Celine Smedley. Kristin's job had given her insight into people's moods and she was not fooled by this client's mask of contentment. Her eyes told a different story when she greeted Kristin at the door of the luxury apartment in the Mid Levels.

"Hello, you must be Mrs Smedley." Kristin's smile was wide and friendly.

"Yes, do come in. Please, call me Celine. Where would you like to do the treatment?" She was in her sixth month of pregnancy and looking forward to having smooth legs as she was finding it difficult to shave with the growing baby in her belly.

"I'll use the bedroom if that suits you. " Kristin looked crisp in her white uniform, which complimented her dark skin, and hair, which was cut in short, layers with a wispy fringe.

Celine thought that she had the most beautiful warm eyes, the colour of mature, polished mahogany. "Of course, come on through. Would you like a drink - some tea or perhaps a cold drink?"

"A cold drink would be great. Thank you."

As if by magic an amah appeared from the kitchen wearing a broad grin. "You like ice lemon squash missy?"

"That would be lovely. Thank you." Kristin smiled at the amah as Celine led the way through the large living room into a bedroom that was decorated in varying shades of blue and white.

"Good, you've let the hair grow. With each treatment they'll grow through finer and sparser. It really is worth going through a little discomfort. You are not very hairy so you'll not find this too uncomfortable." Kristin was applying surgical spirit to the area while Celine looked on with fascination.

The wax, which was made from sugar and lemon juice, was spread on thinly and then a calico strip was smoothed over the area, gripping the wax together with the unwanted hair. Before Celine could brace herself, Kristin had whipped off the strip in one clean movement.

"Ouch! That hurt. Sorry to be such a baby but it took me by surprise." Celine laughed.

"Do you want me to continue?" Kristin rubbed the area to alleviate the sting.

"Yes, yes. I've got the birth of the baby to face, so this is nothing." Celine's eyes were still forlorn in spite of the bright smile. "I'm practising breathing and relaxation techniques for the birth so maybe I should do some now."

"You'll be just fine. Whereabouts in England are you from?"

"Originally from Merseyside but my parents moved when I was sixteen." Celine watched, intrigued, as Kristin spread the wax with a wooden spatula.

"You don't sound as if you come from round there - no accent." Kristin stopped waxing for a moment and looked at Celine.

"I know - people seem to think that anyone from around there should sound like the Beatles but actually we don't. Although the Mersey beat has made it sound fashionable I suppose."

Kristin laughed, "Yes. I love the Beatles. Did you ever get to see them?"

"No, but I did hear Gerry and the Pacemakers at the Cavern Club once. My friend and I played hooky one lunch time and sneaked off from school. We were hoping that the Beatles would be on but I think they were touring. We felt really grown up."

"Wow, how exciting - what was it like? The Cavern." Kristin looked impressed.

"Hot, dark, crowded and very noisy. I remember the walls were running with condensation but we loved it. We did a weird type of dance called the Cavern Stomp. Because it was so crowded we had to dance on the spot with our hands by our sides and just scrape one foot and then the other across the floor. We'd both back combed our hair, put on black eyeliner and pale lipstick and changed out of our school uniforms. We thought we looked great but we probably looked like a couple of emaciated zombies. I've never done anything so rebellious since. It was completely out of character - but my friend egged me on. Luckily we didn't get found out or we would probably have been expelled from school and my mother would never let me forget about it. Mm, my legs are looking better already. Do you like living here?"

"Oh yes, it's very exciting and I love my work." Kristin replied.

The girls chatted easily about life in Hong Kong and Celine seemed interested in Kristin's home life, her husband and two young children. Did Kristin detect a slight look of envy in her client's eyes as she recounted her contented home life?

The treatment complete, Celine told her that she would be in touch but Kristin was not to see Celine for quite some time and under very different circumstances.

In the meantime, she was to meet the Jenkins and life would take one of those unexpected turns.

The next day Kristin set off in good spirits to the Mandarin Hotel and was greeted by an elegant, dark haired lady and her tall husband who had shocking red hair and a booming voice. They were Australians who came from Palm Beach, a suburb of Sydney. Relishing her surroundings, Kristin set to work converting the hotel room, which smelled of wealth and cigar smoke, into a temporary salon. She had become adaptable and was used to sitting in uncomfortable positions giving facials to clients who would lie on the bed with their faces where their feet would normally rest. She warmed the cleanser, which felt like liquid velvet, between her palms before applying it to her client's face and throat. Throughout the treatment Mr J looked on intently and talked to Kristin continuously. He told her that they were visiting the colony to remove some valuable antique Chinese porcelain from a vault so that it could be auctioned. Mrs J didn't seem to mind this intrusion and floated in a sea of relaxation as

Kristin tap, tapped around the eye area using an arsenal of anti-ageing products to help disperse the tiny web of crow's feet.

Mr J tipped her generously as she left while Mrs J remained in her cocoon in the makeshift salon. Not expecting to see the Jenkins again, Kristin was surprised when Jane phoned her the following day and asked if she would give Mrs J another facial. Of course she agreed.

Now it just happened that Kristin and Harry's tour in Hong Kong was about to finish and they were considering emigrating to Australia. Harry, who liked the tropics, was keen on going to Queensland and was confident that he would have no trouble finding a job as a geography teacher there. Kristin had mentioned this to the Jenkins and they had whetted her appetite by describing the wonders of Australia and, in particular, Sydney. Apparently the climate was the best in the world and the lifestyle healthy. It sounded wonderfully freeing after several years in the confines of Hong Kong where a blade of grass was a rarity amidst the concrete skyscrapers.

During the facial Mrs J told Kristin that she had been suffering from Bell's palsy that affected one side of her face. She had noticed a slight drooping there but being diplomatic, had not mentioned it to her. It was hard to put an age on her but Kristin guessed that she was in her early forties. With only the slightest Australian accent she told Kristin that the previous day's treatment had brought about an improvement on the side of her face that drooped. Throughout the treatment Mr J continued his running commentary while Mrs J remained mute. He kept extolling the virtues of life Down Under.

"Whadda yu say to joining Mrs Jenkins and me for dinner tonight? We'd like to meet your husband and talk some more about Australia," Mr J asked as Kristin started to pack her beauty products methodically into her work box in preparation for her next client.

Kristin was surprised that they would want to spend their valuable holiday time with a couple of strangers. The Jenkins were returning to Sydney the following day but were keen to treat her and Harry to a meal in the hotel restaurant. Feeling a mixture of excitement and bewilderment, she agreed to join them and rushed home to tell Harry about the encounter and proposal. Always amenable, he agreed to come along.

"Oh, darling, you'll never believe the opulence of The Mandarin - it's gorgeous. What a malarkey - I'm so excited! I'm going to wear this silk outfit - do you think it's smart enough?" Kristin had been rummaging through her wardrobe that consisted mainly of jeans, shorts, cool blouses and work uniforms.

"You'd look fabulous in a sack. Of course that outfit will be fine. Hurry up, that'll be the baby-sitter." Harry had the air of everyone's favourite uncle with his relaxed manner and easy smile. At twenty nine he was beginning to develop a slight paunch, had thick wavy brown hair and hazel eyes, which were etched at the corners with a few laughter lines.

Dressed in their best clothes, the couple headed for the Mandarin Hotel's carvery. Kristin and Harry were welcomed profusely by their new Australian friends and treated to a delicious meal that was served with deference by an attentive waiter. All the while Mr J chatted about Australia and then, to their complete surprise, proposed a business venture. Mrs J was as enigmatic as a buddha throughout and seemed like an observer rather than a participator of the proceedings.

"We have a large plot of land in the Kangaroo Valley. Would you both be prepared to go out there and start up a health farm for us? You'll have free rein and can design the farm and run it how you like," Mr. Jenkins drawled in his thick Aussie accent.

Kristin's eyes widened in disbelief, her heart fluttering with excitement as a thousand questions ran rampant through her head. She glanced over to Harry who smiled benignly before replying.

"Well, it all sounds very interesting but I'm sure you'll appreciate that - "

Mr J interrupted, "I know, I know - give it some thought, eh? No worries. Mull it over and drop us a line when you've decided. Here have some more champagne. This deserves a toast."

They all clinked glasses and Kristin took a sip of champagne but she was already drunk on the idea of running a health farm.

Addresses were exchanged and Kristin assured the Jenkins that they would write back to them as soon as they had made their decision. They left the hotel in a dream like state as if an unknown hand had sealed their fate.

Harry started to do some research about Sydney and the likelihood of him finding a teaching post, but Kristin would have hopped on the first available plane. They talked well into the night every night and, while still mulling over the proposal, a letter arrived from the Jenkins, out-lining their plans. Kristin, in her usual open fashion, had told them that they had no capital but that Harry would get a gratuity from the English speaking school which employed him at the end of his contract which would pay for their fares back to England. That first letter from the Jenkins read as follows:

"We are so pleased to know that you are interested in coming to Australia and perhaps joining forces with us in some way. This is what we suggest. We have, as you know, a three storey house, divided into three self-contained units in Palm Beach, a rather fashionable area, 30 miles from Sydney and comparable perhaps to the Peak or Repulse Bay in Hong Kong. You might consider taking the middle floor, which is quite large, to live in. The lower ground floor unit would be ideal for Kristin to operate an exclusive salon. We have looked into the prospects of an actual shop or shop site and there doesn't seem to be anything quite suitable, at present. However, it is quite likely that the combined efforts of we two couples, when you have had more time to settle in, become known in Palm Beach, and got some initial business off the ground, may result in us buying a site and building, or buying an established beauty salon. There is no doubt in our minds that you would all love this area and it is quite possible that you would have the property to yourselves most of the time.

You could, perhaps feel that this is an elaborate effort to procure a good tenant in yourselves. Tenants we can live without – in fact we could rent any portion of this property tomorrow if we allowed an agent to get his foot in the door.

There will be a gradual build up of business to assist in gathering a clientele suitable for our ultimate beauty farm project. (Important Kristin earmark one or two European or Chinese operators to either bring down with you or consider for a later date). To accommodate them here in Palm Beach no problem and, if necessary, we could perhaps discuss assisted passage.

Obviously you both are going to need to discuss fully the possibilities of potential business and you could perhaps envisage a thriving business from a population of more than 2 million people, with a reasonable opportunity of getting good business within a 4 or 5 mile radius of Palm Beach. Does this give you sufficient incentive to commence along the lines we now suggest?

For a trial period of, say, six months we would only require the nominal rent for the flat ($30 per week) and all takings from the beauty business end of it to be yours.

Please don't think our enthusiasm for a salon has waned. It is simply that we are such novices ourselves that we need your more professional expertise and your own on the spot deliberations with which to embark on this venture.

We trust you are quite able to follow the contents of this letter and would say in conclusion that we will still be very happy to become involved with you both on a business basis. We hope that you will find plenty to think about in this initial offer of ours – let us know your thoughts and reactions soon."

The typed letter was signed in blue ink with a flourishing hand.

By now Kristin and Harry were ready to move to Australia and so Kristin replied to the letter immediately, accepting the Jenkins' offer. In the meantime, Harry's contract with the school where he taught had finished and the small family packed up their belongings and took a long flight back to England. They left Hong Kong in bright sunshine but were greeted by a dismal British November drizzle at Heathrow airport and shivered as they made their way to stay with Harry's parents. Both Harry and Kristin had written from Hong Kong to inform both sets of parents that within two months they would be on their travels again.

Meanwhile the Jenkins replied to Harry's letter. Using many superlatives, they went on to say that they would launch them into Sydney society with cocktail parties and invite the press to announce their arrival. All this was deliciously intoxicating for a couple still in their twenties.

Maybe fools do rush in where angels fear to tread but they made plans to emigrate. Their scant belongings as well as their car were already en route from Hong Kong to Australia so they could not change their minds at this late stage.

Kristin was close to her parents and found it hard saying goodbye to them. She also felt guilty that she was depriving them of their only grandchildren who they had hardly seen since they'd been born. Her mother could not contain her emotion and cried as she hugged her goodbye.

"Don't worry. When we've made our first million we'll pay for you to come and stay with us." Kristin tried to joke but inside her heart ached and she hoped and prayed that she would see her parents again. It suddenly hit her that they were going to the other end of the earth. This was not the same as a tour in Hong Kong with fares paid for by Harry's employer. They were on their own now.

The journey was long and tiring but worth it - Palm Beach was idyllic. The bay shimmered in the sunlight, white sand almost surrounded this paradise and it was pleasantly hot but not humid like the Far East. Surfers rode the bold breakers, at one with their surf boards until a particularly vigorous wave knocked them into the sea. Luxurious homes, resplendent in their secluded gardens, were dotted along the hillsides that swept down to the bay. To their surprise, there were no shops, offices or restaurants to be seen anywhere.

Josephine and Arthur Jenkins greeted them in the garden of their splendid home which was built to nestle into the slopes of Palm Beach and took them down some narrow stone steps into a two bed roomed apartment which overlooked the bay. A narrow path led from the garden at the back of the house down to the beach. It was like a dream. Everything was perfect and tranquil, except for loud barking from the Jenkins' apartment.

"Take no notice - that's just Fred, our loveable Alsatian." Arthur explained.

"Can we play on the beach now? Please Dad." Ricki implored.

"Yes, please Dad," Nina echoed.

"You just make yourselves at home. But don't let the kids go in the sea. Sharks." Mr J tapped his nose.

Kristin shuddered. She'd have to keep a close eye on the children.

Once over their jet lag, they settled into the pristine, open plan apartment and soon Harry had started work as a teacher in Sydney, which was about an hour's drive away. The children were accepted into the small local primary school in Manly and Kristin was told that a school bus would collect them outside the house and bring them home each day. Everybody looked relaxed, friendly and suntanned. In fact, everyone looked very healthy which was put down to the climate and the outdoor life. Their car was delivered within days and they just had their crate of belongings to arrive and they would have all they needed. It seemed odd not to have a radio or record player and they would have to save up for a television set. But the flat was furnished with the bare essentials and they would manage.

The future was looking bright. They were young entrepreneurs. It all seemed almost too good to be true.

~ ~ ~ ~ ~ ~

I SPY

Josephine asked Kristin to take the short trip up the garden steps to her apartment as soon as the children started school - she was eager to have her first facial in the comfort of her home. Feeling excited that her new career move was in action; Kristin donned a white overall and rang the doorbell. Josephine floated to the door wearing a luscious silk embroidered kimono and ushered her into the sitting room where a couch, covered in white towels was waiting. Kristin enjoyed giving her only client a facial and wondered how long it would be before she would have more queuing at the door of the basement flat that was to be her salon. In the meantime, Josephine made it clear that she would like a treatment every day, except weekends, and she paid generously after each visit. After the first treatment, Arthur ceased his hovering and Josephine and Kristin managed to have the occasional, if stilted chat. Kristin, who normally found it so easy to talk to anyone, felt strangely inhibited by this frosty client's demeanour and she almost wished that Arthur would resume his bustling presence. Meanwhile, she wanted to offer Josephine the best treatments, determined to help her thaw and become just a little more real. As Kristin was removing a face mask Josephine decided to speak.

"As I think I told you at our first meeting in Hong Kong, I was brought up in China. My amah put opium under my thumb nail when I was little. It kept me quiet," she spoke in her usual laconic way.

Maybe it has stayed in your bloodstream, Kristin mused.

"Oh, I hope that Nina and Ricki aren't too noisy. I'm afraid I can't resort to opium."

But her joke was met with a heavy silence.

"Do you and Arthur have any children?" She was determined to be friendly.

There was a pause, "No."

As Kristin applied moisturiser as a conclusion to the facial, she viewed the opulence of the enormous sitting room. It shouted wealth. Under foot, the thick cream carpet was a perfect foil for Persian rugs. Mahogany antiques were strategically placed as if ready for an appearance in a House and Garden Magazine, Chinese porcelain was tastefully displayed and all around oil paintings surrounded by ornate gilt frames adorned the walls. This is more of a museum than a home, Kristin thought to herself. The Jenkins seemed to be very rich indeed, but neither of them worked or mentioned what they had done for a living, although Arthur did make a throw away remark once.

"Josephine is related to an extremely wealthy, prestigious family and still has valuable Chinese artefacts in a bank vault in Hong Kong." He mentioned the name of a famous American family and Kristin was taken aback. This would certainly explain their lifestyle.

Kristin found their behaviour somewhat eccentric as she got to know them better. They rarely went out, except to collect the mail, as they did not like the postman coming to their house. Any unsuspecting visitors would be chased off noisily by Fred, the highly-strung Alsatian with a vicious streak and an alarmingly wild countenance. Kristin had to keep a constant eye on her offspring, as she was terrified that he might attack them. He was not used to company and was especially jumpy around children.

When the family were on their boat trip to Australia they had met a young Aussie guy called Gus. On parting they exchanged addresses and, to their surprise, he managed to get past the hound and ring their doorbell one early evening. He suggested going out for a meal in a few days, to which they agreed subject to finding a suitable baby-sitter. Kristin knew that she could not approach the Jenkins but, on visiting the small supermarket in nearby Manly, she searched the notice board and found an advert.

"Reliable baby-sitter with references available."

She noted down the phone number and called from a nearby telephone box. A friendly voice answered and the two chatted for some time. Bun, as she was nicknamed, had lived in Manly all her life and had grown up children of her own. Then they were all invited to her home that evening for a cup of tea. They were made welcome in her modest bungalow and liked Bun very much. Middle aged, homely and obviously at ease with children, she showed them her hens and they were introduced to her friendly Newfoundland called Chammy. The kids loved this dog and went swimming with him in the warm sea.

"Newfoundlands are natural swimmers and even have webbed feet." She had explained.

"Wow, like ducks." Ricki was impressed.

Chammy was the complete opposite to Fred and was so tolerant that he even let the children hold on to his tail when he swam - taking them for a ride in the sea like a hairy dolphin. The children were in their element as Bun then let them feed the half dozen 'choocks' that provided enough fresh eggs each day for Bun and her family.

"I'd love to go to England one day. Can't see it happening though, we've never been outside of New South Wales let alone Europe. My mum was from here but my dad, who died two years ago, was from the north of England." Bun told them her life story that was that of a typical housewife with grown up children. Kristin was finding her company refreshing after Josephine and the conversation flowed with ease.

"The world's a much smaller place nowadays with air travel. Who knows you may just make it there." Kristin said as she patted Chammy's huge head.

"My hubbie, Geoff, will be home soon. Stay for a barbie." Bun said impulsively.

"Oh, we don't want to put you to any trouble." Harry responded.

"Please, please can we stay?" Ricki pleaded, his eyes bright with excitement.

"Yes. I want to live in 'Stralia forever." Nina sighed.

They all laughed and agreed to stay. Kristin felt at home in Bun's place as she helped her prepare a salad while Harry and Geoff did some male bonding over a cool beer as they chatted and watched meat cook on the barbecue. Kristin viewed the scene with contentment and was confident that they would soon be part of the Australian lifestyle. Perhaps they could put a barbecue on the terrace outside their new apartment and invite the Jenkins along soon together with Geoff and Bun.

As arranged, several days later Harry and Kristin went out for a meal in Manly with Gus while Bun baby-sat. Her husband, Geoff, a local estate agent, dropped her off at the house, as she did not drive. They never did meet up with Gus again as he lived in Melbourne and was only visiting Sydney, but his company was good and they laughed as they recalled their less than luxurious trip from Singapore to Fremantle in the rust bucket cargo ship with its tiny cabins.

"Boy, did I feel crook on that trip. Couldn't eat a thing for days." His eyes crinkled at the sides when he smiled, exposing perfect white teeth. He was the epitome of Aussie youth. Tanned, tall and muscular.

"I know I felt sick most of the trip but Harry and the kids ate everything put before them."

"Was it worth the trip? Do you think you'll like it here?" He asked.

"It's fabulous. I just can't wait to open that salon in the ground floor apartment." Kristin replied.

~ ~ ~ ~ ~ ~

Early the following morning Kristin was summoned, military fashion, to the Jenkins's apartment. Feeling as if she was back at school and about to be reprimanded for a misdemeanour, she obediently entered their apartment wondering what could be wrong.

Arthur lit a cigar while Josephine studied her nails from the comfort of a cream sofa. As usual he was the first to speak.

"I believe you had a visitor last night?"

"Yes, Harry and I went out for a meal and a lady baby-sat for us."

"We would like to make it perfectly clear that we do not allow visitors on our property. That will be the last time anyone comes here - understood?"

Picking up the mood, Fred, the Alsatian growled and for the first time since her arrival in Palm Beach, Kristin felt threatened. She was totally alone in this isolated house. If she screamed no one would hear.

"It's all right. Bun is perfectly respectable. In fact, her husband is a local estate agent."

"Exactly. We don't want estate agents sniffing around our property. No more visitors."

"I'm going to have a lie down now. You'd better go." Josephine had dismissed her.

Feeling perplexed, Kristin decided to walk to the local phone box. She desperately needed a friend to confide in. Relieved to be out of the house, she wondered what the Jenkins had to hide and also what she had let herself in for by being involved with such suspicious people. Two facials and a dinner at the Mandarin Hotel was clearly not enough to form a clear picture, she thought to herself. Were they criminals? That would certainly explain all the money.

Kristin phoned Bun and told her the news.

"Well, they are a weird couple. I wish I could drive, I'd be round like a shot." Bun reassured her.

"Yes, but they'd probably set the dog on you. What a malarkey! I just don't know what to make of the situation. It's just a complete mystery. Why did they make all those promises and then go back on their word? How can I run a salon from the garden flat if no one is allowed to visit?" Kristin was feeling angry and betrayed.

"No, idea. They are a bit of a mystery couple as you say. This is a fairly small community but they never mix and nobody seems to know a thing about them. Come round for a barbie at the weekend and we can chat properly."

That same day Harry had mentioned their plans to some colleagues in the staff room.

"You can't work in Palm Beach mate. It's a holiday place for the rich and notorious. You'll never get planning permission." The maths teacher looked incredulous.

"What, you mean to tell me we've come all this way for nothing." Harry was furious. Surely there must be a logical explanation.

"Sorry, mate. Look, why don't you contact City Hall. They'll put you in the picture."

And they did. The maths teacher was right. Palm Beach was a Grade A residential area and it was impossible to open a business there, especially from a home. So this was why there were no shops or restaurants to be seen for miles around. He bought some flowers on the way home for Kristin. She would have to hear the news first and then he would confront the Jenkins.

"No, there must be some kind of mistake." She wailed after he broke the news, her normally serene face racked with tension.

"I'm sorry, there's no mistake. We've just spent every penny we had to get here - for what?"

"It's all my fault. I wish I'd never met the bloody Jenkins. I'm going upstairs to have it out with them."

"No, you stay with the kids, I'll go up. I can keep my cool. Besides I don't want anything to happen to you."

"What if they are criminals? What if they have a gun?"

"I'll be all right. If I'm not back in an hour, call the police." He tried a weak smile but Kristin was not sure if he was joking.

They hugged each other for comfort before he left - it was time to confront their strange business partners. Harry braced himself as if about to take a dive from a high board, took a deep breath and went upstairs to speak to Arthur and Josephine about the bombshell. To his fury Harry was told that he thought that Kristin would be content with 'pin money' and not to worry about any big business ventures. Arthur fudged and made a few weak statements about a future salon but Harry knew he was lying. It seemed that they knew all along that she could not open a salon in Palm Beach. This explained why they had heard no mention of the prestigious launch into society, the cocktail parties and the press releases. How they could ever have a cocktail party when no one was allowed to visit the premises? They had been conned - but why?

To her relief Harry returned to the apartment angry but unharmed. They talked about moving out and starting a business but they had no capital and Harry was too cautious to ask for a bank loan. Stalemate! Kristin felt betrayed, disappointed and vulnerable – a lonely stranger in a foreign land. The beauty of Palm Beach now seemed to her like a backdrop to a play. It had no substance, just a façade. The place seemed empty – as empty as the Jenkins' promises. She felt like a trapped bird in a luxurious gilded cage.

Kristin tried to find consolation on the beach that she visited each morning. She could feel the Jenkins' eyes on her back as she left the apartment to wander down the lonely path to the beach. Afraid to confront them about her career prospects, she had remained mute. She no longer trusted them or that dog. As she was applying sun tan lotion to her deeply tanned legs, she jumped as the Jenkins approached her. Josephine wore a long silk beach robe, a wide brimmed hat and enormous sunglasses. His unbuttoned red Hawaiian shirt clashed with his hair and Kristin could not help but notice a mat of ginger curls on his chest. This was the first time she had seen them on the beach. Suddenly, the diamond bright day seemed gloomy as they sat down either side of her. The beach was deserted except for a lone figure, sitting not far away.

Her heart thumping in her chest, she attempted to make small talk and found herself babbling about the weather.

"Well, it certainly is a beautiful day again, isn't it? My goodness I'm getting so tanned I could pass for - " She was interrupted at this point by Arthur.

"Do you see that man there - sitting a few feet away?" He said in a stage whisper.

Kristin observed an innocuous looking, elderly gentleman gazing out to sea.

"He's listening to every word we're saying. We have to be careful - people like to spy on us!" he hissed and leaned close to her to make sure she could catch each word.

She said nothing but was anxious to know what it was about the Jenkins that fascinated people so much that they were compelled to spy on them. Making an excuse, she returned to the apartment and locked the door. She had to compose herself - in an hour she would tread the stairs to offer the daily facial - something she now dreaded.

Harry was finding out that this couple had some grandiose ideas about themselves. At 7.30 the following morning Harry was getting into his car to drive to work when, as if on cue, Arthur came out in his dressing gown and started to brush some Mimosa blossom from the bonnet of his car. Staring intently at Harry he remarked, "I'm thinking of getting a Rolls Royce for my princess. Mimosa blossom would look good falling on a Rolls don't you think?"

"Erm, it would look lovely. Well, must be off." Harry couldn't wait to get to school to mix with ordinary people.

Kristin was homesick for England. The silence of the apartment would close in on her once Harry and the children had left for their schools. Wandering over to the window she looked at the beach below and felt desolate. What would become of them all? What had she done persuading her family to travel to the ends of the earth to chase a vaporous dream? Never one to cry easily, she felt her throat constrict as she compared her busy life in Hong Kong to this dead end existence. She had no relatives, no friends except for the baby-sitter, no colleagues and what looked like no future. Why had this odd couple lied to her? Why, why, why?

Harry wanted his old wife back. He had never known Kristin to be lacking in drive and he was concerned that she was becoming depressed. Her usually sparkling eyes and wit had been lost in disappointment. But he also knew that she could be stubborn and so he made some phone calls without telling Kristin what he was up to.

When everything was settled in his mind he broke the news to her one evening as the children slept.

"Darling, I know you're disappointed with the way things have turned out but - "

"That's an understatement!" she snapped at him. "How do you think I feel when you zoom off to work for a full day with plenty of company. I find myself looking at the clock all day, then when the kids get back from school I can't let them out to play in case Fred attacks them."

"We're going back to England." He took her hand.

"What? What do you mean? We've only been here a few months. Just because it hasn't worked out with the nut cases upstairs doesn't mean that we can't do our own thing. I could open my own salon somewhere - we could move out of here and buy a house. We could - "

"We can't, we've got no money. Look, I phoned the Grammar School in Cheltenham and they've offered me my old job back. We'd be crazy to turn down an opportunity like that."

"But, the business. The salon. The health farm. And the kids love it here."

"Kristin, you have to be real about this. There is to be no business here but there's no reason why you can't start something in England is there?"

Kristin walked over to the fridge and poured them each a beer, took a sheet of kitchen roll, blew her nose loudly and said, "Ok, you win. I am homesick and I know you are too. You'll have to tell the Jenkins. We'll talk to the kids tomorrow. At least we've got friends in Cheltenham I suppose. The gestapo upstairs can't stop us seeing them. Harry, we've got no money. How do you propose we get back to England - will we pray to sprout wings?"

"I've spoken to Dad, he can lend us the money for the fares and we'll pay him back in instalments. It's time to cut our losses and just put this down to experience."

The following day their crate of belongings arrived from Hong Kong. Harry did not even bother to collect it but had it sent on to England.

It was time to tell the Jenkins. Once more Harry steeled himself and went upstairs to their apartment while Kristin busied herself with the washing up, praying the whole time that all would be well. The frosty neighbours did not take to the idea very kindly, although they were not out of pocket. Their behaviour was abrupt, impersonal and efficient. The Jenkins had taken a cash deposit when they moved into the apartment to cover any possible damage. Naturally they wanted to get it back, so Kristin made sure that the whole place was immaculate, even cleaning out every cupboard. The Jenkins made a drama out of inspecting the apartment as Josephine sailed around with her nose aloft as if sniffing out any damage. Eventually, looking triumphant, she found a small mark on a blanket in the children's room. Using this as an excuse they retained the whole of the deposit. Feeling that this was unreasonable, Kristin challenged them.

"You can sue us you like," Arthur remarked with a cruel smirk, knowing that the family were now penniless.

The only gain that they had from this experience was that they managed to sell their car at a profit. However, the day they left Palm Beach they found that someone had let their tyres down...

Kristin wished that they were returning to Hong Kong, where at least she knew what to expect and where she had carved out a good customer base.

She did not say farewell to the Jenkins, nor did she look back as they eventually drove away, her dreams lost but not forever.

12

ALL WILL BE REVEALED

They said goodbye to Palm Beach, or Sleepy Hollow as Arthur had fondly called it. In a way, Kristin was sad to leave but, always practical, she was ready to make a fresh start in England. She and Bun hugged each other and promised to keep in touch. Nina and Ricki treated the whole exercise as an adventure and were looking forward to seeing their grandparents again.

On the tedious flight home Ricki made an interesting comment, "Were the Jenkins baddies, Dad?"

"Probably not, son. It just didn't work out as we'd hoped."

"They were not goodies cos they broke our tyres on the car and we had to get new ones. And anyway they hated me and Ricki." Nina looked wistful.

'Out of the mouths of babes,' Kristin thought.

England seemed like a foreign country once again, just as it had upon their return from Hong Kong.

'If only things had worked out differently, we could be enjoying the outdoor life in the sunshine now,' Kristin mused.

Pale complexioned people, grey skies and chilly days made Kristin long for life in Oz. It had not taken her long to become accustomed to the constant sunshine in New South Wales. Kristin wondered at times if they had made a mistake and wished that they had persevered in Australia but she never told Harry. Of course, their parents were delighted to have their children and grandchildren back on British soil after such a short time.

'I will not give up at the first hurdle,' Kristin told herself. She had a plan, but first they needed to find a suitable house. Yes, she knew exactly what she wanted. The house had to have a basement flat so that she could open a salon. Cheltenham had an abundance of Regency properties with unused basements that could be easily converted into something useful. She was optimistic.

After viewing several uninspiring houses, at last Kristin found what she had been looking for.

"Harry, this is it. We must have it." She whispered, pleading with her enormous brown eyes that he had never been able to resist.

"Darling, it's way above our budget and we still owe my father that money. I don't see how..."

"I'll work really hard. We'll manage. We always do. Let's put an offer in and, if they accept, we'll take it as a sign that this is our house." She would not back down.

The clever owner of the property had left them alone to wander around the house as an enticing aroma of brewing coffee wafted throughout while classical music was played softly in the background. The house was typically Regency, situated in an elegant terrace and on three storeys. Enormous sash windows graced each room and to the rear there was a small walled garden. But the main pull for Kristin was the empty basement flat. This would be her salon. She had also noted that there was enough parking outside for clients. In her mind's eye she could see the whole scenario.

Trying not to look too keen, the couple left saying they would think about it.

The family were staying at Kristin's parents' house in a suburb of Cheltenham, having sold their small terraced house before moving to Hong Kong. Fortunately, they had kept their furniture that was in storage.

"We don't have to buy much, the owner's throwing in so many extras, he must be in a hurry to get out." Kristin's old enthusiasm had returned with a vengeance.

"Strange coincidence. When you were looking round the garden he told me he's emigrating to Australia." Harry said drily as they drove past Pittville Park toward Bishop's Cleeve and Kristin's parents' home.

"Hope he's not going to work for the Jenkins. Poor bugger."

"You really want this house don't you? I'll do the sums when we get back and, providing we can get a mortgage, we'll go for it. I can always do some private tuition in the evenings and school holidays I suppose."

"Oh, I do love you." She leant over and kissed him.

"Careful, I'm driving."

Harry's secure job enabled them to get the mortgage and so they put in an offer that was accepted within two days and six weeks later they moved in. The excitement was electrifying when the crate arrived from Australia and was opened in anticipation as if the contents had never been seen before. All was intact and Kristin worked with vigour to make a new home. Fortunately, the previous owner had left behind the curtains and carpets and, although not Kristin's taste, she was glad of them; aware that they had to watch every penny.

Always adaptable, the children settled in well and enjoyed attending their local primary school.

"What do you like best about England?" Kristin asked them one rainy day after school. They were sitting at a pine table in the kitchen eating peanut butter on toast and drinking milk. Both children were still in their brown school uniforms, Nina looked tidy and Ricki did not.

"Fish and chips." Ricki did not hesitate.

"What about you?" Kristin poured Nina some more milk.

"Erm, my new friend Jane. And not living in a flat. And having Jane live near. And my new teacher."

"Quite a lot of good things here then." Kristin was pleased that the children had adapted so well.

"Yes but it's not fair that we can't have satays and gado gado like we used to have at that place in Hong Kong." Ricki loved his food.

"You mean the Indonesian restaurant in Causeway Bay." Kristin loved that place too.

Nina had started a drawing of a house with a tree standing each side. It was neat and she worked with deep concentration.

"A boy at school asked me today why I was so brown. And I told him that we'd been in Australia. Then he said I was posh and he didn't care where I'd been." Ricki was staring at the crusts that he had left on his plate.

Nina stopped drawing and looked up. "When I said that we used to live in Hong Kong, Sarah in my class said that I was la de da. So Jane told her to shut up cos she was just jealous and now we don't speak to her."

Kristin stopped chopping carrots for a moment and sat at the table. "Maybe it's best that you don't tell everyone about us living abroad because sometimes people get the wrong end of the stick and do get a bit jealous. That's a lovely drawing Nina."

"Thanks, Mum. Can I have a cookie?"

"Yes, but we call them biscuits here." Kristin smiled as she put a chocolate biscuit on each of her offspring's plate.

EQUIPPED

Kristin's ambition to open her own salon rose like a phoenix from the ashes of disappointment. A smooth road of success had replaced the stumbling blocks and barriers that she had encountered in Australia as doors of opportunity flew open. She soon picked herself up and, being a natural entrepreneur, enjoyed the preparation needed in order to open her salon in the spacious basement flat. The challenge was nectar to her and she ran her home and business life with efficiency and ease. She and Harry had postponed any decorating that the rambling house needed to get the basement painted first. They decorated the walls in cream and the original cornices were picked out in brilliant white and looked like elaborate piped icing on a wedding cake. New carpets were fitted throughout and mirrors placed on the outside of the louvre panels that formed separate cubicles, giving the reception area a bright, airy feel. She already owned a folding massage couch and had made a batch of her honey wax and so was offering a few basic treatments but she wanted to go all out and offer more. She had a handful of clients after giving some talks and demonstrations at local Women's Institutes but was not content with this. All she needed was equipment and then she could start advertising.

Browsing through a trade journal one Friday lunchtime, she spotted an advert for the entire contents of a beauty salon in Surrey that had closed down. Although it was a long way from Cheltenham, she decided to obey her impulsive nature and phoned the vendor to find out more. After chatting to the salon owner's husband, Kristin told him that she wanted to buy most of the equipment and asked him if he would hold it for her.

"I like the sound of your voice so I'll do just that," was his cheery reply. Kristin had never been one to hang about, believing the motto about the early bird.

Harry was on a course in London that day so she had to hope that he would agree to help her collect this equipment when he got home.

Excited, Kristin managed to hire a Bedford van in which to pile all the goods, hoping and praying that the salon equipment would be in good working order as the advert claimed. It was a long way to travel and a waste of money if the goods were worn out.

When the children got back from school, she told them that they would be going on an adventure.

"Oh, are we going to a fun fair?" Ricki asked.

"No, not that exciting, although I promise that one day we'll go to one." Kristin wished she hadn't used the word adventure.

"Where are we going Mum?" Nina piped up.

"Surrey - to buy some things for the salon. It will mean a very late night but it'll be fun."

"I don't want to go, I want to play with Jane. Why do we have to go to boring Surrey?" Nina whined.

"Is Dad coming? If Dad's coming, then I'll help." Ricki seemed pleased to be included.

"Yes, I'm pretty certain that Dad's coming. Nina, will you stop complaining - I'll ask Jane's mum if you can stay the night. Okay?"

"Yeah! Will you ask now? Please Mum."

"Just be patient - first I have to ask your father if he'll come along." Kristin was sure she could rely on Harry but wanted to keep her options open.

When Harry got home at around 6 o'clock that evening Kristin greeted him with a kiss and a slap up meal, hoping that it would not just fill his stomach but soften his already kind heart. She then broke the news to him that she had hired a Bedford van and would be grateful if he could help her by heading south again. Her enthusiasm was always infectious and, as usual, he agreed.

"Thank you darling. I don't know how on earth I'd manage without you." She hugged him.

"Oh, I'm sure you'd find a way." He said, returning the embrace. "Now, I suppose you want me to collect this van."

"Yes, please - what a malarkey! And just when I needed new equipment."

"Don't get your hopes up - it might be rubbish." Harry hoped that Kristin was not on one of her quests, only to be disappointed.

All was arranged. Jane's mother agreed to let Nina stay the night, much to Nina and Kristin's relief.

So off they went to Surrey, where they found the owner's house in a typical Home Counties area where commuter belt homes with manicured lawns lined the suburban avenues. The vendor and his groomed lady friend greeted them. The wife had left; hence the closing of the salon. Kristin was anxious to see the equipment and was led into a forlorn room, which was once a salon, to inspect the equipment. It was perfect and they managed to get it all into the back of the van. The owner's husband was an affable restaurateur and he said, "Come and see my restaurant before you set off - it's only round the corner."

This they did and, after showing them round the restaurant they got into the van to set off on the long drive home. By now it was gone midnight but, to their surprise, the chef came out bearing three plates of scampi and chips and a bottle of white wine! Full of gratitude they drove off, with Kristin balancing the warm plates on her lap, to find a suitable lay-by in which to eat. Before they knew it they were on the motorway that was fortunately deserted. In a very reckless moment Harry pulled over to the hard shoulder were they scoffed the scampi and chips, hoping that they wouldn't be arrested. They thought it was probably best to leave the wine until a more suitable time.

Ricki thought that all this was great fun and chatted away until he eventually fell asleep in the back of the van while Kristin and Harry took turns to drive. They got home at around 3am and the van needed returning by 10 o'clock that morning. To add to the mayhem, Kristin had invited friends for lunch that day, not knowing that she and Harry would be off on a jaunt and so they didn't get much sleep that night. The couple served lunch to their friends in a semi comatose state. Fortunately their friends were very understanding and seemed to enjoy their meal. Kristin was working on automatic pilot and she had some clients booked in the following day.

The expedition proved to be worthwhile as everything fitted perfectly into the salon and was soon put to good use. Kristin felt as if she now had a proper business instead of a paying hobby. The price lists were amended to include more treatments as equipment such as a G5 massage machine, an infra red lamp, a faradic machine for muscle toning, a paraffin wax heater, a combined desincrustation and high frequency unit for electronic facials plus an electrolysis unit for removing facial hair had been purchased. She had also acquired several trolleys, stools and treatment couches and was in her element.

"Oh darling - this is just as I imagined it would be. We've been so fortunate." Kristin was wiping her new acquisitions with a damp cloth.

"Where do you want this?" Harry was inspecting the machine with interest. It was all foreign to him.

"Just plonk it on that trolley." She waved the cloth in the general direction of the new facial cubicle.

"It looks like something to be used for torture. We have ways of making you talk and all that."

"It's for desincrustation." Kristin replied.

"My point exactly." Harry gazed at the apparatus.

"I can use it on you later if you like."

"I love it when you talk dirty." He pinched her bottom and she pretended to be insulted.

Kristin worked quickly until everything was spotless.

"Where do you want this trolley with the interrogation lamp attached?" He asked.

"Erm, in the same cubicle as the desincrustation machine, please." She was arranging products on a shelving unit. "And it's a cold light magnifier, for your information."

"I know darling, just joking. I must say it all looks very impressive." He just hoped that the salon would be a success after all the disappointment in Australia.

Two hours later she stood back to admire the fruits of their labour.

"Fantastic. Thanks sweetheart. You're an angel." She kissed him on his stubbly cheek.

"All you need now are some victims - I mean clients." Harry chuckled.

An advert was placed in the local paper and she started to give demonstrations to drum up trade and the clients rolled in who, in turn, told their friends about the caring therapist with the magic hands.

Life in Australia was fast becoming a misty memory.

Several months on they were to receive some startling news that would help solve the mystery surrounding the Jenkins.

Bun and Kristin had been corresponding since the young family's return to England and Bun had spotted a newspaper article that she had cut out and posted. Staring out at her was a picture of the Jenkins with the caption Couple Killed in Road Accident in Switzerland. It was such a shock that she had to sit down and read it again for the information to sink in.

The Jenkins had been killed in a car crash while driving a Rolls Royce in Switzerland. They were on a mission looking for 'citizens' for their newly formed kingdom in the Kangaroo Valley. He was the self appointed King Arthur and she, Queen Josephine. They even had their own postage stamps. Suddenly, it all became clear. Kristin and Harry were to have been their first citizens - not in a health farm but a Kingdom!

As soon as Harry put his key in the door that afternoon, Kristin rushed towards him, her eyes flashing with excitement. He braced himself for yet another business brainwave.

"You'll never guess what? I've had a letter from Bun. What a malarkey!"

"Calm down. Give me time to take my coat off. What's - "

"We were to be the Jenkins' chosen ones. They've been killed in a car crash and - "

"Slow down. You're not making any sense. Now start again."

She grabbed his hand and dragged him into the sitting room where the newspaper cutting lay on top of a pile of magazines on the coffee table. She composed herself as he read it.

"Good grief - this explains everything." Harry said in his usual even tones.

"I don't know whether to feel flattered that we were to be the 'chosen ones' or not. It all seems totally bizarre," she said.

"Seems like we got out in the nick of time - although Princess Kristin and Prince Harry has a certain ring to it don't you think? Sad to think that they died so young though. I wonder if Josephine ever got to see any mimosa on her Rolls Royce."

13

ANNABEL

While in England Celine had purchased a book on natural childbirth and had memorised the breathing and relaxation techniques after practising them religiously. The pregnancy was uneventful and she looked blooming in spite of her unresponsive husband.

"Look, James, the baby's kicking. Put your hand here and you can feel it." Celine was determined to make her husband bond with his baby. They were lying on the bed and she pulled up her nightdress to reveal an extended abdomen.

"Yuk, no. It looks revolting. Leave me alone – I'm reading." He sounded genuinely disgusted.

After that Celine started talking and singing to her baby as if making up for James's cool neglect and she began to look forward to seeing the new arrival. She thought about names, writing them down in the back of her journal. James was disinterested and told her to decide.

A room had been booked at a private clinic run by Catholic nuns for the birth. Although not sure if she believed in God any more, Celine was confident that she would have the best possible care and attention. Almost superstitiously, she thought that a few prayers would not go amiss at such an important event. Feeling ashamed that her once strong faith had been reduced to mere superstition, she whispered an apology to God and felt a gentle breeze blow over her as if an angel had brushed its wing against her cheek. Feeling shocked, she checked to see if James had turned a fan on. He had not. Closing her eyes, she let an unfamiliar stillness settle on her.

'All will be well, all will be well,' she whispered.

She did not tell James about her spiritual encounter, fearing that his cynicism might rob her of its reality. The atmosphere between them had become tenser with each passing month.

The baby was late as if in protest. Perhaps it did not want to leave its safe confines and enter a world where conflict was rife. Three weeks after the due date the contractions arrived, at first just twinges but rapidly becoming insistent. Calmly picking up her bag that had been packed for over a month, Celine announced to James that it was time to go to the clinic. It was night but still the heat and humidity hung heavy in the sultry Hong Kong air.

Feeling a mixture of anticipation and dread she arrived at the clinic and was greeted there by a French nun with a face like an angel, clad entirely in white and who spoke not a word of English. As her schoolgirl French was almost forgotten, Celine was slightly concerned as to how they would communicate. The nun assured the parents to be that Dr Cole was on his way and ushered them into the stark delivery room. Glaring lights gave the place the air of an antiseptic interrogation room. The contractions had become insistent by the time the doctor arrived; still sporting his golfing gear that he wore throughout the delivery. A short man, with a ruddy complexion and fingers as fat as sausages, Celine told him boldly that she wanted a natural childbirth and didn't want any drugs. Raising a gingery caterpillar eyebrow, he dismissed her suggestion and mumbled something like, "Mm, we'll see."

"No, really. I know how to do breathing and relaxation exercises and don't want any drugs unless it's absolutely necessary." She insisted.

After a quick examination the doctor told James that his wife could be a while and asked if he would like to join him for a drink. The men disappeared leaving her and the angelic nun to get on with the task in hand. Celine continued confidently with her deep breathing and counting exercises, interspersed with humming a popular song. The nun, who had never seen or heard anything like this before, met this procedure with alarm. Down the corridor they could hear wailing and agonising screams. Celine thought that the midwife would be delighted that she was handling the contractions calmly and quietly; except for the pleasant tune of "The Sound of Silence." Screams this midwife understood - breathing, counting and humming pop tunes were foreign to her. Ignoring her protestations, Celine carried on regardless.

"Arête, Madam, arête," she pleaded, a trickle of perspiration running down her normally serene face as Celine puffed away.

Finally, in desperation and with a determined jaw, the nun grabbed a syringe and pumped a hefty dose of Pethidine into Celine's derrière. Within minutes Celine felt as if she'd had one too many gins as she floated a few feet above the bed. The drug had the desired effect, as she could not concentrate on her breathing. The nun started to relax. Perhaps she'd given herself a quick shot at the same time.

Celine was hoping that she or the doctor would tell her to stop pushing when the baby's head appeared. This would be her cue to start panting which would help to counteract the need to push with the contractions, thus avoiding any unnecessary tearing. She had done her homework and knew just what to expect while James, who always disappeared when Celine was practising her techniques at home, looked bewildered the whole time; ignorance rendering his presence superfluous.

Within ten minutes of the doctor's re-entry into the delivery room the baby was born. What a wonderful moment and what a privilege to bring a new life into the world. Celine was euphoric.

"You have a little boy," the nun announced.

James, looking with intent at his new offspring as if it was a rare species, corrected her and said that they had a girl. They knew that nuns were supposed to be innocent but this was ridiculous. Celine reached out to take her baby but the nun took it away to clean it up.

But her euphoria was short-lived as the doctor started stitching his patient without anaesthetic. It was so painful that she kicked him with the force of a donkey, not caring what injury she might inflict.

"Bloody woman," he barked, "hold her down."

James, obeying the instruction, held her still while the doctor's sausage fingers finished his clumsy work.

However, all the pain was soon forgotten as the new mother held her eight pound miracle in her arms. How such a pretty little doll could be mistaken for a boy was beyond her.

"Welcome to the world, Annabel," Celine whispered, and then, looking at the doctor expressed her concerns.

"I expect she'll need feeding in the night, won't she?"

"Oh yes, every three or four hours." He looked at her quizzically as if wondering why she was asking the obvious.

"What will I do if I don't hear her - if I don't wake up?"

The doctor chuckled, knowingly, "Oh, you will. You will."

The next day she was recovering quietly and wishing that the unrelenting heat would subside. A wave of homesickness for England swept over her like an unwelcome breaker. The nuns had told her not to get out of bed but to press the call button if she needed anything. Glancing up from nursing her daughter, a large brown thing came scurrying across the wall in her direction. It was the biggest cockroach she had ever seen. Feeling trapped, she pressed the call button that was answered by a Chinese orderly who, in broken English, asked her what was wrong.

Celine pointed to the monster that was now just a few inches from her baby, its antennae up as if in search of a victim. Looking at the patient as if her mind had been discarded with the afterbirth, she sauntered over to the offending creature and crushed it efficiently with her bare hand. After making a sickening crunching sound, it fell to the floor where she left it before exiting the room without a word. Her demeanour implied, "Stupid foreign woman."

It was with relief that Celine took her baby home the following day. Annabel proved to be a hungry baby. She woke every three or four hours in the night and exercised her lungs to the maximum, informing Celine that she needed a feed. Celine found herself wide awake within minutes of the baby's cries for milk and was irritated that James never so much as stirred. The doctor was right - she had no problem hearing Annabel cry in the night. It was as if she had left behind the old person and now, since giving birth, a new woman had emerged who would always put her baby first. After a month of this, Celine thought that she would ask her husband to help out with the early morning feed, as she was feeling exhausted and disappointed that she was not enjoying motherhood as much as she had imagined.

"I'll prepare a bottle and put it in the fridge, and then all you have to do is warm it up when she wakes at about five."

James agreed rather begrudgingly.

On the dot Annabel started to scream loudly at five in the morning. Celine lay there waiting for James to feed his daughter. Nothing.

"James, wake up. Annabel needs feeding."

"Spitfires."

"What?"

"They're zooming in fast."

"What?" Celine was now prodding her slumbering partner to no avail.

At 6 o'clock a contented baby was put back in its cot and a tired and crotchety Celine went back to bed.

"What was that about Spitfires this morning when you should have been feeding Annabel?" She asked James over breakfast.

"No idea. Don't remember – must have been dreaming. How do you expect me to feed the baby when I've got to get to work in the morning? It's your job. You can have a nap in the day if you want." And with that he left for the office looking fresh after eight hours of unbroken sleep.

That night he did not come home for his supper and returned late. After putting Annabel in her cot Celine found herself pacing the floor, unable to concentrate on either the television or a book. Each time she heard a car outside in the communal car park she would go out onto the balcony in search of her wayward husband. She felt trapped inside the apartment and, worse still - inside her memories. At midnight she went to bed feeling depressed and knowing that within two hours she would be feeding Annabel again. At 3am James came home, just after Annabel's feed. He was drunk.

Celine's love for her husband was waning as fast as the love for her daughter grew stronger each day. But she was gripped with a consuming obsession with James and his drinking to the point that even the simplest tasks had become a burden. Looking at herself in the mirror she was dismayed to see that her once bouncy hair hung lank and lacklustre and her skin was sallow. She wondered if a beauty treatment would help and remembered the bright eyed therapist, Kristin, who had waxed her legs before Annabel was born. She felt sure that Kristin would be sympathetic but somehow could not summon up the enthusiasm to phone Jane's Beauty Service.

Even Ah Foo was worried about Celine but what could an amah do except household chores? James seemed annoyed that his wife was not bucking up and offered no support, even when she lost the desire to go out or see any of her friends. Celine felt burdened instead of joyful with each passing day of motherhood. Her weight dropped quickly as she lost her appetite and her zest for life evaporated in the tropical heat. Feeling desperate and frightened by these alien feelings, she called the doctor to make an appointment.

After giving her a thorough physical check up, he asked her a few questions.

"How are you sleeping?"

"Not, that well. Annabel still wakes in the night for a feed and sometimes I have difficulty getting back to sleep." She said, omitting the fact that it was when James was out late that she could not sleep.

"Are you eating well?" The doctor viewed her intently over his spectacles.

"Not really – I seem to have lost my appetite."

"Do you ever feel like harming the baby?"

What a question. Celine was horrified. "No, no of course not," she protested.

"I think you have the baby blues or post natal depression. It's quite common and won't last. I'll prescribe an anti depressant but you must stop feeding the baby. Physically, I can't find anything wrong. Come back and see me in two weeks." And with that she took the prescription and left.

Post natal depression. She felt a guilty failure. Her baby was beautiful and healthy but then her marriage was far from perfect, she reasoned. It was as if all colour had been bleached out of her life, leaving a dry skeleton in place of a vibrant body. She felt as if she had fallen into a dark pit with no life line to pull her out, could not concentrate on the simplest of tasks and found it impossible to enjoy a book or even a magazine article as her unruly thoughts of failure and dread of the future obliterated anything that could be a distraction from how she was feeling. Memories of the past few years cascaded through her mind, sometimes as a trickle but gaining momentum until they were a gushing torrent.

Celine was homesick. Although not thinking of herself as a country girl, at this dark time she had a nostalgic longing for the soft rolling landscape of rural England. She would close her eyes and conjure up images of spring flowers, orchards in blossom, birdsong, cattle grazing, mellow Cotswold stone villages, thatched cottages and the smell of freshly mown grass. Her stark concrete apartment block, surrounded by more of the same, made the aching inside her unbearable.

As the depression took hold like a noose around her neck, she remembered vividly her childhood and longed to have a close family member nearby to share in her sorrow. Christmas would soon be upon them and she wanted to make it a joyful time now that she was a mother but wondered if she would ever feel happy again. She recalled her childhood Christmases, the joy that they brought and hoped that one day Annabel would find it as wonderful as she used to.

The sweet memory brought her a morsel of hope and comfort.

"One day you'll hang a stocking at the foot of your bed and, in the morning, you'll wake up to find it full of presents," Celine whispered to her baby as she kissed her on the head. Annabel sighed blissfully, as if in anticipation of such an event.

After two months Celine had recovered from the depression and was weaning herself off the tablets, but her marriage continued to be a strain. She wondered if she would ever be truly happy again or if too much had happened to make that possible.

Her journal was now well used although she did not write in it every day. The writing was therapeutic but she made sure that James never saw it. One night, alone in the apartment, she wrote:

No one ever told me how difficult being a mother would be. Why don't they teach us how to cope with marriage and motherhood at school? What use is maths or geography when a baby is screaming its lungs out half the night? Maybe I'm not cut out for motherhood after all and yet I thought that it was what my destiny held. I wish life was easier than this and that James would spend more time with us. I feel a total failure.

14

CONFRONTATION

Celine stared at the picture in disbelief. She had gone to the Ladies' Recreation Club for an hour's break, thinking that a coffee and a browse through a few magazines might be all that were needed to help her feel human again. Now that she'd stopped breastfeeding, she felt free to indulge in a few small luxuries and Ah Foo enjoyed giving Annabel the occasional bottle. Celine was starting to revel in the solitude of the lounge with its air-conditioning, thick carpet and comfortable sofas and wondered if it was time to invite her mother out to stay now that Annabel was going through the night without needing a feed.

Then, as she flipped the pages of a local society magazine and sipped her coffee, she froze.

The picture jumped out and hit her with a vengeance. There they stood, looking as relaxed in each other's company as any married couple, both with a glass of wine and smiling broadly into the camera. James was wearing a suit and the tie that she had bought him for his birthday and Wendy looked seductive in a revealing top and dangly earrings, her long black hair swept up in a chignon.

As if trying to disprove what she'd just seen, she shut the glossy local magazine sharply, perhaps hoping that somehow the reality of it would disappear. Breathlessly she stared at the date on the front cover. It was six weeks old. Annabel would have only been born two months prior to this wretched photo being taken. Of course, it all began to make sense now. The late nights at the office. The disinterest in both herself and Annabel. The aftershave that he normally said that he hated to wear had appeared once more. Opening the magazine again she stared at the picture before reading the caption. 'James Smedley and Wendy Middleton enjoying a break during a philharmonic concert at City Hall.' The visible screaming facts were that James had another mistress. And with her friend and confident from Amsterdam. It was a double betrayal.

Realising that he would never change, she decided to brace herself for one more confrontation. Ripping the page out of the magazine and stuffing it into her bag she left the luxury of the club sitting room in a white hot fury.

Celine drove back from the club in a dreamlike state, along Conduit Road and turned into her block of flats. She locked the car and entered the lift like a robot. Summoning up self control, she managed to smile at Ah Foo, "Is Annabel still asleep?" she asked.

"Yes missy. She velly good. No wakey." Ah Foo was drying her hands as she spoke. A smell of fried onion wafted in from the kitchen but Celine was not interested in food. She wanted the truth.

Celine murmured something before rushing to the bedroom to compose herself and plan her next move. She needed to be clearheaded and strong. Rummaging in her underwear drawer she found the envelope containing the pictures of the girl in Amsterdam and carefully placed the latest picture on top of them. Seeing the photos taken in Holland brought a fresh wave of despair and all she could do was lie on the bed and let the tears flow as her body convulsed in silent torment.

After ten minutes she heard Annabel cry and she knew she had to be able to cope for her baby's sake; it would be too easy to slip into depression again. Drying her tears, she made her way to the nursery where the cheerful pink striped wallpaper and array of teddies on the window ledge made her feel even more miserable. This should have been the happiest time in her life but once more her dreams of a normal family life had been polluted into a vicious nightmare.

'If we had stayed in England, where the way of life is more staid, this may never have happened,' she thought.

The baby stopped her sobbing and held her hands up in innocent pleasure for her mother as soon as she saw her.

"Don't cry my sweetheart. Mummy's here." She picked Annabel from her cot and held her very close, kissing her damp curls and feeling her heart break for the love she had for her child.

The rest of the afternoon passed in surreal normality. Ah Foo left and Celine fed and bathed Annabel before putting her to bed, somehow resigned to the fact that she and James would soon be divorced. Then the silence of the apartment closed in on her and she was alone with her thoughts. Glancing at her watch she realised that James was going to be late again tonight. She would wait. She had decided what she was going to do.

At 10 o'clock he came home, looking slightly dishevelled.

"I had something to eat with some of the guys from the office. Have you eaten?"

"Yes, Ah Foo left some chow fan which I heated up. James, I have to talk to you." Her words sounded distant and cool but her heart was thudding.

Making his way to the drinks cabinet he started to pour himself a gin and tonic without looking up or speaking and so she continued.

"I'm fed up with your drinking, your staying out late at night, your attitude..."

"You can't tell me what to do. You're not my mother," he drawled like a conceited gigolo.

A simmering fury enveloped her as she thought of her mother-in-law, a woman who would gloat as she told Celine how her son would always be so obedient and would do anything for her.

"I know about you and Wendy." She exploded.

"What are you talking about?" He took a sip of his drink but still avoided her eyes.

"I know about your affair with her." She stood up now and was making her way towards him, energised by her rage.

"You're talking rubbish." He backed away from her.

"No, I'm not. Someone that I respect told me all about it," she lied, "you've been seen together. I've had enough, I'm going to divorce you." Celine was so sure of her instincts that she decided it was worth her while to bluff. Her rage was momentarily cathartic and eased her feelings of helplessness.

James did not respond but pushed her roughly to one side, hurried to the spare room and locked the door. Déjà vu. How many times was this crazy scenario to be repeated?

After ten minutes of hammering on the door to no avail, she gave up. Annabel was screaming, picking up the mood of her mother. Celine backed off, feeling ashamed that her hysteria had woken their baby and she went into the bedroom to take an aspirin to ease her exploding head. Perhaps Annabel would drop off to sleep. But the screaming got louder and, not being able to bear it any longer, Celine went into the hallway to cross into the nursery. On her way she passed the spare room. The door was open and it was empty. James had gone.

'How much longer will this go on? How much is a human being able to cope before cracking,' she thought to herself. Her love for her husband had turned to bitter hatred. She was pleased that he had gone, as she would not be able to trust her shattered emotions.

Picking up the child she rocked her in her arms and smelled the sweetness of her baby. "It's just you and me now Annabel."

To her astonishment, James returned within an hour and humbly asked her forgiveness.

He looked haggard and his devil may care attitude had gone.

"Why did you do it – why?" she whispered.

"I don't know," by now he was sobbing, "I just needed to at the time and Wendy approached me first. You were tied up with Annabel and were tired all the time. She invited me for lunch and - you know the rest."

"So, how do you explain your affair with that Dutch girl? I didn't have Annabel then." She spat at him.

"I don't know. If it's any consolation the cat didn't like her." He looked pathetic, his head in his hands.

"Oh, that makes it all right then?"

"Don't leave me – please don't leave me. I'll kill myself if you do." His sobbing had started again.

"Then come with me for some counselling – if not for us then for Annabel. I'll arrange an appointment with a marriage guidance counsellor. Let's give it one last shot." Celine was confused by James's new approach but still wanted to make a go of her relationship. She wondered if her tenacity was driven by madness or insecurity, or both. For the first time she felt sorry for him. He seemed like the victim now - a victim of his own weakness.

"All right – make the appointment." His head hung in defeat.

An appointment was made for the following week at 6 o'clock in Ice House Street in the Central District, about a ten minute walk from James's office block.

As usual, Celine was early and James was late – but at least he turned up so she was cautiously optimistic. A friendly English woman, Annette, greeted them and showed them into a small counselling room. Celine noticed a box of tissues on the table and wondered how many tears had been shed in the confines of this room.

"Right, let me hear your story first," Annette looked searchingly at Celine. "Then your turn, James."

Realising that they only had an hour, Celine decided to be as to the point and unemotional as possible. She told her story while

James looked impassively at his shoes but her feelings started to erupt towards the end and she took a tissue to wipe away her tears.

"Are you ready to give your account of events now?" Annette looked calmly at James.

"Yes. I don't really know how it all happened..." and he continued to speak robotically without making any eye contact with either Celine or Annette.

The hour passed quickly and Annette smiled warmly at them, "I would like to see you both again if that's all right. Celine, I need to find a chink in your amour and, James, we need to talk about responsibility."

An appointment was made the following week. As usual, Celine was early but James did not turn up. He did not come home until 2am that morning.

The next day she told James that she was going to meet up with Wendy. She was seething with anger that both her husband and her friend could betray her.

"There's no point. She and Duncan have left Hong Kong. He has a posting in Japan."

Celine felt relieved; she was afraid of what harm she might do to her so called friend. At least the woman was off the scene and James could not see her any more - she hoped.

She sobbed silently as she entered a few lines in her journal that night:

Working at the Wiggy Scene during those first few weeks in Hong Kong has, in its way, been a blessing and a curse. Life has a funny way of putting people across our paths, some to bring joy and others challenges into our lives. Friendships bring risk; we never know how things will turn out but unless we open our hearts to others this journey of life can be lonely and joyless. We are not all born to be reclusive like James and I need friends in my life. If I had not gone to work at the Wiggy Scene I would not have met Melissa and in turn Billy and his date, my so-called friend, Wendy. How I hate her now! But if it had not been Wendy, maybe it would have been someone else. And why, oh why did I think that she was a friend when she had designs on my husband? I don't know if I will ever be able to share the secrets of my soul with anyone again if it means that betrayals will arrive at my door to strike such harsh blows. I wish that I'd tried harder to be a respectable colonial wife and then this may never have happened. I feel sure that James will want to return to Hong Kong after this contract ends but I don't want to come back with him.

~ ~ ~ ~ ~ ~

James was apologetic about not keeping his appointment with the counsellor but promised Celine that he would try to be more responsible in future.

"As you know my contract ends in two weeks and I've decided not to renew it, so we'll make a fresh start in England. We'll buy a house and be a proper family. It will be easier without the temptations of this place." He sounded so sincere that Celine believed him and was eagerly anticipating their return to the UK. It was as if living abroad had corrupted her husband and that he needed some stability. He was even starting to take a tentative interest in Annabel, who responded with delight. Celine would gaze at the scene and know that this was her heart's desire – to have a happy family life. She realised that she had pushed any maternal feelings to one side in order to align her wishes with James. Maybe one day there would be a little brother for Annabel to play with.

"I can't tell you how happy this makes me. Maybe we'll be able to recapture those carefree days when we were first married. Remember how settled we were? It was a much simpler life. Okay - we had very little money but it was fun when friends came round for a simple meal and a bottle of plonk." Celine longed for normality again.

"Yes, but you have to also remember that I've moved on."

Celine wished that he had not moved on but was hopeful that once they had left the expatriate lifestyle they could find contentment once more.

"Can you meet me for a last lunch at the LRC today?" Celine asked her husband impulsively the following day. She fancied their delicious black pepper steak and homemade crème caramel for the last time.

"Okay. I'll see you there at 1 o'clock."

As she dressed in one of her cool cotton dresses she was pleased that she could do the zip up with ease. It hadn't taken her long to get her figure back. She spent longer than usual fixing her hair and make-up and it was with a light heart that she drove to the Ladies' Recreation Club.

James was only ten minutes late. They ordered their steaks and a waiter dressed their salads on a portable table next to them making a performance of crushing the garlic and tossing the leaves in olive oil, vinegar and croutons. As they were waiting for their puddings to arrive James pulled some papers out of his brief case and started reading. Celine steadied her gaze out of the widow at the tennis players below and tried to control her anger.

"Do you have to spoil our last meal here by doing office work at the table?" She snapped.

"I'm busy. You're lucky I could make it at all," he replied without taking his eyes off the paperwork.

Resigned to his behaviour, she decided to enjoy her pudding. 'Maybe this is normal,' she reasoned with herself, 'maybe I just expect too much from a relationship.'

They finished their meal in silence before she returned home with a heavy heart.

It was with sadness that she bade farewell to Ah Foo the following week. With tears in her eyes the trusty servant handed Celine a parcel.

"This for you missy." She handed her the present self consciously.

Celine opened the brown paper parcel with care, touched that the servant had spent her hard earned money in such a way. Inside was a pale pink tablecloth, with intricate cut outs and hand embroidered with flowers in pink and blue in the typically delicate traditional Chinese style.

"Oh, thank you Ah Foo. I'll always remember you when I use it. It's beautiful." Celine gasped her approval.

"You no need irony missy. " Ah Foo replied as Celine tried not to laugh at the sweet, thoughtful remark.

Annabel held her arms up to Ah Foo for a kiss as if she knew that she would not see her again.

Celine had almost finished packing their personal belongings with care; delicate jade flower arrangements, china figures, cloisonné vases and ginger jars, snuff bottles, formal Chinese paintings, embroidered silk cushion covers, bronze lamps, silk rugs plus clothing and jewellery purchased inexpensively at what Celine called the Chairman's Shop. She scratched the angry eczema patch on her hand after packing the last item away as she recalled her favourite shop where she had purchased their treasures - the Chinese Merchandise Emporium, an Aladdin's cave of far eastern treasures. Enormous posters of a moon faced Mao smiled out benevolently to his followers in the emporium – the whole shop a shrine to communism. In the food department, Celine had discovered such unusual delicacies as frozen bears' feet and snake. She was hoping that the herbal medicine would cure her eczema; although the assistant had told her it could take some time. It was in the herbalist's department that the mystery of her fellow passenger's treasures on that outward BOAC flight was solved. On display was an assortment of dried objects, each one a cure for anything from indigestion to conjunctivitis. She had watched, fascinated, as the herbalist selected the items required to bring about a cure - roots, flowers, herbs, tree bark, animal parts and other unlikely objects were placed in newspaper. Celine took her strange items home where she brewed up a foul tasting concoction each day. It would have been a delight to Macbeth's witches.

Their acquisitions were shipped back to England and the apartment left soulless. It was with relief that Celine bade farewell to Hong Kong, but she could tell that James did not want to leave.

As he dozed on the long flight home, Celine pulled the secret journal out of her bag and wrote:

I wish I could feel more optimistic about my future with James but so much has happened to sour our relationship and I don't know if I can ever trust him again. But what of Annabel? I will never forget the look in the eyes of Nick's son as he gazed at that picture of Eloise after our chance meeting in the park in Cheltenham. Sometimes I think of the brief time we spent together and wonder if I should have told him my feelings for him. But so many families seem to be fractured these days and the children are the innocent victims - so I will persevere. I will fight for my marriage if only for Annabel's sake. However, this is James's last chance - any more deception and he'll be out of my life for good!

15

PARADISE LOST

Try as she may, Samantha could not forgive Paul for his deception. He, on the other hand, seemed relieved that his secret was out and, now that Samantha knew about his cross dressing, felt that he had to keep talking about it. It was as if a broken water pipe had been mended; such was the gushing of his confessions. He told Samantha that, since returning to England, he had been out a number of times in her late aunt's clothing that he had retrieved from a bag that he was supposed to take to the charity shop. The wig and shoes had been bought by mail order and sent to his office.

"I love you Sam, but you have to understand that I have a need to dress in women's clothes. It started when I was very young," he admitted. "There's no reason why we can't work this out. I love you, tell me what you really feel for me?"

"Nothing. I feel nothing for you."

"But, I thought - " Paul hung his head.

"I did love you, of course I did, but things have changed. Paul, are you - I mean do you like men?"

"If I think what I think you mean, no, I'm not a homosexual and have never been one. Does that make it all right?" he pleaded.

"No, it just makes it slightly less painful, that's all. It's too late - it's over."

He tried to reach for her hand that she withdrew involuntarily as if a snake was about to bite her. The more he talked the more she wanted to cover her ears and block him out. He was a stranger she did not wish to know. Life went on in a dream like state. She was numbed by the prospect of a divorce.

Samantha moved into the spare bedroom with Kim, as she could no longer stand the thought of Paul touching her. Even if he stood near her she felt soiled and each morning scrubbed herself in the shower until her skin was raw. Three weeks later she told Paul to leave. She had calmly decided that she would confront him when their small son was not at home. Already, Kim was behaving badly and had bitten his father in an unprovoked rage.

Kim was spending the day with Samantha's mother, Betty, so the bungalow was eerily quiet and Samantha decided to use this time to tell her husband to go.

"It's no use, Paul. Please just go. Go and get help. I would like a divorce. I already have an appointment at Robinson's and - "

"Please Sam, don't be so hasty. Don't throw all we have away just over a few women's clothes."

"It's not just that," her voice rose in frustration, "you don't seem to understand. If I'd wanted to marry a woman I would have been a lesbian. You are not the person I thought you were. I'm going to see a solicitor tomorrow."

"It's a waste of time seeing a solicitor." Paul could not look her in the eyes.

"What do you mean?" Samantha shivered.

"We don't need a divorce." His eyes darted from side to side like a cornered animal. Then he took a deep breath and went towards her with his arms open.

"Just get out. Don't touch me. Just go and don't come back." She was sobbing now but as he moved towards her to offer comfort she pushed him away.

So he left with tears in his eyes, his shoulders sagging in defeat. He would have to tell her somehow about his other secret. How could he tell her and what would it do to their son, Kim? Why, oh why was he in this mess? They could have been happy together if she'd never found out. Couldn't they?

The next day she found a hand delivered letter on the doormat, begging her to reconsider but, the more he pleaded, the more her love for him turned to revulsion. What would her friends and family think if they saw him out and about dressed like a woman? Her dreams of a happy marriage had corroded away like rusted metal.

Samantha gazed back at the past and wished that she could roll back time to when she stood on that beach in Mauritius in her spotless gown. Feeling lost, she wandered around the bungalow, hating everything about its faded dilapidation. Outside the sky was heavy and it had started to rain and she longed for the blue skies and brilliant sunshine that she had started to take for granted in Mauritius. If only she could return to that time when life offered so much hope, when she was blissfully unaware of the pain that the future would throw at her with such a vengeance. As if somehow it would eradicate the past she went through her wardrobe, wondering if Paul had ever tried anything of hers on. She would buy some new clothes soon, she promised herself. Last of all she came upon her wedding dress, hanging forlornly on a lavender padded hanger. As if possessed, she threw the gown on the bed and rushed into the kitchen where a large pair of scissors lay on the table. Rampant with fury, she ran back to the bedroom grasping the scissors. She started at the hem, and began to hack haphazardly at the silky fabric that had been worn in Mauritius and survived a dunking in the swimming pool. As she cut she started to sob, at first quietly and then, with each frenzied attack, her sobs came out as primal, vicious screams. When the dress was finally in tatters, she grabbed pieces at random and ripped them with her bare hands until, exhausted, she threw the scissors on the floor and ran from the room, slamming the door as if this part of her life was finally closed.

"Why, God, why?" She shouted to the silence, her emotions spent. And, at that moment, it was as if her faith, so strong, so reliable, had died with her marriage.

Two days later she visited the solicitor at Robinson's in a smart part of Cheltenham to start divorce proceedings. She felt driven. In order to survive she was certain that she had to escape the quicksand of her marriage before it choked her.

Mr Hatfield's north facing office was as dark as her mood as she sat opposite him at his mahogany desk.

"I have to inform you that your, erm, partner has already been to see me." He said solemnly adjusting his wire framed glasses.

"Oh, he didn't say. Is he going to make this divorce difficult?" Samantha was surprised and confused that Paul had seen the solicitor before her.

"A divorce won't be necessary. You see you are not legally married. Your marriage in Mauritius is not recognised by law." He paused for a professional moment to let her absorb this news. The poor girl looked so fragile - he hoped she would not cause a scene.

"No, no, you must be mistaken. Paul could never do that." She searched his face in disbelief. He just nodded.

"I'm afraid he could and did. However, your partner has agreed to pay you a generous allowance on the condition that you let him see his son on a regular basis."

"Wait, are you telling me that the whole thing is a sham. That - " her voice trailed off and she started to sob.

"This will come as a shock to you," he cleared his throat, "but the reason that your partner could not marry you is because he is already married. To have married you would have been to commit the crime of bigamy. He has a wife in Scotland who refuses to divorce him."

"Oh, my God. How could I be so naïve? That's why he said to wait until we got to England before registering Kim's birth. Always excuses. Postponements. It's all falling into place now." She scrambled in her bag for a tissue and blew her nose.

Samantha grabbed the desk to steady herself, her sobs becoming louder.

The solicitor waited patiently before continuing. "May I suggest you go home and read his proposals before contacting another solicitor to do the necessary paperwork to draw up an agreement? I am not able to represent your partner and yourself but it shouldn't be too complicated."

She felt as if she was being dismissed into a world that had become cruel and alien to her. She had an illegitimate son and Paul knew about it all the time. How could he have betrayed her like this?

A week later, after seeing another solicitor, it was agreed that Paul would pay her a monthly sum and that they would halve their assets. He confessed that he knew all the time that their marriage was not legal but explained that his wife found out about his cross dressing and left him. A devout Catholic, she refused to divorce him. They had no children, so that made things less complicated. She wondered what lies Paul must have told his parents - they clearly had no knowledge of his marriage to the girl in Scotland. He was certainly an enigma. The very qualities that had drawn her to him - his quiet charm and enigmatic smile had now pushed them irrevocably apart. She had mistaken enigma for secrecy in her innocent quest for love.

Samantha gradually came to terms with the fact that she would have to make a new life for herself without Paul, although she had agreed to let him see Kim on alternate weekends – with one proviso; that he would never let their son see him in women's clothes and that he would attend therapy sessions. He was so desperate to see his son that he readily agreed. As he faced his inner demons for the first time in his life, he became increasingly haggard.

Paul found himself a small apartment in the centre of town and Samantha rented a charming little cottage in a nearby village. She was glad to leave the depressing bungalow with its gloomy decor and gloomier memories. It was time to make a fresh start and offer her young son the security that he needed. A monthly allowance was paid into her bank account and life took on a comfortable routine. Even her health began to improve and she felt a semblance of peace and happiness return. But she never ventured into a church again, somehow blaming God for her misfortune. Rebelliously, she considered having an affair but dismissed the idea when she looked at the innocence of her son. Her life had been complicated enough and she just wanted some normality. The cottage was a comfort to her and she enjoyed a simple life in the village of Wittingford with Kim. She would not let her boat be rocked again, but rock it did when she took her mother to the station one fateful morning.

It was raining hard as she drove her VW across town.

"Don't drive too fast." Betty complained as Samantha hurtled into the station.

Betty was off on a rare holiday to visit a cousin in Birmingham.

"Mum, I'm within the speed limit - stop panicking."

"Don't panic, Granny - you won't miss the train." Kim piped up from the back of the car.

There were just a handful of people on the platform as Samantha saw her mother onto the train.

"Bye, Mum, have a lovely time. I'll collect you next week." She kissed her mother on the cheek.

Betty kissed Kim fondly and gave him a big hug.

"Bye, bye, Granny. Come back soon."

Betty boarded the train, looking worried, carrying a holdall and numerous polythene bags, her newly permed hair protected from the downpour with a plastic Rainmate.

Samantha and Kim waved until the train disappeared out of sight before heading for the car park. It was as they were leaving that Samantha spotted a familiar figure. Freezing with horror, she let out a gasp, tasting the diesel that permeated the air.

He was wearing the navy maternity dress with the red piping that he'd designed in Mauritius. On his head was the same wig that he'd worn that dreadful afternoon when she came home early from church and discovered his secret.

"Paul, Paul," she called out involuntarily, her stomach turning somersaults, but her cries were drowned by the noise of the train as it rushed into the station.

She never did find out if he had spotted her as he grabbed his suitcases and jumped onto the train bound for London.

"Who was that funny lady, Mummy?" Kim asked as the train steamed away.

Fuming with anger, Samantha took control as she looked at her sweet son. So innocent - how could she explain?

"I don't know, sweetheart. I don't know. Just some weird freak." She said with venom as she grabbed his hand and rushed through the rain to the car.

"Why did you call Daddy? Where's Daddy?" Kim persisted.

"I don't know. I don't know. Hurry up, get in - you're soaking." She snapped.

Kim began to cry in the back of the car as she drove through puddles towards home. She would find out what was going on if it was the last thing she did.

"I want Daddy, I want Granny." Kim wailed from the back of the car.

"Well you'll just have to put up with Mummy." She snapped.

"And you're a naughty Mummy." Kim shouted in uncharacteristic rage.

Rain coursed down the windscreen in ever increasing rivulets and Samantha wiped blinding tears from her eyes as she drove through what was now a black storm.

Upon entering the cottage her frayed nerves felt a little soothed. Kim ran in and then turned and hit his mother hard on her thigh.

"Stop it, stop it." She grabbed the still angry child and held him close until gradually he stopped struggling and quietly sobbed in her embrace.

"It'll be all right. Mummy loves you very much. Now, shall we have some toast?"

"Okay and can we watch TV. Together." Kim sniffed and dried his tears with the back of his hand.

"Yes, but first I must make just one important phone call. You go upstairs and wash your hands and we'll have a yummy tea."

Resilient as ever, Kim ran upstairs while Samantha picked up the telephone.

The agent that let Paul's flat was helpful. "I'm sorry but the tenancy has been terminated. He told me that he had taken a job abroad."

"Did he say where? Did he leave a forwarding address or contact number?" Samantha's mind was racing.

"No, I'm sorry - that's all I know," the agent said.

"Okay, thank you," Samantha put down the receiver sharply, washed her hands and proceeded to get Kim's tea.

'What's to become of us? What do I tell Kim? And why did Paul tell me that the therapy was working and that he no longer felt the need to cross dress? How stupid of me to trust him!' She thought.

She felt as if she was lost in a fog of disappointment and confusion and remembered a phrase from a song that she used to sing in Mauritius. 'There's always someone who leaves by train and who will never return.'

16

ART AND LIBERATION

Kristin stood back and viewed her new salon with pride. The basement had been decorated and smelled fresh and clean. Green towels had been purchased in a sale, folded neatly and placed in each cubicle. Beauty products were displayed together with point of sale materials and posters. Price lists had been collected from the printers and she was raring to go. All she needed now were clients so, the next step had to be publicity. There were several other beauty salons in Cheltenham and so she wondered how long it would take to get clients. After working in Hong Kong, she knew that word of mouth was a good way of advertising but, before that could kick in, she needed a strong client base and so placed an advert in the local paper. Never one to procrastinate, she boldly asked for an editorial, which was granted. The journalist wanted her to supply a picture of her to go alongside the write up and so Kristin found a flattering photo and took it along to the newspaper office. She explained that the picture needed clipping as her daughter, Nina, was standing next to her in the photo that was taken on their balcony in Hong Kong. This was agreed upon and a few days later the article appeared in the paper with the headline: 'Kristin looks too young to have a daughter.'

It was with mixed feelings that she gazed at the caption. She could not see the relevance of her being a young mother with opening a new business. However, it was a good editorial and would, no doubt, bring in some business but she was miffed to see that they had not clipped the photo as she had requested. They even mentioned Nina's name in the editorial that she felt was pointless. However, this was soon forgotten as the phone started to ring and bookings made.

She decided not to work on Saturdays if she could avoid it. However, the Saturday following the editorial, she was cleaning the salon, Harry was gardening and the children were playing at a friend's house.

The phone rang and when she answered it the next few minutes stretched into an abyss of fear.

On the end of the phone a man with a husky, breathless voice threatened, "Nina will be fine. I've got her with me here. She's tied up and nothing will happen to her if you do as I say. I want you to answer these questions. Now what bra size are you?"

It was every parent's nightmare. Kristin envisioned her daughter tied up in some stranger's room, her very life endangered. As she tried to keep her composure she offered a silent prayer for help whilst listening to the evil questioning.

Filthy, personal questions snaked down the telephone line and, as her mind was racing and her heart pounding, a miracle happened.

Nina walked into the salon - something she rarely did. The whole ghastly episode was a hoax. Kristin slammed the phone down and hugged her daughter.

"What made you come in - I thought you were next door at Jane's house?" Her words came out like machine gun fire.

"Dunno," she shrugged.

Without wishing to alarm her young daughter she explained the whole scenario and told her to be careful. Nina sniffed, rubbed her nose with her sleeve and seemed to think that her mother was making a fuss about nothing. She took a sticky sweet out of her jeans pocket and went to her room. Maybe it was just bravado.

Kristin phoned the police and was interviewed by a very sympathetic policewoman but they never did manage to trace the caller. Although she did get the odd rude call from dubious characters wanting 'massage', she never did get a call as obscene or gut wrenchingly terrifying as the first one.

Harry was annoyed that the newspaper had printed the photo without clipping it as Kristin has requested.

"Do you know," Kristin told him that evening, "I felt safer in the metropolis of Hong Kong than in this so-called genteel town. I hope that this pervert won't start stalking me, or worse, Nina."

"I'm sure it will be fine. These sort of people usually like to make threats but that is where it finishes." Harry put his arm round her but was not convinced.

It was with a burdened heart and an acute awareness of the frailty of human nature that Kristin returned to her salon the following Monday. Her neighbour had agreed to collect the children from their nearby school each afternoon as her daughter, Jane, was in Nina's class. But Kristin could not relax until she knew that Nina was home and safe. It took her quite a while before she stopped worrying about her.

She worked hard and soon found it a challenge to keep up with the demands of her fast expanding business. It was like a run away horse that she could not catch but, compelled to keep going, she took stock and made a decision to take on her first employee.

Chloe was a local girl, just out of college and keen to start work immediately. She was well groomed, if a little too heavily made up, with grey eyes and dyed blonde hair that she tied back in a neat bun. Her eyebrows were plucked and pencilled in so that she looked perpetually surprised. The interview went well and, as Chloe was the only applicant for the job, she was appointed on the spot. Kristin felt as if she was in heaven as she started to delegate a good proportion of her workload and, three months later, as the business was running so smoothly, she became tempted to do something completely out of character. Yes, it was time for a hobby. A diversion was what she needed.

The seeds had been sown by one of her clients who told her about a new part time course that was starting at the local art college, so Kristin decided to put her name down. It was risky taking time off, but she felt almost compelled to paint. What a marvellous diversion it would be from the constant demands of business and domestic life.

~ ~ ~ ~ ~ ~

Meanwhile, Celine was house hunting in the same area and found a three bed-roomed Victorian semi-detached house near the centre of Cheltenham. Having lived without any greenery for some time, she was attracted to the small south facing back garden with colourful flower beds, and a sturdy apple tree standing vigil in the centre of the lawn. She imagined herself sitting under it with a book on warm summer days while Annabel played close by. Celine had relished every moment of the house hunting and then the furnishing of their new home with antiques that she picked up in auction rooms. When their crate of belongings arrived intact from Hong Kong it was like Christmas. The oriental artefacts blended in well with their furniture and the homemaking was a joy, although, at times, Celine missed Ah Foo, especially on washdays.

She gleaned simple pleasure from household tasks and enjoyed taking Annabel out in the more temperate climes of England. The toddler's waxy complexion turned as rosy as a ripe apple in the fresh air and Celine felt contented for the first time in what seemed an eternity. James secured a job locally and she appreciated the fact that he arrived home each evening for his supper, although he still looked gaunt and was non communicative. At times, Celine missed the interesting expatriates who she had befriended in Hong Kong and who had such outgoing personalities. Then, when winter arrived, she even began to miss the heat and disliked the dark afternoons. But she was content that James seemed more settled.

Then, after a long, gloomy winter, one early morning Celine arose to gentle spring sunshine, daffodils blooming under the apple tree and a child who was constantly smiling. Sasha, the cat, who had been sent to her mother for care while they were in Hong Kong, had moved back in with them and was snoozing on the window ledge. Outside a blackbird sang in celebration of the season. After cleaning the upstairs of the house, she decided to go through her wardrobe and get rid of all the clothes that were unsuitable for England. The brightly coloured dresses that seemed in keeping with the tropics somehow looked garish in the softer light of the Cotswolds. This done, she started on James's clothes. She decided to take his suits to the dry cleaners but first she would go through his pockets in case he had left any money in them. It was then that she found the letter. At first she thought it might be from a girlfriend as it had a Hong Kong stamp on it. She ripped it open, her stomach in turmoil.

At first the contents did not register with her. Then, when the implications hit her, the room started to spin, so she sat on the bed and re-read it. The letter was from a large company in Hong Kong welcoming James to his new post with them the following month.

Next month.

He would be provided with a bachelor flat in an up market area of Kowloon in Hong Kong, together with a driver and a full time amah.

The rest of the day passed in a haze of disbelief. When James arrived home she threw the letter at him.

"What's the meaning of this? Why didn't you tell me you had a job in Hong Kong – and what's this about a bachelor flat? What about Annabel and me – don't we count for anything?" The questions shot out like ammunition until she was breathless with despair and frustration.

James fixed his eyes on her for a moment and then did what he always did under these circumstances – poured himself a large gin and tonic.

"I just can't settle here. I need to be in Hong Kong but I knew that you wouldn't want to come back with me." He said in a matter of fact way as if all this was perfectly normal and that she was overreacting.

"So you want a divorce?"

James sipped his drink before replying, "No. I thought that we could see each other when I come back on leave. This new company offer six weeks annual leave with airfares paid for." He was gulping his drink now but didn't offer Celine one.

"If you think that I want to be a part time wife you are mistaken. That's it, James, I've had enough. Go back to your nice little life in Hong Kong with your tarts and your selfishness." And with that she stormed upstairs and locked him out of the bedroom. He did not follow her.

The next day he was gone. He had packed all but a few of his belongings and disappeared. He had gone from her life forever. He left no forwarding address, no note, no phone call. Nothing.

She was too upset to write in her journal immediately, but took it out of her bag and placed it on her bedside table. The next day she wrote:

I no longer need to hide this journal. James has gone and will not come back - that I know. I had such dreams as a young girl, such aspirations but I never thought that it would end this way. How I despise him! It is finished between us and I can't keep trying - only to be rejected over and over again. I've come to realise that I've wasted the best years of my life on a heartless brute - but I will get over this in time. I have to.

~ ~ ~ ~ ~ ~

Celine thought that she would be able to manage alone but started to have panic attacks in the middle of the night. She didn't want to go back on the anti-depressants but was experiencing the drowning feelings again. Then, to add to the stress, the normally placid Annabel started to scream in the night calling out for her Daddy.

"Instead of soldiering on why not move in with me until things settle down," Veronica offered.

"Thanks, Mum. Just for a week or two until Annabel gets back to normal." Celine was secretly relieved.

But she did not find it a great comfort staying with her mother, although Veronica was a natural grandmother and doted on Annabel. The baby's arrival had filled a void that the death of Celine's father had left in her mother's life. But Celine was mourning a death – the death of her marriage and found herself crying at the least provocation. The slightest prompt like a play on the television would open the door to the grief that she was trying to shut out.

Veronica's only hobby had only ever been her neighbours and their parochial lives. It had always been so, Celine recalled, as she listened to yet another story of the soap opera that was her neighbours' lives.

"Do you know, well - I've heard that a man who dresses in women's clothes has moved into town?" Veronica was in full flow. "He's been seen in Cavendish House, bold as brass and wearing a red wig and high heeled shoes. Well! He's got a pretty wife, apparently, who's left him. Can you blame her? She's a bit of a bohemian, arty type, I've heard. Her mother, Betty, works at the Co-op but I've not seen her there for a while. Anyway, this girl that he was married to has a little boy - poor kid to have a father like that. Whatever next."

Half listening, Celine recalled the mother of her childhood.

~ ~ ~ ~ ~ ~

MUM'S THE WORD

"Well!" Veronica would exclaim indignantly, hands on hips in protest as she savoured the latest morsel of scandal.

She'd be standing at the bus stop, at the fence, in the street; it didn't matter where, as long as she could pursue her only hobby apart from knitting. Gossip.

The best place was the fence, talking to Mrs. Williams, her elderly next door neighbour with the prim perm. Veronica would take two steps back each time she heard something particularly shocking whilst uttering the immortal word, "Well!" This was often followed with, "You don't say," as she egged the news bearer on to say more.

It was Veronica's all-consuming passion. Neighbours and their parochial lives were what she lived for. Celine's long suffering father would come home from a busy day at work and have to listen in dumb silence. He would have his ears blasted by the goings on of

Mrs. Brown, Mr. Jones, whoever. When it got to the juicy bits she'd give the young Celine a sideways glance and continue in a stage whisper.

Having a dark secret in her background seemed to give her an excuse to search for hidden frailties in others. Perhaps discovering other's misdemeanours made her feel more acceptable in those prudish days.

"That Ann Jones has been round next door. I bet she knew Jenny was out. She had Simon all to herself for TWO HOURS. Well!"

"Mm," Celine's father would pretend to show a modicum of interest while trying to lose himself in the sanctuary of his beloved newspaper.

"Pauline, you remember that one with the dyed blonde hair, has just got back from Bahrain. Seems she got herself an American boyfriend when she was working over there." Veronica was fuelled by the tasty morsel of gossip. People in the neighbourhood rarely ventured as far as New Brighton, so Bahrain seemed almost as far away as Jupiter.

Respectability and 'what the neighbours thought' were high on Veronica's agenda. She always agreed with what everyone said, smiling sweetly. Contentious issues like politics or religion were never discussed at home. The family always did the done thing and never challenged the status quo. If the doorbell rang she would whip off her apron with speed and dexterity before answering the door. After her daily chores she would change into a smart dress in the hope that a neighbour would call by. The best china was at the ready in case a cup of tea needed brewing and a home-made cake was always in the tin. Bakewell tart, scones and a variety of cakes – fruit, chocolate, coffee and walnut to name just a few of the delights of her larder. No wonder her trim waist line had disappeared along with her single status.

As well as being on a par with Mrs Beeton, Veronica was also an expert at nagging and was a martyr to back pain. Monday nights were the worst. Washdays made purgatory seem like a holiday camp. First the whites were pushed into the large dolly tub that stood outside the back door. After much pushing up and down with the dolly, a copper contraption on a handle, the heavy laundry was taken out of the scalding water and dragged into the washhouse. This was a separate building with a large sink that stood at the back of the house. The coloured laundry was left to soak in the dolly tub while the whites were put through the hand operated mangle. This contraption stood in pride of place in the wash area next to the coalhouse and outside toilet that was only ever used by the occasional tradesman who was taken short. After the mangle ritual, all the washing was rinsed by hand, wrung again and then hung on the vast washing line in the back garden where the whole area was transformed into a static galleon. Until it rained. Then the lot was rushed indoors and hung on a wooden airer and hoisted aloft to dry above the fire in the warm breakfast room, creating a humidity that rivalled the alleys of Bangkok. Sometimes this was the only cosy room in the whole house. Central heating, along with washing machines and tumble dryers were a rare luxury in post war England. Veronica would light a fire in the sitting room in the afternoon, just in case a neighbour should drop by for a grilling. Or rather a chat.

Upstairs was like entering the Arctic in the winter months. Sometimes toothbrushes would freeze on the window ledge; such were the conditions of the bathroom.

By the time Celine's father got home Veronica would have her hand on her back and regale him with the horrors of washing, mangling and lifting. George never said much. Nor did he ever offer her a hug of encouragement or commiseration. No matter what the weather or the challenges of 'the wash' a cooked supper was offered to George after his commute from Dale Street in Liverpool. He was skinny and would pick at his food as if it had been prepared by an untouchable. Never did he take his plate out to the kitchen but would retire to the sitting room to enjoy yet another cigarette. Chores were clearly defined. There were his and there were hers and the boundaries never changed. No one ever saw him dry a dish nor would Veronica wield a paintbrush. Women's liberation had not been born and Germaine Greer was still a child.

Tuesdays were not much better. Ironing had to be done and what a mammoth task that was. Veronica would sprinkle water on to the offending garment before attacking it with a heavy iron. Many a time she took to her bed with a migraine after suffering at the ironing board. Just before the advent of Women's Liberation, the wonder of crease proof man made fabrics like Crimplene hit the world. Ironing was halved overnight as this disgusting fabric that usually came in vicious colours, caused sweating and felt like cardboard, transformed women's lives.

But, in the meantime, Veronica's suffering continued.

"Those full shirts of yours will be the death of me. The stripes were flashing before my eyes. The aspirins didn't work. Gloria doesn't know she's born not having children." It was the same every week. Celine's aunt Gloria was a woman to be envied according to Veronica.

"That Pauline, you know, the one with the dyed blonde hair, has been ill. Some sickness bug Mrs Adams told me at the Co-op this morning. Goodness knows what she picked up living in Bahrain." Pauline had caused quite a stir venturing so far away.

Celine's mother always seemed old to her. Old and tired with greying permed hair and a plump figure but she loved her dearly and was always seeking her approval.

Then the family acquired a twin tub washing machine and the complaining diminished a little. The old dolly tub and mangle were given away and Celine was allowed to play in the former washhouse - a domain that adults never entered now. It was a secret den where children could have meetings of great importance and it was here that Celine would play house with her dolls away from the watchful eyes of the grownups. Life was on the up for Veronica with the arrival of the washing machine and Mondays were becoming fairly civilised and pain free.

The months went by with uneventful regularity and the gossip continued along with the weekly wash. Then one day the whispering between Gloria and Veronica stopped abruptly as Celine entered the kitchen.

"Pauline had a little girl when she went away to stay with her aunt in..." That's all the young Celine heard but she knew something momentous had happened to poor Pauline, something that would be the source of gossip for many months to come. To have a child out of wedlock in those days was to become a social pariah.

When Celine looked at old photos of Veronica in her hey day she was rather beautiful in a forlorn sort of way. She was slim and wore her hair in a fashionable twenties bob. Her dresses were drop waisted and she wore hats pulled low over her huge brown eyes. She always looked rather sad, unlike her sister, Gloria, who always seemed to be laughing. Perhaps it was because she didn't know she was born.

'Mum drives me up the wall but, at least I don't have to put up with my mother-in-law any more. I think that just might have tipped me over the edge.' Celine thought to herself. Glancing up at her mother, who was staring at her disapprovingly, she enquired, "What's the matter?"

"I don't think you've been listening to a word I've been saying. I was telling you about that man who dresses in women's clothes and has been seen out and about."

"Sorry, Mum, I was just thinking about the old days."

Celine began to develop a trait that her father had perfected – that of blocking out her mother's constant chatter. She would become lost in her thoughts, often wondering how James was getting on without her. She had not heard from him since he left.

Celine's reverie was broken by her mother tapping her on the arm.

"You didn't answer my question. What happened to that wayward wife of, what's his name, Nick?"

"Sorry, I thought I told you - she went to Greece." Celine answered and waited for the look of indignation to shadow her mother's face. She was not disappointed.

"You don't say! Oh yes, I remember now. Well, she'll get her comeuppance; girls like that always do. What I want to know is why you girls just can't be content to stay at home? It was good enough for me and your Aunt Gloria."

Celine felt pensive as she wrote in her journal that night:

Mum is so opinionated - there are two sides to every argument but she is set in her ways. When she was a young woman, Women's Liberation with its so-called freedom and equality had not existed. How our lives have changed! Equality is fine but I'm not sure that women's rights will bring the freedom that they promise. Trying to hold down a career and run a home could take its toll on many women in their search for happiness. The result could be exhaustion and dissatisfaction as most men will not be quick to share the household chores equally. Certainly, James was never willing to help around the home but then I was not a working mother so I can only theorise. However, if James can't be traced or offer me alimony, I may have to be a full time working Mum. Life is so uncertain and why hasn't he written?

17

FRIENDSHIP

Samantha was browsing through an old copy of the local paper that Betty had passed on to her, when her eyes were drawn to a picture of a young woman with a child. She read the editorial about a new salon in town and decided to have her long, light brown lashes tinted. It was about time she had a treat after all the upset over Paul, she decided. Without delay she phoned the number at the end of the write-up and spoke to a cheerful sounding person who booked her in the following day.

"Do you mind if I bring my young son in with me? He's pretty well behaved." Samantha asked.

"No problem. I have two kids of my own and we have a few toys tucked away in the salon so that he can amuse himself. But you have to keep your eyes shut for about fifteen minutes while the tint is on."

"Oh, that shouldn't be a problem if I explain what's going on. See you tomorrow at eleven then."

Samantha bundled Kim into her VW Beetle explaining that she was going to have beautiful lashes and that he must play quietly while she pretended to sleep.

Kristin greeted them at the door and ushered them into a cubicle where she had already placed a box of toys and books to entertain Kim.

As she applied the tint to Samantha's eyelashes she chatted easily to her new client.

"Have you had this done before?"

"No, this is the first time I've been to a beauty salon. I felt like a bit of pampering and thought long black lashes would be rather glamorous."

"Absolutely. Now keep your eyes shut the whole time. That's it. You all right there Kim?"

The child nodded, absorbed in a simple jigsaw.

"How long have you lived in Cheltenham, Samantha?"

"All my life really. Except for a stint in Mauritius where we lived for a couple of years. We've only been back for about six months and, well, it's a long story."

"Mauritius! How exotic. Was it gorgeous there?" Kristin took a piece of jigsaw that Kim handed her and showed him where it should go.

"Yes, it was lovely. Especially the beaches but things didn't work out between Kim's father and me so we're not together anymore. Is the salon doing well?" Samantha wanted to change the subject.

"Oh, yes, we're really busy. I've just taken on an assistant so next week I'm going to start a part time art class - it's something I've always wanted to do."

Samantha felt a flutter of excitement.

"Fantastic. I painted a bit in Mauritius and loved it. In fact, when I left school I wanted to go to art school but I ended up as a waitress instead."

"Why don't you enrol - if you can find someone to look after Kim? It's only one day a week. I've got a leaflet if you want."

So, with her sweeping, dark lashes and Kim in tow, Samantha headed straight to her mother's.

Betty had retired now and was more than ready to help look after Kim while Samantha attended art classes. All she had to do was see if there was an available space for her in the class.

There was and life took on a whole new dimension.

It was at art college that Samantha noticed a good looking Spaniard who seemed to always have his eyes on her whenever she glanced at him. She fought the temptation to speak to him as she had determined to have a life without men but, after a while, she stopped trying. The attraction was too strong.

"I can't help but notice that you look really sad. Would you like to have lunch with me today in the cafeteria? I'm a good listener." His soft brown eyes looked kind and she could do with the company. Since finding out about Paul she had cut herself off from people, feeling ashamed – as if, somehow, it was all her fault. Her confidence had been knocked and she was afraid that she was a bad judge of character. She even doubted that she would be able to find love again and, as an antidote to her disappointment, would daydream that one day, when Kim had grown up, she would live somewhere warm and sunny, become an artist and live alone but never be lonely.

But, now that this attractive Spaniard had entered her world, the day dream had become hazy and out of focus. She looked up at him.

"Yes, that would be good. I'm Samantha, by the way."

"I know - I'm Carlos. What a lovely name – Samantha." He seemed to savour her name, his deep voice and accent making it sound exotic, his words settling on her as gently as a feather and she found herself attracted to him in a way that she found disconcerting.

They made their way to the cafeteria where they drank revolting coffee and ate cheese sandwiches.

"Have you been to my country, Samantha?" There it was again, that way that his voice brushed against her. She found her heart beating faster and her mouth became dry.

"No, I've only been to an island in the Indian Ocean. I lived in Mauritius for two years. We've, er, I've not been back that long."

"Maybe one day you'll visit Spain. It's a wonderful place and the coffee tastes better than this stuff." He laughed. "Now tell me all about yourself."

He was indeed a good listener and before long she was relating her story to him. He wondered why she was smiling while her eyes told a different story. The pain was clearly still fresh. Carlos was the opposite of Paul, constantly joking and open. He had the relaxed manner of one raised in the sunshine. She hoped that he had no secrets – she was tired of living with family secrets. But he seemed friendly and answered all questions without guile. He told her that he was studying art full time but enjoyed the painting classes the most.

"It is because you give me inspiration." He winked and she felt herself blush.

Several weeks later, they started dating but she was taking things slowly. She told him that she just wanted them to be friends - and he had agreed. Carlos had a family in Spain so there was no point getting too serious as he planned on returning when he had completed his studies.

When Samantha first met Kristin at the salon she found her zest for life infectious and wondered if it hadn't been for her influence, if she would ever had joined the art class. She seemed as robust as Samantha was delicate. Soon they became a threesome, as she would often join Samantha and Carlos at lunchtime in the college cafeteria. Samantha noticed that although she was a businesswoman with ambition, she had a strong artistic streak. She and Carlos would outdo each other with their jokes that used to make Samantha feel locked out and a little jealous, as she knew that she was too serious. But it soon became clear that Kristin was happily married and so Samantha's insecurities evaporated like tropical rain on hot stones and was replaced with admiration and respect for her new friend.

Samantha found that painting was therapeutic and she would forget about Paul when she was absorbed in her work. She had a delicate touch, was infinitely patient and loved to merge watercolours and experiment with new techniques. Drawing and painting were all that she had hoped they would be and her contentment showed in her work.

~ ~ ~ ~ ~ ~

CLOSURE

After a few weeks of waiting for James to call or write to her, begging her to return, Celine realised that she was denying the truth and had to make a decision. At last she accepted that her marriage was over and so, with apprehension, she visited a solicitor to apply for a divorce. The papers were sent to a forwarding address in Hong Kong that James had eventually posted to her. No other information was forthcoming, just an address in an affluent area of Kowloon. She thought that he might fight her and refuse a divorce but he did not and everything progressed smoothly. He had decided to stay permanently in Hong Kong, as he liked the life out there. Most of all he liked his freedom, Celine suspected. Marriage and children were not for him. He had never dared to rebel against his mother and so he rebelled against Celine, knowing that she was no match for him and loathed confrontation. Always a misogynist, James hated women – especially the mother who had controlled him with such success.

Annabel thrived with all the attention she received from both her mother and grandmother and was a great comfort to Celine. She had started to walk and talk from an early age and Celine was a proud mother. After the visit to the solicitor Celine felt a calm envelope her and she knew it was time to move back home – the panic attacks gone. Deep down she knew that she could never have been happy with James and had been fighting a losing battle. With acceptance came serenity. Gradually, she began to adjust to being a single mother and started to enjoy the home and garden once more. She did not contact any of her old friends or colleagues but decided to make a fresh start, thinking that as a single woman, she would have difficulty fitting in with married couples. Always an avid reader she joined the local library and, when scanning the notice board there, was drawn to an advert for painting classes at the nearby art college. Remembering her dream of becoming an art student she approached her mother for support.

"Mum, now that Annabel and I are settled I wondered if you wouldn't mind baby-sitting for me once a week so that I can go to an art class? I thought it would be good to have an interest outside the home and I noticed that the local art college are doing a part time course."

Uncharacteristically, her mother paused before replying, "Art school - you don't say? Yes, I'll baby-sit for you, I suppose, although if Annabel plays up you'll have to give up the course. It will be good for you to do something new, although in my day the home was quite enough. But why art school? What about sewing – you never did get the hang of it for some reason. Heaven knows you could do with some sort of distraction after all you've been through." Veronica spoke without any real understanding of the trauma that her daughter had endured, her own life being a steady flow of routine with a reliable husband.

It was with excitement that Celine enrolled at the college and purchased her brushes, pads and paints. She had let her hair grow longer and lived in jeans – as if recapturing her teenage years. The classes were a success and she lost herself in creating drawings and paintings. Rather than feeling miserable when her final divorce papers came through, she felt free. Free to be herself for the first time in years. Or maybe for the first time ever. With each brush stroke she felt as if she was recreating herself into the woman she wanted to be and not the one she was expected to be.

~ ~ ~ ~ ~ ~

Soon Samantha approached Celine, the quiet student, who liked to work in a corner at the back of the studio. Samantha thought that she was beautiful in a mysterious sort of way and decided that it would be good to break through the invisible barrier that seemed to surround her. It appeared that the barrier was fragile and easily broken and she, Kristin and Celine found the art class to be a lifeline.

"You have a very distinctive style – really free. Have you been painting a long time?" Samantha asked as she gazed upon the painting of a skyline in Hong Kong.

"No, I've only just started really. Although I always wanted to go to art school."

"How funny - I wanted to do the same. Look, are you doing anything after the class – fancy a coffee in town? Perhaps you'd like to join Kristin and me." Samantha glanced over at Kristin who had just packed her brushes away.

Celine thought that Samantha was pretty in a delicate way and liked her bright manner and bird like way of holding her head to one side when she asked a question. Her long fair hair was tied into a loose ponytail with a purple silk scarf and fine fronds of hair strayed about her face and neck. The only makeup she wore was a little kohl pencil around her large grey eyes. She wore silver drop earrings, an ankle length denim skirt, a peasant blouse and a colourful waistcoat. Her frame was slight and she had long, artistic fingers.

"That would be great – my daughter is with my mother today and she said there was no need to hurry back, so why not?" Celine never liked the art class to finish and this seemed a good way of prolonging the enjoyment.

A tall woman in her late twenties strolled over, a rucksack containing her paints on her shoulder. Her dark hair was cut in a sharp bob and she wore black jeans and a red smock. She had a sudden smile that was open and wide and honest eyes that were so dark as to be almost black. Full of zest, she sparkled with humour and had an air of competence about her. Celine looked at her intently as she tried to recall where she had seen the face before. It had been puzzling her since joining the class but she just could not remember where she had seen her, other than at art school.

"Kristin, meet Celine. Celine, this is Kristin who has also just taken up painting. Kristin and I only met at her salon a few weeks ago but we feel as if we've known each other for ages." Samantha explained.

"Hi, you look familiar. Have we met before?" Celine asked.

"I've been thinking the same. You haven't been to my salon have you?" Kristin was intrigued by this girl, with the thick hair and familiar deep eyes.

"No, but I must get your number. I could do with a leg wax. I was going to have it done regularly but reverted to shaving again."

Kristin had sudden recall. "Of course. I gave you a leg wax in Hong Kong. Remember?"

"Yes, of course!" Celine's eyes widened with surprise, "what a coincidence. Your hairstyle is different - longer. Yes, you did a great job and I was going to call you again but my life had become rather complicated and leg waxing was not a priority. What are you doing in Cheltenham?"

"It's a long story. I'll fill you in on our way to the cafe."

The young women did not know it at the time but they were to become close friends and confidants. It was as if fate had flung them together for good reason.

They piled into Samantha's rather battered car that had been painted bubble gum pink, chatting all the while as they made their way to the Montpellier area with its caryatids that stood in stony splendour at the fronts of the shops. Feeling liberated, Celine enjoyed sipping her coffee without having to worry about Annabel wrecking the place. The song "Yesterday," was playing in the background and Celine's memories of sad times were sharpened by the lyrics. She wondered if she had ever really loved James. If she had, surely she would be missing him now but maybe it was not James that she loved, only the idea of marriage and a home of her own. She had been swimming against an unrelenting tide for a long time.

"How old is your daughter?" asked Samantha, brushing cake crumbs off her embroidered purple waistcoat.

"She's almost two. I'm a single parent. My divorce came through last month."

"Snap, me too. My son's three now. He's with my mother today. Where is your ex living?"

"He's in Hong Kong and has no intention of returning to England so I'm very much on my own – except for my mother who has been great."

"No wonder we click, it seems that we're all expatriates. I was sort of married and lived in Mauritius before I found out about Paul's lifestyle and we split up. Actually, I never fitted into colonial life abroad, although it was a beautiful place to live." Samantha looked pensive.

"I was a misfit too as a colonial wife. It was as if I was trying to fit into a time warp. It didn't matter though as I met some young interesting people who were of like mind. And although life was difficult at times, I hope that I've learned something from it all." Celine was delighted to have so much in common with her new acquaintances and felt comfortable sharing her heart with them; something that she had sworn she would never do again.

"Well, I didn't even try to be a colonial wife in Hong Kong because I knew it was not for me and started working pretty much straight away as a beauty therapist so perhaps I had a lucky escape," Kristin said, folding her paper napkin absentmindedly.

Samantha nodded, "My time was marred towards the end of our stay in Mauritius because I contracted a tropical illness which left me feeling weak and, when I returned to England, I ended up in hospital for tests. I just thought that the heat was getting to me but it was more serious than that, so I'm still in recovery mode. It was horrible in hospital. The first few days I was in isolation in case I had something like typhoid. When that was ruled out I had to go through a lot of unspeakable tests - tubes in every orifice. I'm glad that's over and done with. Any boyfriend on the scene?" Samantha asked Celine, eager to change the subject to a lighter topic.

"No – I'm off men at the moment. Besides, I don't go out at night so don't have any opportunity to meet anyone."

"I know what you mean. Actually, I rather like the independence that I have – now that I've got used to it. At first, I found it lonely and a bit scary but now I enjoy not being beholden to any man. At least we have choices now. In my mother's day they would put up with anything for the sake of respectability. Perhaps I'm just being selfish." Samantha looked even more ethereal than usual as she meditated on her life.

"Now don't get all cynical. One day you'll probably be swept off your feet and live happily ever after. Providence probably has just the right partner waiting in the wings for you." Kristin interjected with a chuckle.

"Now you know I lost my faith when I found out about Paul so there's no point trying to convert me. You're lucky being married to Harry; he's so dependable and kind. Now if only I could find someone like him. Happily married to Mr Wonderful with 2.4 children and running a business. You have it all." Samantha said this in a matter of fact rather than a jealous way.

Celine wriggled in her chair wondering if a disagreement was about to ensue but Kristin was not the touchy type and brushed away the comment like a wayward fly. To her the remark was inconsequential and, always ready to jump into another person's shoes, she was understanding and non judgemental.

"It hasn't always been plain sailing. When we went to Australia on a business venture that failed it seemed that we'd thrown all our savings away for nothing. Sam - I'm really sorry to hear about your ordeal in hospital. It sounds ghastly." Kristin was serious for a moment.

"Well, it could have been worse. As it happens, I had tropical sprue, which gets better in a temperate climate. If I'd had malaria it would have been a lot worse. Oh, tell us about Australia next time we meet." Samantha asked, aware that it was getting late.

"Yes, next time. I really ought to be getting back," Celine glanced at her watch and was surprised to see that they had been chatting for almost two hours.

"I'll drop you off at your mum's place on my way home. Why don't you bring Annabel round for tea on Saturday? Kristin and I have already met up on several Saturday afternoons as Harry usually takes the kids out and we can have a good natter. I've got a tiny cottage in Wittingford." Samantha smiled revealing small white teeth.

"Yes, please. That would be great. I've put a deposit on a second hand car so I'll be mobile again soon." Celine was pleased to have new friends who had so much in common with her.

"So, it's tea at Sam's then!" Kristin announced as if declaring an important piece of news. And in a way it was.

Samantha dropped Kristin off in town and then headed for Pittville, where Celine's mother lived. Annabel was thrilled to see her again and squealed with delight when she picked her up for a kiss.

"Have you been a good girl for Granny?" Celine lifted Annabel above her head and swung her around which produced giggles and more squeals from the toddler.

"She's been as good as gold, haven't you Annabel? Although my back's starting to play up so it's best you don't dilly dally after class. You're a bit late - what happened?" Celine's mother always had a worried expression on her face.

"Sorry, Mum. I shouldn't have taken advantage. I'll come straight back next time but I've met some new friends at college and we had a coffee afterwards. One's married with two children and the other's a single parent too." Celine enthused.

"Mm, you don't say."

Was Celine imagining it or did her mother look disapproving. Art school was not quite like the Mother's Union and she didn't want Celine to become bohemian now that she was no longer a respectable married woman. It had taken a lot of persuading to stop Celine attending Art College when she left school and she hoped that she would not become wayward. Respectability was important to Veronica.

Celine's brief journal entry that night read simply:

Art College is even better than I had hoped. I love it and I have met two wonderful new friends. Can't wait for tea at Sam's on Saturday.

18

TEA AT SAM'S

Samantha had left the back door open for Kim to run in and out to play in the narrow cottage garden where flowers grew haphazardly as if a packet of seeds had been scattered at random. Her neighbour had just finished mowing his lawn so that a lingering green sweetness filled the air. She had picked some yellow roses that morning and arranged them in a jug where they stood on the table as if emitting sunshine next to some homemade scones that she had removed from the Aga and which lay cooling on a rack. Next to them, a tray had been set with a mismatch of delicate china cups and saucers. Samantha loved to bake and was looking forward to her two new friends' arrival for tea that afternoon. This was to be the first afternoon tea at Sam's place and she sang quietly to herself as she put the kettle on the Aga, listening out for the sound of a car parking outside.

Tea at Sam's place was to be like breathing sea air after being incarcerated in a stuffy prison. Samantha's tiny cottage, the end of a terrace, was built in butter yellow Cotswold stone in the village of Wittingford in Gloucestershire. The village boasted a thatched pub, the Dog and Duck, and a small grocery store. Samantha's cottage overlooked a village green at the front and a farmer's field at the back where cows grazed on the sweet emerald grass. On either side of her front door, hollyhocks grew beneath a climbing rose. Inside was quaint and smelled of mown grass, fresh flowers and home baking. The ancient front door opened into a single downstairs room that was warmed by an Aga, which also served as a well used cooker and nearby was a deep, old fashioned sink with a wooden draining board. A green and white gingham curtain was fixed under the sink where Samantha kept her assortment of pots and pans. The room was simply furnished with an antique oak dresser; a matching drop leaf table and four ladder-back chairs. In the lounge area a small cast iron fireplace nestled in the wall, it's hearth filled with pine cones. On one side was a two-seater sofa and, on the other, were two old wing chairs, each covered in different fabrics in matching hues of green and pink. At the tiny open windows, flowered chintz curtains flapped in the breeze. An array of mismatched antique china filled the dresser and a worn Persian rug lay on the cottage's original flagstone floor. Two pictures hung on the uneven white walls; one of a Creole girl wearing hoop earrings and the other a bold beach scene that looked as if it had been painted with a palette knife; both reminders of Samantha's time spent in Mauritius. The low ceiling had weathered beams running across it and a narrow staircase led up to the two tiny bedrooms and a bathroom with somewhat unconventional plumbing.

If it hadn't been for the art class the new friends might never have met. It was a new decade and a new season.

Celine and Annabel arrived first.

"Hello, you must be Annabel." Samantha greeted her guests, thinking what a pretty child Celine had.

"Yes, be." Annabel rushed in, looking for Kim. She had heard about him and was excited at the thought of meeting him.

Kim came in from the garden, shuffling his feet and looking shy.

Annabel, sensing this, took his hand and asked, "Will you be my friend?"

Kim nodded and the two children went off to play while Celine drank in the atmosphere of the cottage that had a comforting ambience. "Oh Sam, this place is wonderful. What a find! It's like a picture on a postcard."

"I know. I'm so fortunate to have found it. I've always dreamt of living in an old house in the country."

There was the sound of a car outside, doors slamming, and children chatting excitedly. Kristin, Harry and the children had arrived together with their Labrador.

Kim and Annabel rushed in from the garden, not wishing to miss out on anything. They could have been related with their startling blue eyes and tumble of blonde curls.

By now the cottage was overflowing.

Kristin introduced Celine to her family and then Harry offered to take all the children to the park for a couple of hours.

"I couldn't possibly ask you to mind Annabel, she's into everything." Celine was viewing Harry with the eyes of a woman who had been married to a man who would not have been willing or able to take on a brood of children. She found herself staring at his kindly face in admiration.

"It's up to you but really it's not a problem. Nina is great with young children and will help," he replied as he grinned at his daughter.

"Yes, I'll mind her for you. She won't cry." Nina went over to Annabel and put her arm around the child's shoulder.

"The girls can play and Kim and me'll fly my kite." Ricki said, aware that he was the eldest and not interested in playing with girls, even though Nina was a tomboy and hated to wear dresses.

"Well, if you're sure - thanks." Celine was looking forward to chatting to her new friends without the interruptions of children.

Harry did seem like everyone's favourite uncle with his relaxed manner and easy smile.

Annabel ran up to him and held her arms up to be carried, "Carry me," she implored.

Harry picked her up and she snuggled into the warmth of his chunky sweater that made Celine feel a tinge of sadness as she realised that Annabel might never have a father figure in her life.

"If she really misses you, I'll just bring her back." He stated in his matter of fact way. And with that he left like the Pied Piper, the noisy children in tow.

Samantha busied herself in the kitchen area while Kristin and Celine chatted from the comfort of the sofa.

"Want some tea?" Samantha took an enormous earthenware pot from the Aga where it had been keeping warm.

"Yes please." Both girls responded at the same time and then laughed. Samantha poured into the fragile cups, her thin hands trembling slightly.

"Did you say that you'd not long been back from living abroad?" Celine asked her hostess.

"That's right. We lived in Mauritius for two years but, well, things haven't worked out since we got back. I think I told you that Paul and I are separated." Samantha replied. She was not yet ready to discuss Paul's secret, the memory of which was like a recurring nightmare, but she knew that it would not be long before she could tell her new friends about it.

It was their first get together at the cottage and the conversation flowed along with the tea.

"Seems like we've each got a lot in common. From what you said your time in Amsterdam was a bit of a nightmare." Kristin smiled at Celine, her expression that of sympathy.

172

"Tell us about your time in Amsterdam." Samantha was curious to know everything about her new friend with the sad hazel eyes.

While she handed round a plate of home made, thickly buttered scones she marvelled at these new found relationships. The three young women had just been launched into the deep waters of their companionship. Celine settled into the sofa and began her long discourse. She found it cathartic to share the sorrows of her heart, which had started in Amsterdam. The two hours flew by as she shared her secret heartache with two friends who she instinctively knew she could trust. At one point Samantha handed her a tissue as she shed a few tears. Too soon, Harry returned with the children and it was time for Celine to take a tired but contented Annabel home.

"Thanks, Sam. It was great to see you again." Celine had enjoyed each moment of the afternoon.

"You'll be coming to the next Saturday afternoon meeting at my place, I hope." Kristin looked at Celine expectantly.

"Yes, please. I'm looking forward to it already."

"I think we should call our meetings SAMs for short in honour of the one who started them," Kristin chuckled.

She hosted the next SAM the following week. Just a short distance from the centre of town, her terraced Regency house had an air of faded grandeur, and was a reminder of the days when servants lived in the attic while the lady of the house would never consider work of any description. A discreet brass plaque on the door and a small window sticker were the only evidence that a beauty salon existed in the converted basement flat, which was once a kitchen and scullery, where maids once worked from dawn to dusk.

Kristin served tea and flapjacks in her spacious sitting room that was graced with its original cornicing and ceiling rose. Large sash windows looked out onto a busy avenue and, once again, the girls had fun chatting while the children went with Harry to the park. The following Saturday the girls met at Celine's house and so it became a pleasant routine that the adults and children enjoyed.

Soon the friends became close and, as well as the Saturday afternoon ritual, would sometimes take the children to play in the park where Celine had met up with Nick that summer afternoon. She had tried phoning him but the operator said that the number no longer existed. Once, as she was walking past his flat, she decided to call on him but a stranger answered the door and said that he didn't know of anyone called Nick. Philosophically, Celine decided it was just as well there was no man in her life, as she needed time to heal.

Saturday afternoons became the highlight of Celine's week. As each girl shared her story with the others, the bonds of friendship strengthened like a steel rope.

"Tell us about your life in Mauritius," Celine asked Samantha one afternoon.

"How long have you got?" she replied.

"As long as it takes. We're all ears. And, if there's time, you must tell us all about Hong Kong and Australia," Celine said, looking at Kristin.

And so their stories unfolded.

Sam and Kristin are the kindest and most interesting girls I've ever met. I'm so pleased that Sam approached me that day at class. We have so much in common and already they feel like sisters to me. Celine wrote in her journal that night.

~ ~ ~ ~ ~ ~

It was several weeks later, during one of their Saturday afternoon tea sessions, that Samantha told Celine and Kristin about Paul's secret. Kristin was shocked and Celine sympathetic. As memories surfaced, Celine decided to tell them about her family secret.

"When my grandmother died a few years ago, I inherited her engagement ring." She began her story as the others listened intently. "It has a row of five diamonds set in antique rose gold. This ring has sentimental value, so I would never sell it. Well, not unless I absolutely had to. However, I don't suppose I'll ever know which of my grandmother's two husbands gave her the ring. I think it will always be one of those frustrating, unsolved mysteries. It was by accident that I found out that the old man who I loved and called Grandpa was not my real grandfather." Celine gazed into the distance as she recalled her relative with affection, sighed and continued her story.

"It was during a particularly thundery evening that the phone rang in our flat in Holland. As was often the case, I was alone. I jumped out of bed and was surprised when I heard my uncle's voice - I should have known something was wrong. Well, something was very wrong - my Dad had died suddenly."

Kristin and Samantha said that they were sorry to hear this. Celine thanked them and continued.

"I caught the next flight back to England. James said that he couldn't take the time off work and so I went alone. Mum's letters had arrived each week keeping me abreast with her and Dad's lives. They enjoyed an uncomplicated routine. I couldn't wait to get to the sanctuary of the home where I'd spent my teenage years, although it would never be the same without Dad. The house felt empty when I arrived and Mum seemed distracted. She talked constantly about the neighbours but didn't mention Dad once. Denial was her coping mechanism for a while, I suppose. Somehow we got through the funeral and Mum was remarkably strong. I remember my legs feeling like jelly and singing The Lord is my Shepherd. It felt as if the whole scene was part of a tragic play and when the curtain went down we could go home and everything would be back to normal again. My father would be in his chair eating a bar of chocolate while he watched the news on the television. My sister had travelled the much shorter distance from Cheshire to Cheltenham to attend the funeral. She was certain that Dad would have written a will, although Mum insisted that she didn't know of one. Before returning to the north of England, my sister asked me to help her search for this elusive document. It was as we were rifling through cupboards like a couple of burglars that I came across Mum's birth certificate - which I was just glancing at casually before tidying it away again. My eyes stopped and were riveted to one line - Mother's maiden name - Scott. I'd never even heard the name mentioned before. Mum's maiden name was Hart - we all knew that. So, I asked my sister what the name Scott was doing on the birth certificate. She said that she thought I knew and that my Aunt Gloria had let the cat out of the bag when she told her that our grandmother was divorced and remarried. Apparently, it was a scandal at the time and even made the front page of the newspapers.

I remember sitting on the counterpane as this piece of news sank in. Why hadn't Mum ever told me such important information before? And why, if Janet knew, had she not mentioned it to me? I was stunned. Longing to find out more, I asked my sister when this happened and who our real grandfather was. She didn't know but thought that the divorce was in 1909. People just didn't get divorced at that time, which was why it was such a scandal. It was a very rare and expensive thing to do. It would also have meant that my grandmother would be forever stigmatised. Hence the secrecy, I suppose. Then she told me that this Mr Scott was the father of my mother and her sister, but not their brother. He was the offspring of husband number two, my Grandpa Hart - the kindly man who was my grandfather, or so I thought. She said that she didn't know the reason why the divorce had taken place but Gloria had said there was a rumour that Grandpa Scott was a gambler or a womaniser. The family had lost all trace of him as he had emigrated to Australia soon after the divorce. Janet said that my grandmother moved back home with her parents and, eventually, met a kindly Yorkshire man who became her second husband. He was a good step father and my mum and Aunt Gloria loved him. I was still trying to come to terms with the loss of my father and now I felt as if I was faced with a double bereavement. I remember crying a little. My sister, being typically British, did not let the luxury of such feelings get in the way of searching for what she considered to be the all important will, which never did turn up. This was because it didn't exist. Anyway, the next day my sister went home, leaving me to comfort Mum and help her sort out her affairs. But, before returning to Holland, I asked Mum the burning question about her father. She looked shocked that I knew about her past and was not forthcoming with any details. All I could find out was that she had never met her real father. She hadn't wanted to. She felt it would have been disloyal to her mother. When I asked her why there had been a divorce she simply said that she didn't know. It was no good pressing her any further as she made it clear that the subject was closed. One day, I promise myself, I will travel up to Liverpool to get information for the Scott family tree. Grandpa Scott, without doubt, was a black sheep. In the meantime, I have a lovely diamond ring that's a reminder of what I hope were happy times for my grandmother. Whether this lovely piece of jewellery was given to her by Grandpa Scott or Grandpa Hart I still don't know." Celine looked wistful and drained her tea as she completed her story.

"So, you say that your real grandfather emigrated to Australia and that his name was Scott?" Kristin had been listening with care but wanted to get the facts right.

"Yes, it's all very complicated." Celine responded.

"It seems a lot of families have secrets." Samantha said looking at Celine's hands.

"Yes, and a lot never get discovered. No, I'm not wearing the ring but I'll show it to you next week when you come for tea. It will give me an incentive to give myself a manicure." She told her as she too looked at her smooth skinned left hand that was simply adorned with a gold wedding band. Her eczema had disappeared since James had left so she put the condition down to stress.

Kristin had started to lean forward in rapt attention towards the end of Celine's story and promised herself to write to Bun in Australia. It was probably too much of a coincidence but she was curious to find out more about Celine's family. She was unusually quiet after hearing about the mystery grandfather and seemed lost in her thoughts. Her reverie was broken by Samantha's question.

"Have you noticed that I've been keeping my nails really short lately?"

"I always notice things like that – it's my job." Kristin informed her as she nibbled on a piece of fruitcake.

"Well, it's because I've started to play the guitar again. Carlos is really good and he persuaded me. I'm a bit rusty but I'm enjoying it. Paul was never interested in my music, so it's good to have someone to share it with. Did I ever tell you about the time I went on the stage to perform?" Samantha brushed a stray lock of hair from her eyes with her long fingers.

"No. Really? Come on, tell us about your showbiz career." Celine was intrigued as well as being ready to sit back after her long discourse.

"Okay. It all started in Mauritius after I'd decided never to be a colonial wife. We were meeting some interesting people there. While most of our friends were Mauritian, we did know a handful of Brits. One of my closest friends was Louise. If it hadn't been for Louise Armstrong I might never have thought about singing. I certainly would never have got up on a stage if it wasn't for her encouragement. She had a sort of joie de vivre. The Armstrongs were really different from any other family that I'd ever met before, or since. They were Christian Scientists and didn't believe in pain or illness. Once, when discussing the birth of one of her children, Louise described the process as 'moving sensations'. Quite an understatement I thought, having just given birth to Kim."

Celine and Kristin heartily agreed with this observation. Samantha carried on with her story.

"They lived with their large family in an old colonial house in a quiet area. Louise was artistic and rather eccentric. She was also hospitable and invited me to her house to paint with her new acquaintance, a Mr Singh, the Indian High Commissioner. He was an accomplished artist and I picked up a few tips from him as we each produced a portrait in oils of the daughter of Nancy, Louise's maid. Monique was a Creole girl with gentle brown eyes and was about eighteen at the time. Once or twice, Cedric Lim, an exceptionally tall Chinese man would join us. The first time I met him he bowed.

'Charming ladies,' he said, looking suitably enigmatic at Louise and myself.

We were delighted and I think I detected Louise blushing, but I'm not sure to this day if Cedric was sending us up. He sounded just like Charlie Chan. Cedric kindly gave me the painting that hangs in the living room - you know the one of a beach scene. He'd worked quickly and loosely with a palette knife in a relaxed technique which I envied." Samantha paused, sipped her tea and looked at her two friends intently.

Celine was the first to respond, "I've always admired that picture and wondered about the artist and, presumably, you painted the picture of the Creole girl that's in your sitting room? It's very good."

"Mm, thanks. I've got happy memories of both of those pictures." Samantha looked thoughtful, her large eyes misty. "Oh, and then there was the dance. Louise had a large mirror and ballet bar in her dining room. She took a ballet class once a week and got me hooked too. I was becoming quite cultured. Next came the music. David, Louise's rather ethereal looking husband, played the guitar and Louise the piano. One day, they asked me to sing while they played a piece. Feeling rather foolish, I squeaked out a few notes.

'No, not like that. You must learn to breathe,' Louise said with great enthusiasm and then took a large gulp of air in order to demonstrate the technique.

After teaching me how to breathe she had me hooked as the notes coming from my mouth sounded unexpectedly clear. It was as if someone else was doing this and I was just an observer and soon I found out that I loved singing. It's a way of releasing what's in the soul; an experience that I found to be emotionally freeing. I even acquired a second hand guitar and learnt a few chords to accompany myself. It was through Louise that I met Valerie, a beautiful South African ballerina. She too was a novice guitar player and we would meet and practise our chords and sing together. Most of the songs were French, mournful and heartrending. My favourite song at the time was Ticket de Quai."

"Oh, can you sing us a bit?" Kristin asked.

"Okay," Samantha cleared her throat and sang in a clear, sweet voice, "Car y a toujours quelqu'un, Qui reste sur le quai des au revoir, Y a toujours quelqu'un qui part, Et qui ne revient pas."

"Oh, that's lovely. So what happened next?" Celine asked.

"You've got a lovely voice. Can't say I understood the lyrics but they sound mournful." Kristin nodded her appreciation.

Samantha had a sip of tea and continued. "It means that someone is always waiting on the platform to leave by train and that there's always someone who never returns. Well, that song has proved to be prophetic as that is exactly what happened when Paul left. " Samantha looked dewy eyed as she spoke, remembering happier times. Times of innocence and optimism. She composed herself and continued her story.

"I missed the Armstrongs when they left Mauritius to return to England. Their maid, Nancy, came to work for us and loved little Kim, who had got to know her when he visited the bohemian household. We kept in touch and I managed to stay with them in Devon a short time after Paul left, before I met you two. Louise had opened an art shop with a studio at the back where she threw pots. She was in her element. It was quite healing staying with them and she taught me some new songs. When David came home from work, she asked him to accompany me on the guitar in a sad song called 'Morning, Please Don't Come.' It told the story of a woman about to say goodbye to the love of her life as he departed – probably to war. Louise told me that I was brilliant and announced that she was going to see if I could perform at a show that had just come to town. She might as well have suggested that I had my teeth out without anaesthetic such was the effect this had on me."

The girls laughed out loud.

Samantha continued, "I told her that there was no way that I'd go on the stage!

'Nonsense, you'll be fine,' Louise said with alarming finality.

She arranged it all and I was scheduled to sing on stage the following Saturday. I was beginning to think that perhaps we were all slightly unhinged. David and I were third on the bill. I looked out from behind the curtain and wished I wasn't there - it was packed. What had I let myself in for? I decided that I would just look at Louise sitting in the front row and pretend that no one else was there. Then I might somehow get through this terrifying ordeal. Two rather brassy looking females who seemed to be in competition with each other as to who could sing the loudest performed the first act. I wished I could have had an ounce of their confidence. Next on the bill was a slapstick comedian who managed to raise a few laughs. I hoped that my performance would not have this effect on the audience. The thought crossed my mind that I could bolt or feign a sudden heart attack - but too late. Before I knew it, David had pushed me onto the stage to perform Morning Please Don't Come. I wished that morning had come and that this whole ghastly experience would be a thing of the past. My knees felt like blancmange and my stomach was gurgling with fear."

At this they all laughed again.

"So, you actually did it then?" Kristin looked impressed.

"Yes," Samantha continued, "holding my head high I took a deep gulp of air, remembering to breathe from the diaphragm and, fixing my eyes firmly on Louise, I started to perform. Immediately she started to make some strange gestures with her hands and was mouthing something incomprehensible to me. This had an extremely unsettling effect. I was already in a state of shock and this just added to the trauma. The short song seemed to be endless as I tried to decipher the semaphores that Louise was demonstrating. To my surprise no one laughed and there was even a ripple of applause as I finished the song. On a sort of adrenaline high, I floated off the stage in my gypsy dress and felt that I could have done the whole thing again. That's showbiz! Soon after Louise joined us back stage. I asked her what all the gesticulating and mouthing was about.

'I was trying to get you to go nearer to the microphone,' she explained.

I hadn't rehearsed on the stage or used a microphone before and so she thought she had been helping me. I decided that for my next performance I would not look at the audience but focus somewhere just above their heads. Of course, this never happened. That was to be my first and last stage appearance for which I and, I am sure, many others are very grateful." Samantha's story was complete and she grinned at the recollection of her time with Louise.

Each was becoming an expert raconteur and loved to tell their stories in an environment of mutual trust and affection.

"You never know – maybe you and Carlos will sing Morning Please Don't Come at some time.' Celine told her, half joking.

"Never." Samantha was adamant as she helped herself to more tea.

"Never say never. Seems like you and Carlos make a good duo." Kristin said.

And then Samantha eyes became dreamy and she wore that secret smile that was becoming a habit since she started to become attached to Carlos.

~ ~ ~ ~ ~ ~

Tea at Sam's, or SAMs as Kristin loved to call them was born and life seemed complete. She had a loving husband, two healthy children, a thriving business, an enjoyable hobby and two special friends. What more could she ask for? One afternoon, as the girls were enjoying tea in Kristin's large, comfortable sitting room with her Labrador, Bess, asleep in front of the fire, they got to chatting about animals.

"I don't think I could have managed without Sasha's company when James left for Hong Kong. She's the most affectionate cat and loves company. She hates it when I go out and gets Annabel's soft toys out of the nursery and places them in the hall." Celine commented.

"Oh, how cute! She's a lovely cat. I'm more of a dog person but Sasha's different to other cats - she's so friendly. We had a couple of dogs in Mauritius," Samantha said, "but they were full of fleas so they lived in the garden. It was always warm so they didn't suffer. People there didn't allow animals into the house and dogs were used to guard property more than to be pampered pets."

"We got Bess at the animal shelter as soon as we moved into this house. She's about two year's old and the children adore her. When I was a kid I used to raise money for the PDSA doing bazaars, carol singing - well, anything that raised money. I must have been a bit bossy because I loved all the organising. My friends must have got sick of me." Kristin said.

Samantha laughed. "You see you've always been a business woman."

"I suppose so. Don't know whether that's a good thing or not. Sometimes Harry has a job to keep up with all my ideas. There's one brewing at the moment but it's too soon to share." Kristin looked mysterious.

"Let poor Harry recover from the expedition to Surrey to get all the salon stuff first!" Celine found it hard to keep up with Kristin's zeal and energy.

"Yes, you're right. I really must rein myself in a bit more." Kristin said flippantly and her friends knew that she did not mean a word of it. "Have you heard from Paul?" She asked, her eyes settling on Samantha.

"No, he's just disappeared off the face of the earth. But at least he puts enough into my bank account each month so that I can pay the bills. The amount I earn from the baking is just for the odd luxury like new clothes." Samantha replied. "What about you, have you heard from James?" she looked at Celine who was patting Bess on the head.

"He never writes and, in a way, I hope he doesn't. I want to put all that behind me. Annabel never mentions James - I think she must have forgotten about him. No doubt he's enjoying the bachelor life." She sounded cynical, her gentle mouth turned down temporarily at the corners.

19

THE LETTER

When Annabel was two she started to attend a nursery school in the mornings and, soon after, when she was confident that Annabel was happily settled there, Celine found herself a part time job as a window dresser in an up-market boutique. It felt good to be back in the world of fashion again and she was able to channel her artistic streak into unusual and creative displays. She felt like a malleable piece of dough, shaped into a new and happier person.

Samantha, Kristin and Celine got to discuss the business of working mothers and nursery school at their now regular Saturday afternoon meetings.

"Nina and Ricki both went from the age of two and so they had no trouble settling into primary school when they reached five. I personally think it's a good idea to send Annabel." Kristin advised her friend.

Samantha, who was over protective of Kim since the discovery of Paul's cross dressing, was not convinced. "I don't want Kim to go to nursery school – you just don't know how good the carers might be. It's not that I wouldn't like a break sometimes but I want to make sure that he's all right and the only way I can do that is if I can keep an eye on him." She fiddled with her cheesecloth dress as she spoke, pleating and un-pleating it between her fingers.

"I was so over protected by my parents that my first day at school was a nightmare. I told the teacher that I was leaving so that I could go to my Dad's workplace. My parents had me late on in life. They were always warning me of the dangers of this and that. No bicycle, no swing, watch you don't fall over. It's a wonder I ever managed to leave home and get married." Celine sounded irritated.

"Some parents have a unique way of messing us up, it seems." Samantha remarked with a tinge of resentment. "I still blame Paul's mother for his behaviour. Apparently, he was left in his cot to cry a lot and he told me that he remembers reaching through the bars and touching her clothes." She shuddered as she recalled her ex-husbands emotional attachment to female attire.

183

"I know what you mean. James's mother was so manipulative and strict that I'm sure that's why he was weird." Celine sympathised with her friend.

"There's only one way to move on, in my limited experience, and that is to forgive." Kristin's manner was consoling, her gaze without guile.

"Thank you, but could you please just straighten your halo?" Samantha seemed irritated by Kristin's remark.

Sensing the tension, Celine came to the rescue. "Shall I make some more tea; this pot is stewed by now?"

"What a good idea. I'll make it." Kristin jumped up.

"Do you ever wish you'd waited until you were a bit older before marrying James?" Samantha asked Celine while Kristin was making the tea.

Celine paused for a moment. "Yes, I do wish that I'd waited. I've so many regrets. I wish I'd left home and gone to university or, even better, Art College. If I'd gone to the same college as Nick it might have stopped him going off the rails. My mother was so controlling when I think back. But, when I was a kid, I didn't realise what was going on. I just accepted that her control and my Dad's overprotection were normal. If I'd gone away to college I'm sure it would have given me more confidence and I think I would have done quite well. The trouble is my Mum was from a completely different age. Women got married, stayed at home, looked after the family and then occupied themselves with crochet or a touch of weeding the garden. By the time they reached fifty they seemed like old women. It's as if choices were made for them and they never questioned the alternatives."

Kristin breezed in with a pot of tea, just catching the end of the conversation.

"I had a client in yesterday who goes to these new Women's Lib meetings. She asked me to go and I might - just to be nosy."

"Really. I've heard that they burn bras and hate men." Samantha giggled.

"This lady seems quite happily married and, I happen to know she wears a bra, because I wax her underarms! Actually, I probably won't bother to go because I feel liberated enough. Harry doesn't try to put me in a box - far from it. He even encourages me to do what I want. This client is all fired up though. She says that women in the Middle East and Africa have a terrible time compared with us in the West." Kristin was thoughtful.

"I'd like to feel more liberated but I don't hate men and couldn't part with my bras. It sounds silly but sometimes I feel as if I haven't grown up even though I always seem to be sensible." Celine said.

"It's never too late to start again you know. You've got your whole life in front of you. Plenty of time to grow up." Kristin remarked sagely.

Their meeting brought with it a tide of questions and Celine wrote with feeling in her journal that evening:

Growing up takes a long time. Even when we think we have reached maturity, there are still more steps to take before we arrive, if we ever really do. It is like crossing a river from the bank of childhood to adulthood on the other side. We can't get across with one giant leap. The journey is taken from one steppingstone to the other. Progress is slow and often slippery.

~ ~ ~ ~ ~ ~

Although James paid her alimony, Celine felt that she had made the right decision to take a part time job, she enjoyed the company and the extra money went into a savings account. Annabel was an energetic, strong willed child and the stimulus of nursery school fed her inquisitive nature. Celine had been concerned that her only daughter would be clingy and not wish to be parted from her but the opposite proved to be true. Each afternoon when she was collected, she chatted brightly about the amazing things that she did each day at her little school.

"Did you have a good time today?" Celine would enquire, knowing that she'd get an enthusiastic response.

Annabel would nod her head with vigour, her curls bobbing, and regale her mother with the wonders of the morning. "Did. Like it cos I got my own peg. I made biscuits and looked after Annie cos she cried."

"That was kind of you. Why was she crying?"

"Cos her mummy's gone away for ever." Annabel announced this with drama and wide eyes.

Thinking some tragedy must have hit the family and wondering if now it was the time to explain about death and heaven, Celine enquired what had happened.

"Her mummy went to Co-op. But when I did give her my biscuit she stopped crying." Annabel sighed. "Then we played in the garden in the sand pit."

185

"And what did your friend Fiona do today?" Celine enquired as they turned the corner of their road.

"Screaming. And she did drink fuzzy juice with bubbles. And, my Daddy's gone away forever." This was announced in a matter of fact tone that concerned Celine as Annabel rarely mentioned James.

"Yes, you know where he is but that doesn't mean that you won't see him again." Celine braced herself to explain to her once more about the absentee father who never wrote or sent a card.

"He's gone Kowloon side," Annabel said ominously as she paused for a moment and squeezed her mother's hand, "so you won't be pleased. Mine starving – can we have spangled eggs?"

Celine's heart swelled with love for her daughter and she couldn't help but think what James was missing not being there to see her grow up. She didn't know how Annabel remembered Kowloon but presumed that she'd been listening in on adult conversations.

"Of course we can have scrambled eggs. You are the most precious girl." She squeezed Annabel's hand in response.

"I know." Annabel said with conviction.

So life had developed into a busy and satisfying routine. Each morning a cheerful Annabel was dropped off at nursery and then on Mondays, Wednesdays and Fridays, at 10 o'clock, Celine would arrive for work at the shop in Montpellier. Time flew by and at 1 o'clock she would collect Annabel and stroll home for lunch, followed by a nap for her daughter while she caught up with household chores. The weekends were special thanks to Saint Harry as the friends soon named him. Each Saturday afternoon he would take all the children out so that the three friends could meet. Celine felt that the only thing missing from her now settled life was the art class but had little time to paint now that she was working. The six month course had finished and she would have to wait for six weeks if she was to resume her studies.

~ ~ ~ ~ ~ ~

It was on a lazy summer afternoon as the friends were sunbathing in her cottage garden with its fragrant tumble of roses and honeysuckle that Samantha broke the news to her friends.

Samantha had checked her bank details that morning, and to her horror, discovered that Paul had not paid anything into her account that month. Bracing herself for the worst, she phoned the manager who informed her that Paul had stopped all his standing orders as he had left the country. He was sorry, but he had not been given a forwarding address. By now she was engulfed in panic. What was she to do? She had very little savings and the whole food baking would not pay all the bills.

"I've got a dreadful situation here," she said to her two friends, "this is probably our last Tea at Sam's. I'll have to leave the cottage. As you know, Paul disappeared on the train that day but, until now, he's kept up his standing order at the bank so we were managing."

"This is terrible. You'll have to see a solicitor." Kristin was shocked.

"There's no point - no one knows where he is. I'll get a full time job and move to a cheaper place. If necessary, I'll ask if I can stay with Mum for a while. The landlord provided all the furniture here, so I haven't got much stuff of my own. I'll manage. Bang goes my dream of living in a country cottage." Samantha looked at her feet.

It was a moment before Celine responded, "Why don't you move in with me? I've got plenty of room. It'll be great and we know that we get on really well."

"Oh, do you mean it? You're not just feeling sorry for me are you? What about rent? And Kim is noisy sometimes." Samantha looked unsure.

"I wouldn't have offered if I didn't mean it, silly. We can help each other with the kids." Celine was excited at the prospect of Samantha's company, especially on those long winter evenings when Annabel had gone to sleep.

"I think it's a marvellous idea. Probably meant to be." Kristin enthused.

Samantha, her eyes shining with hope for the first time that afternoon, rushed over to Celine and gave her a bear hug. "Thanks a million - you really are a great friend. I can't believe it."

So it was settled. The following week Samantha, with the help of her friends, packed her few belongings and moved in with Celine. She said a sad farewell to her friendly neighbours before leaving the cottage that had brought her so much happiness. Stoically she shut the heavy oak front door behind her for the last time.

"Goodbye house." She whispered as she brushed a few tears from her eyes and climbed into her pink car that was loaded with an overflowing toy box, bedding and two suitcases.

Tea at Sam's continued but not at Sam's place anymore.

Samantha was given a large spare room overlooking Celine's back garden with the sturdy apple tree, while Kim shared the other, smaller bedroom with Annabel.

"You can be my brother and you'll sleep in that bed but you must be good or you'll have to go back to the other house." Annabel bossed Kim around.

"Can I share your toys?" Kim had his eye on a few things.

"Yes, but you mustn't break them. My Daddy's gone Kowloon side. Where's your Daddy?"

"I heard Mummy tell Auntie Kristin that he was from another planet."

"What's a planet?" Annabel asked as she searched through her toy box.

"I asked Mummy and she said a planet is up in the sky, like the moon. So, I suppose he's gone back to the moon or something." Kim looked serious.

"Oh, he's the Man in the Moon. At nursery they did tell us bout him. Maybe we'll visit. You can have that clown doll if you like." She thrust the cloth toy at him as if this would take away his sadness. The moon was a long way off and so he might not see his Daddy anymore.

"I want a space ship for my birthday." Kim took the clown anyway.

Downstairs, Samantha and Celine were rearranging things.

"Put all your baking stuff in here. You'll soon get used to the kitchen and I've cleared a space in the bathroom for your bits and pieces." Celine busied herself, pans clanging, dishes scraping as she moved utensils from one cupboard to another in the spotless kitchen.

"I'll try and keep things as tidy as you. Look, I love cooking. How about I take over all the food shopping and preparation as payment for our rooms? I don't mind cleaning and ironing too if it helps. And baby-sitting if you need a break."

"I expect things will evolve as we get used to living together. I quite like cleaning so I'll continue with that but I'm not that keen on cooking any more. It's probably best if we do our own ironing but it's not cast in stone - let's just see how it goes. This could work out really well and Annabel is so excited to have Kim to play with. There - a whole cupboard just for your whole foods. Shall we have a cup of tea?" Celine smiled triumphantly.

"Good idea - I'll put the kettle on. This kitchen is great - so much space. I can't wait to start cooking." Samantha filled the kettle and took some mugs from a cupboard. "Shall I do a spaghetti Bolognese tonight?"

"Lovely. There's some mince in the fridge. It's great to have you here." Celine gave Samantha a hug.

Samantha went to the fridge for milk and checked for onions, garlic and peppers.

"There's enough mince here for me to make a chilli con carne and a moussaka for the freezer. I'll get cracking after we've had a cup of tea. We're meeting here this Saturday aren't we?" She said.

"Yes, we'll continue of course. I couldn't - "

"Oh, yes we must never give up our SAM meetings. Never. I'll make a cake later. I want to try out a new recipe." Samantha took the tea into the sitting room.

Any unspoken misgivings that Celine felt after asking Samantha to stay soon evaporated. The arrangement worked well and the girls enjoyed each other's company. Kim had started the same nursery school as Annabel and was enjoying it. Samantha had managed to finally let go and trust others to look after her son. She took both the children there and collected them, giving Celine time to work a few more shifts. Celine happily baby-sat several nights a week while Samantha went out with Carlos. Samantha said that she was happy to baby-sit for Celine in the evening but her offer was not taken up. Where would she go - a single mother on her own?

With a more reliable oven and a larger kitchen in which to work, Samantha enjoyed experimenting with new recipes and started to supply a newly opened cake shop in the town. Soon her nightingale voice wafted about the house as she sang unselfconsciously while she cooked.

Meanwhile, the SAM meetings continued.

As they were sipping Earl Grey and eating some home made lemon drizzle cake one afternoon in Celine's lounge, Samantha posed a question.

"Just say no if you can't. Carlos has asked me to go on holiday with him to Spain for a week. And, while we're there, he wants me to meet his family and I wondered if you could look after Kim for me. I don't think he will be too demanding and Mum said she'll have him at the weekend, but I do understand if you can't..." she looked beseechingly at Celine.

"Hey, Carlos must be serious if he wants you to meet his family. Will you be sharing a bedroom with him?" Celine was slightly jealous of the way the relationship was developing and wished that she could meet someone like Carlos.

Samantha blushed, "I doubt it very much - his family are old fashioned. Besides, I keep telling you that this is more like a friendship than an affair but, for some reason, neither of you believe me."

"Of course we don't believe you - Carlos is gorgeous. How could any girl resist him?" Kristin teased.

"Well, you'll just have to believe me. This visit is more for Carlos to see his huge family. The Spanish are very family minded and see each other all the time - I think he misses them quite a lot. So, Celine, can you look after Kim for me? Please."

"Of course, I'd love to look after him, he's already settled and thinks of this as his home. Kim and Annabel get on so well. Just let me know when and I'll start taking the vitamins." They laughed and Samantha gave Celine a hug.

"Thank you so much. Oh, I can't wait. Look, if you need a holiday you know I'd do the same for you."

'A holiday. This sounds too good to be true,' Celine mused. She had saved more than enough to take a package holiday somewhere and decided that she would call into a travel agent when she was next in town.

But, the following week, her spirits were soon to crash. It started as just an ordinary day. Samantha had dropped the children at nursery school and was to spend the day and evening with Carlos. It was Celine's day off work and so she had done a supermarket shop. When she got home, a letter from Hong Kong was waiting for her on the doormat. The handwriting on the envelope belonged to James. Holding her breath, she opened it and then sat down, her heart pounding.

He had met a Chinese girl whom he wished to marry. He sounded smug as he announced that he had at last found what he was looking for. No other details were given.

Swearing to herself, she ripped the letter up and burst into tears; just as she had thought that there were no more tears left to cry. How long would the pain go on? What did this girl have to offer him that she could not?

Curious to know more, Celine wrote to Melissa, who was still in Hong Kong, asking for details. She had a letter back by return informing her that James had cut himself off from his friends and frequented the red light district of Wan Chai in Hong Kong. It was there that he met up with a twenty year old bar girl whom he was to marry. Celine knew that in Hong Kong a bar girl from Wan Chai did not just serve drinks.

As she read the letter again, all the old feelings came flooding back. It was as if the knife that she had used to open the letter had stabbed her in the heart, reopening a wound that she thought was healed. Why had James, who prided himself on his private school education and was well read, decided to marry an uneducated bar girl who probably spoke little or no English? Celine could only imagine that the girl looked up to him and this, in turn, was a boost to his ego. She longed for Saturday afternoon to arrive so that she could share her feelings with her two friends. In the meantime, she had the telephone as a lifeline. Hoping that she'd be in, Celine dialled Kristin's number. After what seemed an eternity the phone was answered.

"Kristin, it's Celine. Have you got time to talk? I've just had a letter from James. Sam's with Carlos so I don't know when she'll be back." She found her words spilling out like rice from a burst sack. Halfway through her story Kristin butted in.

"Don't wait till Saturday. Harry will baby-sit the kids. I'll be round after supper at around half seven. I'll bring a cake so make sure the kettle's on. And don't worry. Everything will be fine. Okay?" Kristin reassured her friend in a calm, steady voice.

As arranged, Celine collected a chatty Annabel from nursery mid afternoon. Samantha was nowhere to be seen as she and Carlos had already picked up Kim for their afternoon outing. Feeling bereft, Celine could not wait until evening when Kristin was to come round with cake and consolation.

True to her word, she arrived on the dot bearing a ginger cake. Ten minutes later, Samantha got home, her guitar in one hand and with a tired Kim grasping the other.

"Hi, where's Carlos?" Celine asked.

"He's got a college assignment so he dropped us off at the door. What's wrong - has something happened?" She looked intently at Celine, sensing that all was not well.

"I've had a letter from James and - "

"Hang on, Kim's really tired. I'll get him to bed and then we'll have a long chat." Samantha hugged Celine before taking Kim up to his bedroom where Annabel was already sleeping soundly, looking angelic as she cuddled her favourite teddy bear.

Kim fell asleep as soon as his head touched the pillow, so Samantha rushed downstairs to find out what was wrong. After a tearful explanation of the day's events, Celine felt better.

"You know this already but you are better off without James. You have had so much patience with him and given him enough opportunity to change his ways. The trouble is we can't change people – we can only change ourselves." Kristin said.

Celine nodded, grateful for Kristin's nuggets of wisdom.

"You have been much more forgiving than I ever was with Paul. Try to forget him like I am doing with my ex." Samantha's words made sense to Celine.

"I know you're right. Sorry to be such a bore - I just get cross with myself for not getting over him sooner. Thanks for listening. How was your afternoon?" She smiled at Samantha.

"Really encouraging. Carlos is making such an effort to get to know Kim who adores him. For some reason, Kim thinks that Paul's a spaceman, it must be his way of coping, so we tried to explain to him this afternoon that Paul might not come back."

"How did he take it?" Kristin asked as she picked up the last crumbs of the cake and put them in her mouth.

"It's hard to tell. Sometimes he gets a bit withdrawn. But Carlos is brilliant with him and told him that Paul still loved him even though he may not see him anymore."

"Paul could just turn up at the door one day - that would be a shock," said Celine.

"Yes, especially if he was dressed as a spacewoman." Kristin quipped and the subsequent laughter broke any lingering tension.

"I'm looking forward to going to Spain. It'll be fantastic to have a break. Carlos says his family are really easy going but I'm a bit nervous about meeting them. He's got a sister, Ana, and a brother, Luis, who speak a little English but the rest of his family don't know any. Apparently, his brother went to Barcelona but hasn't been seen since – bit of a crisis I think. Anyway, Carlos has taught me a few words of Spanish, but we always end up speaking English so I bought a phrase book this afternoon. I'm worried that I'm going to say the wrong thing and put my foot in it. It's so funny, this afternoon he was

192

teaching me how to say 'Have you any post for me, and I said, have you any horsemen for me?'" Samantha giggled and fiddled with the large topaz ring that she wore on her right hand.

"You're a scream. Look, you'll be fine - they'll adore you. Why don't you pop into the salon and I'll give you a lash tint before you go. On the house, of course." Kristin helped herself to a sliver of ginger cake.

"We're still meeting this Saturday afternoon, aren't we?" Celine asked.

"Of course, come to me. Only an earthquake or an outbreak of plague would make me cancel a SAM afternoon." Kristin was adamant.

It was past midnight when Celine snuggled up in bed that night, but she was too preoccupied to sleep. An owl called outside as she began to write in her journal:

What would I do without my friends? James never ceases to hurt me - his letter was a bombshell - but, now that Sam and Kim have moved in, I don't feel so lonely. It's working out better than I thought and even the children seem happier. Sam's cooking is amazing and she really enjoys it. She's a bit secretive about Carlos though and insists that their relationship is not serious - I'm not so sure.

20

KRISTIN'S SEARCH

Kristin had not written to Bun for several months but was motivated to do so by the comments that Celine had made at the recent SAM meeting. She was intrigued by Celine's story of her unknown grandfather. It was a bit of a long shot but definitely worth looking into, she reasoned. So, the following evening, as Harry was watching a football match on television and the children were asleep, she took pen to paper.

Dear Bun,

Sorry for not writing sooner. I have no excuse except that life is hectic, as usual. Remember I told you about my new friends who I met at art school? Celine Smedley was telling me recently that she has a grandfather who she has never met. Her mother, Veronica, will not tell her any facts about him but says that her mother left him when she was a toddler around the year 1912. The reason that I mention this is because his surname was Scott; he was born in Liverpool and emigrated to Australia, never to be heard of again. I remember you telling me that your father was originally from Liverpool and that your maiden name is Scott. Could he be a relation, I wonder? Please let me know if you have any details.

Kristin continued with news of her family and salon before signing off.

Two weeks later she had a reply from Bun.

The letter read:

Dear Kristin,

How lovely to hear from you. Glad that you and the family are well.

I was excited to read about your friend's grandfather and I think I have some interesting news for you. I can't remember if I told you or not but my father died several years ago. What I have not told anyone was that he made a confession to my mother on his deathbed. It seems that, as a young bloke in Liverpool, he had a wife and two young daughters who he left when he had an affair many, many years ago and a well-publicised divorce followed. Then he emigrated to Australia where he met my mother. Running away, I suppose. He told her that the girls were called Gloria and Veronica and his ex-wife, Elsie. My mother did not know anything about his family, presuming that she was his first wife. What a shock it must have been for her! We think we know people, don't we? After he emigrated to Sydney they married and had me. I am sure that your friend's mother and I are half sisters! My father was called Gerald Scott. He was a quiet man who kept himself to himself but he was a good enough father, I suppose. I don't recall him ever talking about his life in England – it was as if it never happened, although I was aware that he had an English accent. Perhaps Celine could check with her mother if he is indeed the same man. I am sure that he is. Being an only child, it is lovely to think that I may have a half sister - even if she is the other side of the world. I do hope we can get in touch with each other.

Life goes on much the same here. The chickens are laying well although, now that I'm getting older, I find the garden is harder to manage and it has become a bit of a wilderness. Chammy enjoys his swim each day. The heat is shocking at the moment and I never seem to get used to it. Maybe it's my English blood!

Try not to work too hard!

Love to you all,

Bun

~ ~ ~ ~ ~ ~

Kristin broke the news to Celine the following day at their SAM meeting which was to be at her house. She waited until Celine was sitting comfortably in a squishy armchair and Samantha had popped to the loo.

"I've got some news for you which you may want to keep private." She whispered to Celine.

"Oh, is it about the salon?"

"No, it's about your real grandfather," Kristin took a deep breath and continued, "I think I've managed to trace him through my friend, Bun, in Australia."

"Really? Oh, tell me. I don't mind if Sam hears - we've no secrets."

At that point, Samantha came in, having just heard the last part of the conversation, "What secrets? There can't be any more, surely?"

Kristin went over to the bureau, pulled open a drawer, produced Bun's letter and handed it to Celine.

"This is incredible. My grandfather is Bun's father. I can't believe it." She passed the letter to Samantha to read.

"You'll tell your Mum won't you?" Kristin asked.

"Of course, but I'm not sure how she'll take it. You know what she's like - hates any scandal. But, she needs to be told. Wow, this is such a strange co-incidence. You've mentioned Bun before but tell me what she's like so I can let Mum know all about her?" She was flushed with excitement.

After Kristin had gone into great detail describing Bun, Celine was fired up to speak to her mother, so she dropped Samantha back at her house and drove straight round to the little semi in Pittville.

Veronica answered the door expectantly. She loved having visitors, especially if it opened the door to some juicy gossip. She looked slightly disappointed when she saw Celine standing there.

"Oh, it's you. Come in. I've just made some tea. I thought you were Joan from opposite."

"Sorry to disappoint you, Mum, but I've got some important news." Celine smiled but was bracing herself for Veronica's reaction.

"Nothing bad, I hope. I've had enough bad news to last me a life time what with that husband of yours and everything." She always used every opportunity to have a little dig at her younger daughter, but Celine was impervious to her remarks by now.

"Let's have that cuppa first." Celine went into the kitchen and poured Veronica some tea. "Sit down, Mum."

It felt strange but now she, Celine, was in charge instead of the other way round. Veronica sat down obediently at the kitchen table looking worried.

Sitting herself on the opposite chair, Celine took a deep calming breath. "It's good news - I think that I have managed to trace your father."

Veronica gasped, her hand to her mouth. Then, shaking her head from side to side, she whispered, "No,no. My father must be dead by now."

"Yes, I'm sure he is, but, apparently, he confessed on his deathbed to his second wife that he had left a family behind in Liverpool."

"But, but – how did you find out? Lots of people emigrated to Australia." Veronica looked agitated and fiddled with her pearl necklace.

"I know, but this one was called Gerald Scott and had a wife called Elsie and two daughters called Gloria and....Veronica." Celine was not sure that her mother was taking the news well.

"My God, it must be the same person. His name was Gerald, although Mother never talked about him. How did you find all this out?" Veronica was talking rapidly now, her cheeks flushed, her neck mottled with angry red blotches.

Celine proceeded to tell her mother about Kristin's news and her friend Bun. All the while Veronica gazed out of the window as if a passing neighbour would rescue her from this unfortunate revelation. She got up, turned her back on Celine and stood at the window before responding.

"Then this woman, Bun, is my half sister. Oh, I wish Gloria were alive to know about this." Tears filled Veronica's eyes as she digested the news.

"Mum, Celine tells me that Bun would like to write to you. May I give her your address?"

"Oh, I don't know. I don't know if I want anything to do with the daughter of the man who broke my mother's heart. I just don't know." Veronica was clearly in shock so Celine decided to let things settle down before pressing her mother to get in touch with Bun and, as expected, it was not long before Veronica had changed the subject to a more comfortable topic, the neighbours. Sighing, Celine poured herself a cup of tea and prepared herself for the inevitable gossip. Gossip and trivia did not sit well with her.

It had been another momentous day and Celine wrote in her journal that evening some of her thoughts.

Poor Mum - she was in such a dither over the news of her father. I wish I could have met my real grandfather. What was he really like, I wonder? And what unspeakable traits have I inherited? I hope Annabel grows up to be normal - what with this Gerald Scott as a blood relative and James as a father? More than anything in the world I want her to be happy.

~ ~ ~ ~ ~ ~

Celine decided that she would only have another child if she was married to a man who could turn his hand to anything remotely domestic. Although she enjoyed looking after Kim, she was feeling rather drained when a tanned and bright eyed Samantha returned after her holiday in Spain. Apparently, the trip had gone well and Samantha had enjoyed meeting Carlos' family, although only his sister spoke English. She, Celine, was glad that she had been busy, as she had not had much time to think about James and his new girlfriend – soon to be wife. The house looked as if a bomb had hit it, but Celine decided to have a lavender scented bath and an early night before starting any housework. Domestic chores had become less of a priority to her these days and she was glad. At one time, she would have tackled the housework even if she had been worn out and then felt a tinge of resentment. As she soaked in the fragrant water she was reminded of Kristin's salon that always smelled delicious, as if the plant oils had been permanently absorbed into the walls.

SAM meetings were being held more regularly at Kristin's elegant Regency house now that she had a phone extension from the salon. Buoyed up by success, she did not want to miss any business opportunities. Sometimes a client would ring the doorbell on her day off but she was quite happy to answer any calls if it meant extra appointments. Although the downstairs salon was always immaculate, there was a type of organised chaos in the living quarters upstairs. The large rooms were scattered with mislaid homework, books, toys and old newspapers. Although the drapes and furniture were well used and faded the house had a welcoming homely atmosphere.

Wearing a black shirt, black jeans and black sandals, Kristin welcomed her friends, "Come in, come in. Sorry about the mess – just step over it. I haven't had time to tidy up yet. This week has been frantic what the cleaner off and the kids on half term."

Kristin looked tired - usually life's little trials just bounced off her like a rubber ball against a wall. Her usually sleek bobbed hair looked a little dishevelled, she was not wearing makeup and had dark circles under her eyes so that, all in black, she looked like a Sicilian widow.

"Where would you like us?" Celine asked, wondering what could be wrong.

"I thought we could go into the conservatory as it's sunny. Go on through. You look great Samantha – you've put on a little weight."

"Yes, it must be all the cake we eat on Saturdays. I don't mind though. Carlos said I was too skinny before."

"What's all this about being an independent woman?" Kristin laughed as she made her way to the kitchen to put the kettle on. In spite of her laugh she looked haggard and was clearly worried about something. "I'm going to perk some coffee for myself - I need the extra caffeine - but you two have whatever you like – would you prefer tea?"

"Coffee would be great, please." Celine replied.

"Herbal tea, please, anything you have." Samantha was on a healthy eating regime and had started to supply a newly opened health food shop with some of her homemade bread and cakes. Her eyes glowed and she looked relaxed in a long batik skirt and embroidered white top. On her slim wrists she wore several Moroccan bangles that jangled when she moved and her fair, sun streaked hair fell loosely against her shoulders. She looked younger, more carefree.

The old conservatory led onto a neglected but lovely garden with established rosebushes and wisteria growing against an ancient brick wall. Celine felt herself relax as she sank into a wicker chair with soft cushions and closed her eyes for a few minutes as the stress of the week seemed to fall off her like dead leaves from a tree in autumn. A watery sun crept through the large windows and the smell of freshly ground coffee wafted in from the kitchen. She hoped that when Kristin visited her that she felt the same solace in her home.

Looking worried, Samantha scanned the conservatory for any lurking spiders before perching on the edge of a chair.

"Is anything wrong?" She asked Kristin as she jumped up to help her wheel in a trolley. She flitted like a colourful butterfly handing out plates, chocolate digestive biscuits and paper napkins.

Never one to evade an issue, Kristin replied. "I sacked Chloe yesterday."

"But Chloe seemed to be such a hard worker, why did you sack her?" Celine was surprised.

"I thought something was up. Oh dear, what's been happening while I was away?" Samantha got up and hovered by Kristin as if her presence could somehow alleviate the problem.

Pouring coffee for herself and Celine and dunking a chamomile tea bag for Samantha, Kristin began to tell her friends what had happened.

"After I took Chloe on, my life was so much easier. I could finish work early and be there for when the children got back from school and I was able to have the odd morning or afternoon off for things like taking the children to the dentist, which was great. Most of my wealthier clients, who always used to ask for me, had started to book in with her. They'd been with me for ages. Then, when I queried it, Chloe told me that they no longer wanted me to do their treatments but had asked for her instead. I suppose I should have been suspicious but I was too trusting and, for some reason, believed her. So, one by one, she was treating my best clients. This had been going on for several months but I'd tried to make light of it. Then, the other evening, a client phoned me at home. She told me that Chloe was going to start her own salon and had been telling my clients. I thanked her for telling me and put the phone down, stunned and feeling betrayed. It was my own fault, I suppose, for being so naive. I knew that it was time for damage limitation and so I wrote Chloe a letter of dismissal, deciding to pay her in lieu of working out her notice before she could do any further harm. Knowing that she had access to my entire client list of addresses and phone numbers, I just hoped that she had not written all the information down. Anyway, the next morning, Chloe breezed confidently into work and I gave her notice. She looked shocked. When I confronted her, her eyes became hard and she wanted to know how I knew."

"Oh, no - did you tell her?" Celine looked aghast.

Kristin shook her head, "No, I did not. So, she took her money and flounced out! I was left with a full appointment book and no therapist. With a little rescheduling, I managed to fit everyone in and just worked longer hours. Mrs Matthews, the client who informed me, brightened my day by calling in with some flowers." At this, Kristin wiped away a tear. The girls had never seen her like this before. She was always the strong one who was available to offer sound advice. Samantha listened, still standing, with her mouth slightly open in surprise while Celine got up and gave her friend a hug; she knew how hard Kristin had worked to build up the business and how much it meant to her. Kristin pulled a tissue out of a pocket, blew her nose and continued.

"I spoke to a lot of clients yesterday and they all knew of Chloe's plans. Apparently, she'd been sitting on a wall outside on her days off handing out her price lists to clients as they left the salon. She's undercut me with her prices, of course. But the worst thing is that she's telling a pack of lies about me. She's telling people that Harry and I are getting a divorce and that I'm closing the salon. It's the first

200

I've heard of it! Can you believe she'd do such a thing? It really hurts as I've been good to her and treated her like one of the family. She had access to the house by the spiral staircase into the hall and often sat in the lounge to eat her lunch. Apparently, she has premises lined up just around the corner and is to open in about six weeks. Oh, and you know that I have the sole agency for the treatment and products that I use? I had a feeling that she would try to get the agency. So, I phoned the company and asked if Chloe had applied for it. You guessed it - she had."

"What a bitch," Samantha interjected.

"Well!" Celine exclaimed, realising to her dismay that she sounded just like her mother.

Kristin continued, nodding her head and speaking with breathless rapidity.

"She'd told the company the same story - that I was about to close the salon and move away. I assured them that this was not true and they said that they'd cancel her order. It was about to be dispatched that week."

The girls tut-tutted in disbelief and offered their commiserations.

Kristin looked relieved to be able to talk freely about her woes. "Now I know why Chloe had been saying that my best clients wanted her to do their treatments. Goodness knows what else she's told them. Then I found out she had written to them all, sending them a price list. So she had gone through my client list after all." With that Kristin slumped in her chair as if all her energy had been spent telling the story.

"You mustn't worry. Her tactics won't impress people. I bet you won't even notice any difference in your business." Samantha consoled her friend and then added, "I never did trust Chloe - she always seemed a bit two faced to me."

"She seemed all right to me, just a bit pushy and over confident. But don't worry, you'll find another assistant soon enough. But maybe next time write it into her contract that she can't open a salon within a certain radius. And don't be so trusting." Celine knew about betrayal.

"Thanks for your support. I'll cope, I know. It's just so upsetting. I've got an advert in tomorrow night's paper for a therapist, so maybe the right person will come along. What a malarkey! In the meantime, I'll just have to work even harder." Kristin's already strong jaw was set with determination.

As the girls nibbled their biscuits, Samantha brought up the topic of painting, "I don't know about you but I'm really missing the art classes. We seemed to be able to paint away our troubles," she sighed.

Celine nodded in agreement, "I keep meaning to get started again but, somehow without the class to give me motivation, I always seem to find something else to do."

"Now that I'm baking for the health food shop, I don't have that much time, but I feel that, if I don't start painting again soon, it will be something that just becomes a distant memory." Samantha said.

Kristin joined in, "I miss the classes too but there's no way I can take any time off work at the moment. Unless..." She paused, gazing into space as if she'd just seen a vision. "How about this; come with me." She got up quickly and marched into the hall on a mission.

Intrigued, the others followed her down the spiral staircase leading from the hall into the salon. They breathed in deeply as a reflex to the lavender, orange blossom, jasmine and woody aromas that permeated the air. The atmosphere was a quiet haven of peace for clients, if not for the busy therapists. Kristin was like a swan gliding across the water; the movement looked effortless but unseen feet were paddling furiously below.

Kristin led them through the salon into a small staff kitchen that held a wall unit, sink, table, three chairs and a kettle. At the back was a door leading onto a room that Celine and Samantha had never ventured into before. It squeaked as Kristin opened it and ushered them in. A large room was revealed that housed a boiler, some shelves and a myriad of junk; trainers, tools, rusty cans of paint, and an old bike lay cluttering the space.

"Behold, the Art Room." Kristin announced with a flourish of her hand.

Celine just stood staring while Samantha started to skip around the room like a child at Christmas, "This is great, this is absolutely great," she enthused.

"It won't take long to clear this room. Picture this – the junk removed and we have all the space we need. There's enough light coming from that window. You can set your easels up and leave everything here. Look, this old trestle table can be set up and we are away." Kristin always made everything sound so easy. She was smiling broadly, her hands on her hips, all worries forgotten in the excitement of the moment. "The room is cosy in the winter and we can open this back door for air in the summer."

"I agree, the room would be perfect but it's just time that I don't have now that I'm working," Celine sounded disappointed.

"Then why don't we make our SAMs into Saturday Art Meetings? We can still drink tea and chat but, while we're doing that, we can paint. What a malarkey! Now that the kids are getting older there's no reason why they can't join us from time to time. We can all paint together." Kristin put great emphasis on the word paint when she used it whilst spreading her hands in Mediterranean drama.

"What do you think, Celine? I think it's a great idea but you may prefer to relax more." Samantha fixed a steady gaze at her friend as if willing her to agree to paint again.

"I think it's a brilliant idea. We'll help you clear the room. Harry won't mind us using it will he?" Celine was bubbling with excitement now.

"Is the Pope a Catholic – what do you think?" Kristin remarked as she started to pile up junk into a corner, her old energy and drive restored.

"What about any mess that we might make?" Celine asked.

Kristin laughed, "Any paint spillages on this old lino flooring will only enhance it. I now rename this room The SAM Studio."

~ ~ ~ ~ ~ ~

So, the SAMs took on a new format when the friends moved into The Studio. They had decorated the walls with some of their past work and all the junk had been cleared out. Although the girls started off chattily, as they became absorbed in their painting, the atmosphere became like that of a silent order. Kristin had discovered that her forte was portraiture and had sketched her daughter before beginning an oil painting of her. She paused, stood back from her work, looked satisfied and was the first to speak.

"I've got a new therapist called Fran starting on Monday. She's older than Chloe and has a much gentler manner. She's agreed to sign a contract about not opening a salon within a five mile radius. The other good thing is that she's worked at a top health farm and so has lots of experience. I feel quite positive that things are looking up." Kristin, true to form, still retained a sparkle of optimism.

"Oh, that's great news. Did she answer the advert in the paper?" Samantha asked as she worked delicately on her watercolour, tipping her pad to watch the colours merge into a haze of blue and pink, creating a watery mauve sky. She found this her favourite medium and produced impressionistic pictures of flowers and landscapes.

"No, actually she's the niece of one of my clients and has just moved into the area. She lives in Gloucester and was able to come for an interview straight away." Kristin was mixing her paints now with a palette knife to get the correct flesh colour.

"Fantastic! You know what they say about one door closing and another opening," Celine said philosophically.

The painting resumed for a good while until the silence was broken again.

"Did you get an invitation to the end of year art exhibition at college?" Celine spoke to whoever might listen as she concentrated on her work. She was painting a dramatic landscape in bright, acrylic tones from a photo that she had taken in the Cotswolds.

The others said that they had and all decided it would be good to go along and see the full time students' work.

"Now that we are official artists it will be good to compare our work with theirs don't you think?" Kristin was already talking about exhibiting their work much to the alarm of the other two friends.

"Yes, it would be good to visit the college again. I'll ask Mum if she wouldn't mind baby-sitting for us." Celine was delighted to be painting once more.

Reluctantly, Veronica said that she would baby-sit, something that she had never agreed to do before in the evening. At least if she baby-sat she could have some residue of control over Celine. Secretly, Veronica was concerned that Celine might meet up with a fellow artist, like her friend Samantha, and had stipulated that Celine must be back before 10 o'clock. She didn't want her to get into the habit of going out at night - especially if it meant going to any pubs. Anything could happen and probably would.

Samantha and Celine set off in high spirits as Veronica sat in the lounge with her knitting. Both children had gone to bed early and promised to behave. As arranged, Kristin was waiting for her friends in the lobby looking stunning in a white trouser suit and black high heeled shoes. She was talking with animation to a student and handing out one of her price lists to another visitor when the girls arrived at the college.

"The more I learn about art, the more I feel that I know very little." Celine mused as they wandered around the familiar rooms, drinking in the atmosphere.

The exhibition was even more inspiring than they had expected, although some of the work was a bit too abstract for the friends' taste.

"We could do better than that," Kristin remarked as she viewed what appeared to be three cubes in different shades of blue. It was called 'Slow'.

"Shh, someone will hear you." Celine was looking around in embarrassment.

Kristin laughed unashamedly, "It must have been his blue period, I suppose."

"Hey, have you seen this?" Samantha was reading a poster on the notice board.

PAINTING HOLIDAYS IN ANDALUCIA. STAY IN A GENUINE SPANISH FINCA, ENJOY HOME COOKED LOCAL FOOD AND RECEIVE PROFESSIONAL TUITION.

"Now this looks as if it's right up your street. Why don't you make some enquiries – look there's a local phone number. You must go - I'll look after Annabel for you." Already Samantha was rummaging in her copious patchwork handbag for a pen and paper.

As Celine wrote the number down she felt the same excitement that she'd experienced when she first bought her paints and brushes. On the dot at 10 o'clock Celine and Samantha arrived home, having chatted non stop in the car about the holiday.

"Thanks, Mum. How were the kids?" Celine studied the pained expression on Veronica's face and hoped that they had not played up.

"Annabel took a while to settle - she kept saying that she was thirsty and wanted a drink of water but eventually nodded off. She was just trying it on with you out. Kim was good though." Veronica stifled a yawn.

"Thanks so much. I'll run you home if you're tired." Samantha smiled kindly but wished that she'd asked Betty to baby-sit as she detected a tinge of resentment in Veronica's demeanour.

Veronica hoped no one would see her getting out of the battered pink car but accepted the lift anyway. Celine certainly had some rather eccentric friends - what would the neighbours think! She had not brought her up to be like this with such strange ideas and hoped that Samantha would soon find a place of her own in which to live.

She was sure that the girl with the unusual clothes would be a bad influence on her daughter. It was only a matter of time.

The following day, inspired by the art exhibition, Celine plucked up the courage to phone about the holiday.

"Hello." A croaky female voice responded.

"Hello, I'm phoning about the painting holiday in Spain. Do you know if there are any spaces left?"

"Yes, there's one space left in the group and it's for you!" The voice at the other end laughed and then started to cough with a chain smoker's raucous spluttering.

Celine waited patiently for the rasping to stop before asking more about the holiday. It was to start in three weeks and was within her budget. Not wanting to miss out, she booked it on the spot and then started to have misgivings. She would not know a soul, had never been on holiday alone before and was concerned that Annabel would miss her. Wondering if she had made a mistake, Celine shared this with her friends the following day.

"Don't be daft – you'll be fine and so will Annabel." Kristin reassured her. "It's not as if she doesn't know Sam. Now that you all live together she's like a second mother to her and she enjoys having Kim to play with. If you don't go you'll always be wondering what you'd missed. I have a really good feeling about this. Go for it!"

"Yes, you may not get this sort of opportunity again, you know." Samantha nodded in agreement.

Celine wished she could be sure but decided to go anyway.

Veronica's demeanour was disapproving. She didn't need to say much; her pursed lips spoke volumes. Eventually, she uttered, "Mmm. You don't say. Well, I hope you know what you're doing. Funny lot these artists – make sure you lock your bedroom door at night. I've heard it all now. Art holiday, indeed! Whatever next? I expect your new friends put you up to this. Just don't ask me to look after Annabel while you go gallivanting off to Spain."

"It's all right, Sam's going to look after her. No need to worry." Celine told her with a degree of satisfaction.

21

THE HOLIDAY

In spite of the early hour, Gatwick Airport was busy with holidaymakers waiting to board their flights. Celine wondered if she was destined to wait for planes on her own or, if one day, she would have a man to go on holiday with. It was ironical that Samantha, who said that she never wanted anything to do with men again, had found Carlos. Of course, she was happy for her friend, but Celine had always felt the need for a partner and no one new had come across her path.

Celine checked her watch. She had another hour to wait before her plane would leave. As usual, she was too early. Unable to concentrate on her novel, she sipped a cup of tea and decided that she disliked airports.

'No man's land,' she thought as she viewed the departure lounge in preparation to take her flight to Malaga.

A crying child broke her reverie and she wondered how Annabel was getting on with Samantha. She was already missing her young daughter. Now feeling grumpy, hot and tired, she rubbed her gritty eyes and wished that she had not needed to be up at 2am to get to the airport in good time. Dear Harry had insisted on driving her there, forfeiting his sleep, but at least he didn't have to work that day and so she didn't feel too guilty accepting his offer. She would rather be painting in Kristin's house, listening to her sensible advice or hearing Samantha extol the virtues of Carlos. Instead, she was embarking on this mad venture. Perhaps her mother was right and she had let her new friends influence her too much.

There was little chatting on the flight as people tried to sleep. Having such long legs, Celine found it difficult to doze off, as the seat in front of her dug into her knees. As she stared out of the window, she thought about the events of the past few years and wondered what the future held for her. She came to the conclusion that she had never been allowed to think for herself. First, her mother dominated her and then her husband. She wondered if she had been attracted to a control freak because it had felt familiar, but she decided to stop analysing the situation and try to enjoy the moment. She had spent too long regretting the past and worrying about the future and would not allow self pity to poison her. The past was gone and the future unknown – all she had was the present.

Suddenly, a vivid, surreal sunrise splashed across the horizon as if an unseen artist had flung paint onto the canvas that was the changing sky. It was a reminder to her that everyone is so very small in the great scheme of things. That, in spite of all human frenetic activity, and amidst life and death, the sun goes down and rises each and every day - slowly and magnificently. As Celine beheld this spectacle, hope bubbled up inside her like fermenting wine and she started to look forward to the holiday.

Then, as daylight illuminated the sky, almost instinctively she closed her eyes and prayed, "God, please make this holiday a happy one." A deep peace enveloped her as her dormant faith awoke and immediately she had a flashback to when she was seventeen. She and Nick were at a youth club, dancing. It was a happy, uncomplicated time. A time before she met James who mocked her child like faith as something that only an unsophisticated or rather simple person could possess. He prided himself on being a rational, thinking person. Gradually, her faith had eroded along with her confidence.

Feeling deeply moved, she took her journal out of her bag and wrote:

I think that I believe in God after all. This has been quite a revelation! Now that I am alone on this adventure I feel free to explore my true feelings. My faith was probably there all the time but circumstances had tried it to the limit. I must not blame him for what has happened, as I made my own choices and then bore the consequences.

As the plane landed at Malaga Airport, Celine had an uncanny feeling that a new phase of her life was about to unfold. Perhaps Kristin would prove to be right once again. It was as if the past few years had melted into oblivion. She was slowly becoming a new, confident and creative woman and was even contemplating reverting back to her maiden name.

Passports inspected, a rush ensued to be first to reach the luggage carousel, only for passengers to stand and stare, tight jawed, willing it to start. 'More, quicker, faster,' the carousel seemed to hum as it lurched into action. Eventually, the luggage tumbled through the hole in the wall and people jostled each other to grab their cases. The first person to leave the carousel wore a look of triumph as if he had just won a gruelling marathon. At last, her case appeared. Now she had to search for the stranger who was to collect her. Feeling excited, she strode out to look for him wondering what he would be like.

She had been told by the 'rasping one' on the telephone in England to look out for a sign being held up at the arrivals lounge with her name on it. Someone would be there to meet her and drive her to the farmhouse.

Sure enough, as she wheeled her case into the throng in the arrivals lounge she saw her name on a board and looked up to see – Nick. Nick, looking tanned, handsome and wearing a broad grin.

"Welcome to Andalucía, I've been expecting you."

~ ~ ~ ~ ~ ~

It was love at first sight.

As they left Malaga, Nick drove along bumpy, deserted roads past orange, lemon and olive groves, proud mountain ranges and white villages perched on hillsides like pristine sugar cubes. They passed several men with ramrod backs on horseback and children waved as they drove through the villages. The sun beat down from a cornflower blue cloudless sky so that the colours of the landscape seemed clearer and brighter than any Celine had experienced before.

On the long drive to the house where Celine would be staying that week, Nick filled her in with events from the past year. He had sold his flat in England to an investor who rented it out and he, Nick, bought himself an old farmhouse near Ronda in southern Spain. After renovating it, he started to advertise rooms to rent before deciding to offer painting holidays. His aunt, a retired school mistress, took the bookings for him. Yes, she was the one who Celine had spoken to, and yes, she was a chain smoker. Jeremy, Nick's young son, had started to attend the local village school and was already fluent in Spanish. Nick told her that he was happy and loved living in Spain, with its relaxed way of life, friendly people and wide open spaces. Celine realised that this was the first time that she and Nick had been completely alone for a long time and she found herself short of breath to be so close to him. His strong hands, hands that were used to hard work, held the wheel loosely and she remembered how she had wanted to touch them when they had been sitting together in his flat after that chance meeting in the park. Or maybe it wasn't chance after all.

"As soon as I saw your name on the booking form I was delighted but decided not to get in touch with you in case you changed your mind. Instead, I thought I'd surprise you. I didn't want to frighten you off by letting you know I would be your art teacher." Nick laughed that low laugh that Celine had always found so earthy. Now she found it exciting.

"Fancy a coffee? This is a good venta." Nick drove in before waiting for Celine's reply.

"I could murder a coffee. The stuff on the plane tasted like dishwater," she told him.

As she got out of the car the dry heat caressed her. Bougainvillea in variegated shades of pink, orange and purple mingled across the doorway of the country restaurant. Inside, it was dark and moody with barrels of wine and sherry piled up against the stone walls. Brightly coloured tiles decorated the bar area and tapas were displayed invitingly on the counter, glistening olives, meatballs, slices of cheese, tuna and Spanish omelette. A huge Serrano ham, that treasured Spanish delicacy, hung above them ready to be carved into thin slices. Off the bar area, a large restaurant was being prepared where a waiter was setting tables with check table cloths using a matador flourish.

"Buenos dias. Dos cafes con leche por favour." He greeted the waiter in what sounded like perfect Spanish. In the dim light he looked like a native with his dark hair and eyes and his tanned, olive skin. Nick had a serenity about him that comes when a person finds their destiny in life.

"Si señor, dos cafes con leche." The waiter took their order with a serious air and proceeded to work a complicated and noisy coffee machine.

"Would you like anything to eat? It's a bit early for the Spanish – they don't start lunch until 2 o'clock but we could have a tapa or two. Just choose something from the display and they'll serve it with bread." Nick seemed to be looking intently at Celine as if he'd seen her for the first time.

"Yes, please. I think it was breakfast that they served on the plane but I couldn't be sure and that seems a long time ago now." She returned his gaze and his eyes crinkled up at the sides as he smiled at her.

"Would you like another coffee or a glass of something?"

"I could do with another to keep awake. It's the best coffee I've ever had." She replied.

They ordered some more and Celine decided on a slice of Spanish omelette. Nick ordered the meatballs and a plate of chips.

"Spanish coffee is good and so is the food. Simple, but fresh. I love it." He sipped the brew without taking his eyes off Celine. "You look different. I know you've grown your hair but it's more than that. You look peaceful. Last time we met you looked tired and careworn. I take it you don't regret leaving James?"

Celine was savouring the delicious tapas, "It's the best thing I ever did. The only good thing about being married to James is that I have Annabel," she said.

"That's how I feel about Jemms. They're hard work but worth it. By the way, I didn't tell you but Eloise and I are divorced. It was what she wanted. She found herself a German guy and they are travelling around India. Calls himself Jazz. His real name's probably Wolfgang or something. She doesn't even contact Jemms which is sad as he still asks about his mother." Nick drained his coffee cup.

Celine shook her head in sympathy, but her heart leapt at the news. He ordered the bill - it was time to leave and Nick seemed pleased to change the subject.

The road to the finca became a dirt track and she understood why Nick drove a Land Rover. As they bumped along, Celine gazed at the stunning countryside and understood why Nick loved the place. She had fallen in love with it too.

Soon, they came to an old house set in an olive grove. It was painted in the traditional white and had terracotta roof tiles. A large wooden pergola covered in a creeping vine graced the front of the house and under it stood a rustic wooden table and chairs. It looked inviting and Celine could imagine large groups of people sitting there on balmy nights, eating leisurely meals and drinking wine. And everywhere palm trees grew, some small and spiky, others tall and haughty. At the border of Nick's property fat cacti grew, some displaying red fruit. Chickens roamed the grounds, pecking at whatever they could find, their feathers glistening in the sunlight.

"Here we are - Casa Bonita. It means Pretty House but sounds better in Spanish somehow. Mi casa es tu casa. Welcome home. Don't worry about the dogs, they look fierce and keep the gypsies away but they're friendly. The other five guests arrived yesterday and

211

have gone to explore the village so I'll introduce you when they get back." Nick took Celine's bags from the boot and led her into a huge living room with beams and uneven white walls. Everywhere Nick's paintings were displayed, somehow looking more in keeping here than they did in Cheltenham. She did not notice the one of Eloise though and wondered if it hung somewhere else in the house. Off the living room was a pebbled courtyard where a fountain stood, its water sparkling in the afternoon sun. Swallows swooped down from the rafters to drink and everywhere exotic flowers grew in the borders, graceful birds of paradise, hibiscus, datura, oleander and delicate jasmine. And geraniums flourished in pots in varying shades of pink, coral and red.

"This is heaven, Nick. What a wonderful house. I love the fireplace. Do you have open fires in the winter?"

"Yes, believe it or not, it gets very cold in the winter and we have a log fire burning day and night. I'm very fortunate to have found this place. Come through the courtyard and I'll show you your room. You've brought your own painting materials, haven't you?" His manner had suddenly become business like and Celine felt disappointed that this was not going to be a week of two friends reminiscing as Nick had a job to do.

Her room was small but pretty with blue painted shutters at the windows that looked past the olive groves to a valley. Nick put her bags down on the single bed that had an elaborate wrought iron bed head. A painting of the finca hung above her bed, the bright colours in competition with the bougainvillea that was peeping in at the open window.

"Because everyone here is English we'll have afternoon tea at 4 o'clock in the courtyard. You'll have plenty of time for a siesta. Sorry, but you'll have to share the bathroom but it's next to your room, so you won't have to go far."

Nick left her to unpack and she felt suddenly drained, so decided to take a nap before showering. She fell onto the comfortable bed and was asleep within minutes, sunlight from the open window caressing her face.

When Celine joined the other guests later that afternoon she heard voices emanating from the kitchen, interspersed with laughter. Then she was surprised and disappointed to see a stunning Spanish girl, together with Nick, leaving the kitchen with the tea things on large trays. They seemed at ease with each other as they chatted together in Spanish. About twenty two years of age, the girl had black hair that hung past her shoulders like a thick curtain, flashing brown eyes and an arrogant arch to her back. She had the high small breasts of a dancer and, Celine noticed, did not wear a wedding ring.

"Everyone – this is our new guest, Celine. I'll leave you to introduce yourselves while I get the cake. Oh, Celine, this is Ana who comes in to help every day. She only speaks a little English but is learning fast."

'I'll bet she is,' Celine thought unkindly and immediately hated herself for it. She knew that she had changed since finding out about James's infidelities but sometimes she felt that she had no control over her thoughts. Looking over at Nick and Ana again she tried to read any hidden messages between them. They were in a secret world amongst the English guests and Celine wished that she could speak Spanish. Nick was still sounding business like and Celine looked to see if there was anything between him and Ana. She could not tell.

22

NICK

There were only five other guests staying at Nick's finca; two middle aged couples that seemed rather straight laced and a single man called Justin who had recently taken up painting. The two couples, Greg and Michelle and Martin and Heather were friends who had been watercolour painting for a number of years. Apart from Justin, the others didn't seem serious artists but just wanted a holiday with a difference. Nick's son, Jeremy, mixed with the adults well but didn't remember Celine. He was open faced, like his father, with a quick smile and twinkling eyes that still held the simple trust of the young. He seemed close to Ana and Celine noticed that they chatted and laughed at lot together in Spanish – the guests excluded from their seemingly carefree world. Celine hoped that Ana had not become a mother substitute for Jeremy.

Ana had cooked an estafado, a hearty beef stew cooked with cloves, onions and garlic, which everyone enjoyed late that balmy evening, sitting under the pergola, just as Celine had imagined. Nick had put a tape of wailing flamenco music on the stereo, which added to the atmosphere and, in the background; crickets serenaded them as if in competition with the music. The wine flowed and the conversation was easy. Celine dropped into bed past midnight and fell into a deep, contented sleep.

The following day, after a breakfast of fruit from the garden, fresh bread rolls and strong coffee, Celine, wearing a large brimmed hat to guard against the sun, found a quiet spot in the grounds of the finca and prepared to paint. The artists had been instructed to split up and get a feel for their surroundings before starting their work. Celine gazed upon the valley with its orange and lemon trees thriving in the sunlight and wondered why she felt so at one with Spain even though it was her first visit. She had never had these feelings for Holland or Hong Kong. After about ten minutes she began to work, at first tentatively as if daunted by the sight of the blank canvas, but soon she was making flamboyant strokes of bold colour using acrylic paints and large brushes. As always when at work, Celine was transported to another world as she lost herself in the painting. After about an hour Nick drew alongside her.

"So the real Celine is emerging!" he said with enthusiasm.

"Is that good or bad?" Celine chuckled.

"It's very, very good. You paint with a freedom and maturity that usually only comes with years of experimentation. At this rate, you won't need any tuition. The only advice I can offer you is to be a bit bolder with your shading. Mmm - it's coming on really well. I know you are absorbed in your work, but we're all going to have a coffee break in the courtyard. Want to come? You can leave your paints here, there's no one around to disturb them."

"Okay, just give me a few minutes and I'll join you." Celine put her brushes in a jar of water and stood back to look at her painting. She couldn't believe that she had produced such an effect. Spain must have inspired her. Or maybe it was being with Nick again. She heard bells tinkling in the distance and, glancing up, spotted a herd of goats being shepherded across the valley, a sight that had probably not changed in centuries. And, as a breeze wafted across her face she caught an unfamiliar aroma of wild thyme and rosemary. Everywhere there was the sweet smell of a lingering summer stretching into autumn.

Everyone was gathered in the cool courtyard as Ana served coffee and local almond biscuits bought at the village shop. Justin sidled up to Celine and sat a little too close. Instinctively, she moved away a fraction.

"Wonderful here, isn't it?" He looked at Celine with serious grey eyes. His fair skin was beginning to turn red in the unaccustomed sunshine.

"It is very special, yes," she observed.

"How about a stroll around the olive groves before commencing our painting?"

"That would be nice." Celine heard herself say. Immediately, she regretted it and hoped that Justin didn't get the wrong idea. Besides, she wanted to have some time with Nick. She craved time alone with him with a deepening intensity. It was with longing that she remembered his teenage kisses and wished that she had never met James.

They walked slowly through the ancient, gnarled olive trees and Celine listened as Justin told her his life story which gathered pace like a runaway train the more he spoke, his eyes wild and darting. He was a salesman in his mid thirties from the Birmingham area and looking for a soul mate he told her.

'Unusually open and chatty for a man, but a bit intense.' Celine thought to herself. She had gradually become more discerning since being married to James.

Wondering if he actually just wanted a sounding board, Celine broke into the conversation.

"Well, I think it's time to get back to some work. Nice talking to you. See you at lunch."

Justin made a point of sitting next to Celine each mealtime. Perturbed by his attentions, she was polite but did not encourage him. He seemed to be troubled and had a haunted look in his eyes.

"I feel as if I've known you all my life." He told her towards the end of the following day as they viewed each other's work, which was displayed in the courtyard.

She just smiled blandly in response and wondered if she should tell him to back off. As usual, being non-confrontational by nature, she thought it better to just be polite.

Celine took a long shower that evening in the guest bathroom with the cheerful yellow and blue hand painted tiles. As the warm water caressed her she started to sing, all inhibitions evaporated in her new surroundings. Wrapping herself in a large towel she emerged from the bathroom, distracted by thoughts of Annabel and realising how much she missed her.

"Whoops, sorry." She bumped into Justin, resplendent in a Chinese brocade dressing gown, standing quietly in the passageway off the central courtyard that linked the bedrooms.

"Enjoy your shower?" Justin's eyes seemed to devour her, leaving her feeling uncomfortable.

"Yes, thanks," she muttered as she hurried to her bedroom feeling somehow soiled.

~ ~ ~ ~ ~ ~

The gondola was painted in bright colours. Celine was reclining against some cushions and gazing up at Nick as he rowed along a wide river. It was as the olive groves disappeared and they reached the smooth open seas that he joined her on the cushions and kissed her lingeringly on the lips as they drifted. And drifted. Suddenly, a large bird swooped down from a darkening sky and, on its back, Ana rode wearing a flamenco dress, its red flounces flapping in the breeze like blood soaked wings. She and the bird seemed merged into one threatening, screeching being and started to peck noisily at the side of the boat. Water leaked through the side of the boat, making it sink and still the bird pecked. Tap, tap, tap.

She awoke feeling disorientated and then remembered she was in Spain.

'Nick, it's Nick,' her heart swelled with desire, 'he still loves me after all.'

The tapping was persistent. Still feeling a memory of his lips on hers she called out, "Come in."

She had no idea of the time but it must have been the early hours of the morning. Footsteps on the tiled floor and then he pulled back the sheet and lay next to her. By now, her heart was fluttering with the expectation that her lover was back in her life again.

"Nick. Oh, Nick," she breathed.

"You're my soul mate. You're the one I've been waiting for."

Celine froze. It was Justin. Her heart began to hammer with fright and she felt sick.

"Get out. What the hell do you think you're doing?"

"All right, all right. I thought you felt the same way. I thought you fancied me."

Celine pushed him away, fearful that he might force himself on her.

"No, I do not fancy you. Get out, we're not alone in this house – I'll scream." She meant to shout but her voice came out in a hoarse whisper, as if it was trapped in a cage of terror.

"But - you smiled at me in a special way. I did not imagine it." He tried to kiss her but she slapped him hard against the cheek.

"You bitch." He had her by the wrists now and Celine's panic was choking as she struggled.

Outside a dog barked and Justin became still, as if he had suddenly realised the consequences of his behaviour.

"I mean it - I'll scream and the police will be here before you can - " She threatened, her voice now surprisingly strong.

He went limp, let go of her wrists and started to shake, "Okay, okay - I'm going."

And with that he slunk out.

Celine pulled her nightdress down and raced to the door on unsteady legs, her heart still pounding. Should she awaken the house? In the meantime, afraid that Justin might return, she placed a heavy chair against the door and fell back into bed where she cried tears of fear, disappointment and frustration. In that moment, she knew that she was deeply in love with Nick – that he was her soul mate but had he found his in Ana?

Later that morning, Celine got up with a headache. She'd had difficulty getting back to sleep after her unwelcome visitor and was dreading seeing Justin again.

By the time she reached the breakfast table the two middle aged couples had started to eat. As she entered the room they stopped their chatter and looked embarrassed. Then she heard angry shouts from outside. It was Justin and Nick.

"Are you crazy? What are you playing at daubing paint on my jeep and how dare you say these things about Celine." Nick was uncharacteristically angry.

"What's going on?" Celine looked at the four at the table for an explanation.

"You'd best go and see for yourself." Heather told her gently while the others made a point of studying the table cloth.

Rushing out of the front door, she was greeted by red graffiti on Nick's jeep.

CELINE IS A WHORE it shrieked.

"Nick, what's going on? Who wrote this?" She stared in disbelief.

"I'm sorry – this idiot took it upon himself to daub a load of rubbish on my car."

"She egged me on. Flirted with me and then pushed me away. She's a tease and a whore." Justin's eyes were flaming with vitriol, his strident voice hammering at Celine's already sore head.

"I did not encourage you. You're imagining the whole thing." Celine was furious and hoped that Nick did not believe Justin's story.

Standing between them, Nick took Justin and frogmarched him into the living room.

"Pack your bags, you're not welcome here."

"Gladly, I've had enough of you all." Justin spat as he ran across the courtyard to his room like a petulant teenager.

Celine sat at the table and poured herself a cup of coffee in a state of shock. She felt strangely guilty and wondered if she had encouraged Justin without knowing it.

"That went well." Greg said drily and they all chuckled. Celine wondered if she was on the edge of hysteria as she heard herself laughing loudly.

Nick managed to clean up his jeep and, wanting to make sure that he was away from the area, took a sullen Justin to Malaga where he could try to get a flight. As she watched them drive away Celine relaxed, determined to enjoy the rest of her holiday. The remainder of the group decided to take a trip to nearby Ronda and asked Celine if she would like to join them. She jumped at the opportunity and grabbed a camera before heading off to the village to catch a bus.

The ride had taken under an hour along precarious hairpin bends that looked down onto a checkerboard of plains surrounded by craggy mountains. The raw beauty filled Celine with wonder and her incident with Justin was pushed to the back of her mind as she revelled in the landscape. They arrived in Ronda late morning and descended from the bus by the famous Puente Nuevo bridge that straddled the enormous El Tajo gorge where dissidents were once flung to a gory death. The Moorish influence was everywhere in the old town and Celine decided to split from the rest of the group to get inspiration for her next painting as the others wanted to go shopping. As she wandered the narrow pebbled streets, she once more felt at home in this foreign land. Enthralled, she took many photographs in the hope that she could use them as a prompt for more paintings.

Cafés would soon be full of customers enjoying a meal but, in the meantime, waiters stood on the pavements like wax works staring into space, in their own private worlds, waiting for some lunchtime activity. The shops in the Old Town were small and exclusive; jewellery twinkled on rich dark velvet and on display were leather handbags, belts and shoes plus tourist items which somehow looked incongruous amidst the traditional buildings with wrought iron balconies like heavy black mantilla lace. The narrow streets, designed for donkeys and pedestrians, were crowded with traffic and there was much tooting of horns.

Suddenly, bells sang out. A middle aged woman, dressed entirely in black emerged from one of the many ancient churches. She shuffled along, her back bent prematurely as if she had forgotten to leave her burden at the altar. An older lady reverently decorated one of the many shrines to the Virgin, using fresh flowers, each one a tender offering.

Celine meandered contentedly into a restaurant, just off a square. There were no tourists to be seen and it was cool and welcoming inside. Crisp yellow tablecloths matched the shirts of the staff. Behind the bar bottles were lined up like soldiers and reflected the light from above. Sitting down on a softly cushioned chair she glanced up. Rustic beams stretched across the white ceiling and three enormous metal paella dishes were suspended from the wall, whether for use or ornament she was not sure. Pictures of bullfights graced the walls and Celine hoped that she would never have to witness such an event. One painting of a matador, the epitome of machismo, grabbed her attention. There he stood in his gold embroidered waistcoat ready to face danger or death for the sake of honour and Celine understood that this was a very different culture to her own. Andalucian lanterns hung festively around the bar and ceiling; the Moorish influence once more evident and the background Flamenco music made her feel oddly at home, once again. She wondered what Nick was doing and hoped that Justin would not cause any further trouble. Most of all she prayed that her encounter with Justin would not spoil her tenuously rekindled relationship with Nick.

Waiters dressed in black aprons with matching bow ties busied themselves behind the bar as lunch time approached. Olives were being dispensed from a large plastic container into small terracotta dishes and tapas stood in the chiller on the bar ready to be devoured.

One of the waiters approached her with a haughty half-smile, notebook poised.

"Buenos dias, señora." He bowed slightly, revealing shiny black hair combed over a bald patch.

"Buenos dias. Un café con leche, por favor." Celine remembered a little of the Spanish that Nick had taught her on their trip from the airport and she hoped that she wouldn't need to say anything else.

Soon a rich coffee aroma filled the air as the noisy machine went into action, first grinding the dark roasted beans before steaming water mingled with them, creating a divine infusion The coffee ceremony completed, her drink was placed with pride in front of her.

"Café con leche, señora," he said solemnly.

"Gracias." Celine said with unaccustomed confidence.

She took a sip of the strong warming drink. As a bonus, a chocolate had been placed in the saucer. She let it melt slowly in her mouth until she reached the hazelnut and then, crunching it, savoured the flavours and textures.

A middle aged man, dressed in navy blue and wearing a walrus moustache was sitting at the bar doing a puzzle, oblivious to the outside world, absorbed in his conundrum. He stopped occasionally to swig his brandy.

Soon, a young man strolled into the café and had an animated discussion with the waiter. There was much waving of arms. They were probably just discussing the weather. The young man wore a defiant pony tail and tight jeans. He had deep lines at the sides of his mouth.

'Perhaps the consequence of hard living,' Celine thought.

He appeared careworn as he began to pace the floor, hand on his mouth. Deep in thought, he produced a tape measure and started to measure the bar.

The puzzle man never looked up.

A thick set woman wearing an apron and cap walked purposefully to the kitchen chewing her bottom lip and carrying a ladder. She headed for the kitchen where noises of activity had begun and a smell of garlic and onion frying permeated the air.

The maitre d' wearing a black suit lifted the best wines with pride into a display cabinet and then stood back to admire his work. Satisfied, he made his way to a swarthy man with long sideburns. More animated discussions were loudly pursued.

An older waiter with a thick shock of white hair started to put the olives on the tables in preparation for the lunch time trade. It was 1 o'clock - an hour before the Spanish would arrive for the most important meal of the day.

The man sitting at the bar must have finished his puzzle. He ordered another brandy and flicked through his paper in a desultory manner.

The waiters pursued their work with purpose and seemed to be enjoying the routine. All over Spain the same ritual would be repeated. Table cloths changed. Coffees served with pride. Lunches prepared. Wine poured. Olives displayed. Everything going like clockwork. At that moment, a familiar face appeared at the café door. It was the middle aged woman who left the church looking so worried. She made her way to the puzzle man. There was much agitated pleading from her as the volume of her voice increased with each sentence. Her dark eyes were shadowed as if by a secret tragedy, her face a spider web of lines. He avoided her gaze and looked only at his paper.

An unwilling eavesdropper, Celine felt a mixture of compassion and embarrassment.

"Porque, Enrique?" The woman questioned, her voice now a wail.

He did not answer but kept his gaze on his glass.

"Yes, why Enrique?" Celine wanted to ask him but knew she could not.

Resigned, the woman left the bar, her shoulders a little more stooped.

He ordered another brandy. And Celine thought of James.

The waiters carried on as if nothing had happened. They worked on automatic pilot. They had seen it all before.

Realising that had she stayed with James she could be this woman and feeling an empathy with her, Celine wanted to go to her and say something comforting. But what could she say? An invisible foreigner sipping coffee in a corner. Their lives separate. For the first time Celine was truly convinced that it was for the best that she and James had parted. Parted before she became a stooped woman with a burden too heavy to leave at the altar.

Celine paid her bill and went out into the startling sunlight to meet her companions.

On the bus back to Casa Bonita, she reached into her bag for her journal and jotted:

Today, I have come to understand that for a brief moment in time peoples' lives are tenuously intertwined. Connected but separate. Each of us will go home to a different complex scenario - including myself. The woman pleading with her husband today was like a vision of what I could have become if I had stayed with James. My future is still so uncertain and, after that scenario with Justin, I know that I am vulnerable. How could I be so stupid? I should have seen what he was after! And did Nick believe his lies about me?

~ ~ ~ ~ ~ ~

The week progressed in a lighter vein. Several paintings were finished, much food and wine was consumed and still Celine had not managed to have any time alone with Nick. She began to wonder if he was ignoring her. Perhaps he did have a thing going with Ana.

Then events escalated with rapidity. It was their last night and the other guests had gone to bed after a delicious meal of paella followed by fresh fruit salad. 'Ana's a good cook as well as being beautiful.' Celine thought with dismay. How could she compete with such a girl, especially now that she had a child in tow? She had found that men cooled off rapidly when they found out about Annabel. Wanting to make a lasting impression on Nick, as it was perhaps to be their last night together, she had taken a lot of trouble getting ready for dinner that evening. Her lightly tanned skin was complimented by a white sleeveless dress and she wore amber beads that matched her large eyes. It was time to remove her wedding ring that she had worn almost as protection. She hoped that this might signal a message to Nick, but, at this late stage of the holiday, she had her doubts as to his interest in her.

"Let me help you with these dishes." Celine viewed the detritus on the dinner table.

"Leave the dishes. Let's talk. Want some more wine?" Nick held an opened bottle of Rioja.

"Why not? It's my last night and I don't want to go home." Running her fingers through her hair, she could not hide the disappointment in her voice.

"I don't want you to go. I wish you could stay here too. It's been hard this week what with the other guests and everything. Until I found out about Justin, I thought that you two might have become romantically linked and I didn't want to get in the way. I was jealous to be honest but, now I know the truth, I want to ask you something." He poured her a glass and topped up his own.

"Fire away." Celine's heart was pounding and she felt light headed. Was it the wine or Nick that was having this effect on her?

The cicadas kept up their racket in the background and the air was sweet with the perfume of the jasmine, datura and dama de noche blossoms. Nick drew her to himself and kissed her softly on the lips, and then holding her face gently in his hands, he spoke slowly and solemnly as if his words had been well rehearsed.

"I love you, Celine. I always have and this week has proved it to me. Being with you has brought back so many good memories. Remember how happy we were when we went out together? That day that we met in the park was wonderful and disappointing at the same time. I wanted you back but realised that you were intent on saving your marriage. I've never told you this before but I was heartbroken when you married James. I suppose we've made a lot of mistakes since then but we both deserve a fresh start. Will you consider coming out here and - " he paused and took her hands in his. "My darling, please, please marry me? We could - "

"Nick — it's not that simple. I have a child of my own now," Celine's heart was soaring but she interrupted him before he could go any further.

"Of course I've thought about that. I've always wanted a big family, as you know. We talked about it often enough. Remember we said that one day we'd have four children. Well, we still could. I promise to be a good father to Annabel and love her as if she was my own. Please marry me, Celine."

"I love you too but, I -," she paused and closed her eyes as she remembered that fateful encounter with Eloise, "I don't know if I can ever trust a man again. I've never told you this before, but Eloise came into the shop once. It was when we were engaged and you were at college. She told me that you had a lot of girlfriends, implying that you slept around and that you took drugs and - "

Nick gasped, "What! She told you that? I don't believe it - my God, she had it in for you. She told me that she'd heard rumours about you - that you did all those things once I went to college. Then I got your letter telling me that you'd met James and that seemed to confirm what she'd said. Eloise could see that I was broken hearted and she was so kind to me - cooked me meals and offered comfort. The rest is history. It was all a front but I was taken in by her lies. She even proposed marriage to me - what a fool I was to even consider it. I was on the rebound, I suppose, and fell for her charms. Once we were married I saw her true colours - she was a total bitch. Selfishness personified! The marriage wouldn't have lasted as long as it did but for the fact that she was pregnant with Jeremy. You know the rest - she left us both to go travelling. You must believe me, my darling, I didn't sleep around, nor did I take drugs - although a lot of the students did experiment. Please believe me when I say that you can trust me in the future. I will be a faithful husband to you - I promise with all my heart. Marry me, Celine."

Relieved to hear his account, she smiled into his eyes and they kissed hungrily as she cherished the moment so that it might be indelibly printed on her memory. Then her old insecurities started to seep into her consciousness like a deadly poison and she wondered if she would ever be able to trust a man again.

"Tell me about you and Ana. Are you lovers?" She had to ask him or the question would continue to fester.

Nick's mouth fell open with shock and he shook his head.

"What! Oh, good heavens no, no – she means nothing to me. Ana is an employee who I get on well with, that's all. Besides, she's engaged to Pablo. Celine, forget about anyone else, it's you I love. I can't imagine life without you."

At this news Celine put her head on Nick's chest and sighed with contentment and relief. He stroked her hair and rocked her in his arms as if she was a child. Then he held her head in his hands and, looking into her eyes, said, "You don't have to give me an answer right now. I know you've been through a lot. Take your time." Nick stroked her face with such tenderness that tears pricked her eyes.

"I don't need to. I'll be back. And, of course I'll marry you. I love you too. And, I promise to be a good mother to Jeremy. Annabel's used to having a sort of brother in Kim, so she won't feel as if her nose is being put out. I've got a lot to tell you about my new friends. Oh Nick - this has turned out to be the happiest night of my life." Celine told him without hesitation, a smile of surrender breaking through her tears.

As if on cue, Nick took a small box from his pocket and took out a ring. Celine gasped as he slipped a tiny cluster of diamonds set into white gold onto her bare finger, replacing the gold band that she had put away in her suitcase.

~ ~ ~ ~ ~ ~

Veronica took the news of Celine's move to Spain remarkably well, although she admitted that she would miss Annabel. Celine could not wait to tell her friends what had happened in Spain. She had deliberately kept the news in her heart and waited until the next SAM meeting. The joy and excitement was electric. They hugged and laughed and shed a few tears as Celine recounted the events of the week with Nick.

"You look absolutely glowing. Isn't it amazing the way things have worked out? Oh, I'm so happy for you. When do you plan to get married?" Kristin found the entire story of the week magical.

"In about six months so that I'll have time to sort things out here. Let's hope that this wedding will go better than the last one. Thank goodness I haven't got a monster mother-in-law coming to put the mockers on things." Celine commented.

"It will be lovely. Nina will be so excited about being a bridesmaid for the first time and I'll actually be able to get her to wear a dress!" Kristin bubbled with delight when she heard Celine's news of her wedding in Spain to Nick.

Samantha looked wistfully at her two friends. "This may never have happened if we hadn't decided to go to Art College. It's as if a plan was laid out and we just had to take one step at a time and it would all unfold. I expect Annabel will be a bridesmaid too won't she?"

"Oh yes. She doesn't really understand but knows she'll have a special dress. I remember when I was a bridesmaid for my sister. It started off well but ended in tears." Celine announced. She could feel a story coming on, and as it was a Saturday afternoon, she didn't want to break any traditions.

"Do tell." Kristin pleaded.

Celine recounted the time that her sister married, had a wonderful reception and a big party in the evening.

"I loved being a bridesmaid, but when it was time for the party, I had to go to the old lady next door where I spent the night."

"How old were you?" Samantha asked.

"Oh, I was fifteen. In retrospect, quite old enough to go to the party. All the family were there - except for me."

"That's awful," Kristin interrupted. "No wonder you married young – you probably wanted to get away from home."

"I never gave it a thought but maybe that's true. I'm sure Dad would have wanted me there so it was either my sister or Mum who wouldn't let me. And my wedding to James would have been wonderful except for the monster-in-law." Celine laughed as she recalled James's mother, glad to have her out of her life.

"The next wedding will be different - you'll see." Kristin reassured her.

~ ~ ~ ~ ~ ~

James had been informed of Celine's impending marriage but did not respond to her letter personally, choosing instead to have a solicitor write to her demanding half the proceeds from the house sale. This Celine arranged without bearing a grudge. However, there was still a mortgage on the property and so she was not a rich woman. Samantha was sad to leave the Victorian house that had offered her succour at a time when her life was in a state of flux. She had made plans, but before they could come to fruition, she and Kim moved in with her mother, Betty. It was with mixed feelings that the friends packed a crate of belongings to be shipped out to Spain and watched a removal lorry take the furniture away to be sold at auction. The home where so much had happened in such a short time became an empty shell and Celine felt a tinge of sadness as this part of her life closed. She was missing Sasha but knew that Veronica would give the cat a loving home.

Annabel had attended her final nursery school class, the girls had met for their last SAM meeting and Celine was almost ready to move to Spain. It was an emotional meeting that Saturday afternoon at Kristin's place and not a few tears were shed as the three friends reminisced about their treasured times together.

Celine started to pack her suitcases in preparation for her and Annabel's flight to Spain and, as she was going through her underwear, came across the brown envelope stuffed with pictures of James's previous mistresses together with the long black hair.

Feeling nothing but pity for him, she took the items into the sitting room, placed them in the small fireplace, struck a match and watched with relief as they burned. It was time to bury the past for good and move on.

"Goodbye, James. Be happy." She said to the flames before returning to finish her packing. She had an important journey the next day. Her journal entry that night was upbeat.

As I watched the flames dance around those almost forgotten photos, I realised that it is not what happens to us in life but how we deal with things that is important. It has taken me a long time but my hatred and bitterness have become ashes and have no power or life of their own to destroy unless I allow them. I am a stronger and more empathetic person because of the trials and, I hope, have enough love in my heart to overcome the hurts of the past. I have finally forgiven James and feel such a freedom in releasing him. Tomorrow is a new day. A day of fresh beginnings. A new season.

23

THE WEDDING

"You look like a fairy princess," Kristin's daughter, Nina, told Annabel as she helped her into her bridesmaid's dress. It was the same colour as Nina's – a pale aquamarine blue, but more flouncy.

"Yes, and I've got a new brother now. This is my room and he's got another one." Annabel was matter of fact.

She swirled in front of the long mirror in the same guest room that Celine had first used at the finca and that the bridesmaids were now using to get ready. On the bed Annabel's favourite teddy sat with a look of astonishment on his face. The excitement in the air was tangible and infectious.

Downstairs the noise level was rising as the boys played football outside. Kim and Jeremy had overcome their initial shyness and played boisterously together while Ricki supervised. Nick and Harry chatted on the veranda with Simon, a retired pastor who used to run the youth group that Celine and Nick attended as teenagers. Delivery men arrived at the door with groceries while Betty, Ana and some of her friends chatted enthusiastically above the blare of the radio as they prepared salads. To add to the cacophony, Nick's two dogs, both rescue animals, barked louder than usual, sensing that today was to be different and the cockerel in the chicken enclosure was crowing over his brood of contented hens. The only exception amidst the hullabaloo was the feral cat that had adopted Nick and which lay on a sun kissed wall in a deep, indolent sleep.

"It's so good of you to make the trip to Spain to conduct our marriage service." Nick smiled at Simon.

"Oh, it's my pleasure. I remember thinking that one day you two would marry. Besides, how could I refuse a holiday in Andalucía after all the rain we've had in England this year?" Simon responded, running a finger under his dog collar that was chafing in the heat.

Upstairs was a little more sedate, the fervour more contained. Kristin worked with alacrity, the tools of her trade laid out in a neat line on the dressing table. There seemed to be a brush in every shape and size.

"It would take me a week to put my makeup on using all this clobber." Samantha joked.

"You look fabulous," Kristin complimented Celine after she had worked her artistry with her professional makeup kit that she had brought out especially for the occasion. Samantha's makeup had been done, she was already dressed for the ceremony and, as a finishing touch, had applied a little of her perfume so that the room was filled with the gentle aroma of apple blossom and vanilla. Kristin noticed that she was wearing a cross around her neck but did not comment, as she knew that Samantha liked to keep her spiritual life private.

Celine had treated herself to the works before leaving for Spain, "I'm a product of your beauty salon," she responded to Kristin's comment as she inspected herself in the mirror. "It's so good that Fran is popular with the clients and that so few of them went to Chloe's salon."

"Yes, I needn't have worried but at the time I didn't know. Fran is actually a better therapist than Chloe and has a great manner with the clients. The business is flourishing and Top Health magazine has given me a super write up about the oils that I mix for clients to use at home. Now people are ordering them by post and they're flying off the shelves. At this rate, Harry will have to give up his job and help me keep up. I've also met up with a cosmetic chemist and we're talking about him starting to formulate my own skin care range. All very exciting. I know exactly what sort of products I want. Don't breathe a word. All very hush-hush at the moment. " Kristin was her usual dramatic self and was revelling in the adventure, her skin glowing as if in an endorsement of her hand blended oils.

Samantha's eyes widened, "So, that's the mystery that's been surrounding you recently."

"Yes, I didn't want to tell anyone until I was sure that it was feasible." Kristin confessed, looking embarrassed on account of her uncharacteristic secretiveness.

"No one deserves it better, you work so hard." Celine told her friend. "Will you still talk to us when you're rich and famous?"

"Sometimes I feel as if I'm in a fantastic dream and I don't want to wake up. Isn't it great the way it's worked out for us all?" Samantha looked wistful.

Before Kristin could answer her, Annabel, wearing the frilly confection ran in, followed by Celine's mother.

229

"I'm a fairy," the little one chimed as she spun round and round until she fell over.

Celine looked at her daughter with pride, "You are a gorgeous bridesmaid."

"I'm not a maid, I'm a fairy," Annabel protested, her bottom lip pouting in protest.

Samantha took the wedding dress, a simple affair in cream silk from its hanger, handling it as if it was as precious as a designer gown and helped her friend into it, pulling up the zip over Celine's slim body. Freshly picked jasmine flowers from the garden were woven into her hair; a simple but effective foil to the dress.

"I can't believe this is happening – it's like a fairy tale." She stood back to admire the dress.

"Tis a fairy's tale and I'm a fairy." Annabel started to spin again.

"Please stop her, Mum or she'll be a sick fairy." Celine looked at her mother, willing her to take Annabel away so the girls could continue their feminine activities for just a while longer in peace.

"Come on – let's find Nina and Auntie Betty." Veronica, looking florid in the heat, picked up the toddler. "This place should be called Casa Crazy with all that's going on. I've never known anything like it."

Then, within half an hour, all became tranquil. Nick, Harry and Simon had left in good time for the church with the spruced up boys, followed by Ana, Betty and Veronica with the two young bridesmaids. The dogs had become quiet and the radio switched off. The girls revelled in what was probably to be their last time together in this way with a glass of chilled white wine.

"Here's to us. Happy wedding day," Samantha raised her glass.

"Here's to Tea at Sam's!" Celine clinked her glass with first Samantha, then Kristin.

"Here's lookin' up yer nose as they say in beaut Australia," ever the mimic, Kristin raised her glass in a Down Under toast as they waited for the expected sound of hooves outside.

"I hope Antonio will be on time. Everyone seems to be about an hour late in Spain." Celine voiced her concern as she sipped the cold, sweet wine.

"Don't panic. I've just spotted him coming along the lane." Kristin was glancing out of the window at the scene below for what seemed the hundredth time that morning. "Here, take your bouquet – it's time to tie the knot."

Outside the sun was searing hot as the friends walked carefully in their high heels onto the cobbled drive to meet Antonio, Ana's father, who had arrived from the village.

"Hola. Listas?" He greeted them with his gravelly voice as he helped the three friends into his horse drawn carriage. It was only a short drive to the church along an unmade road through an orange grove. The friends sat in uncharacteristic silence with just the clip clop of the horse's hooves ringing in their ears.

It was the most joyous day of Celine's life. She had recaptured a love that she thought she had lost forever. She had finally buried the past, found her destiny and was grateful to be given a second chance.

Celine's heart was replete; such was her happiness, as she walked up the aisle to be joined to him, unaware of anyone else but Nick. She felt full of light. The tiny church felt comfortable, like a homecoming after a long absence, the ancient stonework trapping the cool air inside. Behind her, the bridesmaids followed, Nina looking demure and Annabel waving to the congregation as she recognised people, as if the whole affair had been laid on for her. The boys, Kim, Jeremy and Ricki stood silently at the front of the church in their best clothes, overwhelmed by the reverence of the scene.

Nick seemed to have a permanent grin etched onto his already cheerful face and he gazed at Celine throughout the ceremony. He had won back the woman he had always loved and was glad that he had been patient and waited for her. Like a frightened bird, she would have flown away if he'd tried to capture her too soon. He kissed her after they had said their vows and she breathed in his aftershave. It was fresh and smelled of lemons and she knew that he was wearing it just for her.

It was quite a fiesta – the party in the grounds of Casa Bonita that followed the church ceremony.

Ana and Pablo cooked meat and fish on a brick barbecue that Nick had built, Ana all the while talking loudly as she gave him instructions, to which he responded with his banter as if in rehearsal for married life. It seemed as if all the villagers were there in their best attire, some of the women wearing traditional flamenco dresses in bright primary colours. No doubt there would be dancing later on. A few chosen friends and family had arrived from England. They seemed reserved and lacklustre next to the vibrant Spanish guests who didn't need an excuse to party nor a drink to lose their inhibitions.

Celine's sister, Janet, and her husband, Richard, were there looking bemused by all the activity. This was not like any wedding that they'd been to before and they looked as if they were in shock.

The finca had been decorated with garlands of flowers and the table under the pergola was heavy with barbecued fish and meat, salads, bread, olives and wine. In the centre, a three-tiered wedding cake stood - its snow-white icing incongruous in the early afternoon heat. The air was filled with joyous sounds as food was consumed amidst music, chatter, laughter and the innocent sound of children playing. The sun shone brightly that glorious day as if it too was celebrating life, its heat coaxing the fragrance from the abundant flowers.

"To the newlyweds. Cheers everybody." Harry raised his glass and everyone joined him in a toast.

As the guests were sipping their drinks Kristin sidled up to Harry and whispered, "Have you noticed how much Celine's changed? She's stopped her constant tidying up. The place is in chaos and she hasn't even noticed."

"A miracle indeed." He remarked dryly.

Kristin continued, "I don't think our surprise guest is going to appear. I hope I haven't made a mistake persuading her to come. Do you think she's changed her mind? And what if she turns up and it doesn't work out. Do you think I've been meddling?"

"Don't worry; she's probably just missed a connection. She'll be here and it will be fine." Harry, always steady, placated his wife.

Children ran in and out of the olive trees, the Spanish kids mingling happily with the English, the older ones looking after the toddlers.

Celine threw her wedding bouquet over her shoulder to whoops and claps from the noisy and exuberant guests. Ana caught it with triumph, smiling coquettishly at Pablo. She coughed nervously and spoke first in Spanish and then in faltering English.

"I wants to felicitate the wedding of Nick and Celine and also to my brother, Carlos, for the marriage to Samantha. I wish them all to be very happy. I am just sad that our brother, Luis, cannot be here, but we have lost touch with him since he left to go to travel. I know he would be happy for you all. Bueno. Salud." Glasses were raised again as Carlos gazed at his new bride and Nick at his.

"Speech!" Kristin called out, banging a spoon against her glass.

"This is such a happy day for me to be marrying the love of my life, Samantha. I thank God every day that He brought us together and that I went to England to study art for it was there that I met her – and, of course Kim. We are looking forward to our new life here working with Nick and Celine as they expand the business. This is a special house. A house of restoration and peace where, I hope, we can work together to help those seeking a holiday with a difference. Thank you all for coming along to make this such a marvellous day. " Carlos announced with conviction before translating his speech into Spanish.

They made an attractive couple, Samantha with her delicate features and Carlos with his dark Andalucian appearance. She looked ethereal, almost angelic in her cream dress and he a strong caballero. The past was such a far off, alien place to her that she was now able to embrace the future with optimism.

Ana and Carlos' father, Antonio, brought out a guitar, which he strummed and then started to sing flamenco, all the while tapping his foot to the vibrant beat. Others started clapping in time to the song and Celine and Nick, followed by Samantha and Carlos danced, the crowd clearing a space for them in the shade of the trees. Ana and Pablo followed, the rhythm of the flamenco a part of their heritage, their eyes flashing with the passion of the dance. An older Spanish gentleman, who had been sitting alone watching the proceedings, got up and made his way to Celine's mother.

He bowed formally, "I am Pedro – please to dance with me?"

"Erm, oh er, thank you. I'm Veronica," she rose to her feet, buoyed up by all the excitement, and danced a type of self conscious tango as onlookers called out "Olé."

Later on, Celine made her way over to Kristin who was wiping a few tears from her eyes as she stood in the shade of a Jacaranda tree, its blue blossom almost matching her dress.

"You will come out and visit won't you. Just because Samantha and I are now married women doesn't mean that we can't have the odd SAM meeting."

"Just try and keep me away. Who knows, I may need to open a health farm in Andalucía one day." She winked and Celine's eyebrows shot up. She had learned that what sometimes started with an idea with Kristin had the habit of turning into reality.

Then the tempo of the music changed. The girls looked over to see Samantha and Carlos singing together. He plucked the guitar as both of them sang in harmony, her voice sweet and his deep and melodious.

"Look at those two. They must have been practising - they sound wonderful together." Kristin gazed in amazement. At the end of the song Carlos handed the guitar back to Antonio amidst applause.

"Will the two happy couples stand together for some more photos? Yes, next to the bougainvillea." Harry had to shout to make himself heard over the noise of the party. "This is a double wedding with a difference and must be recorded for posterity. Where are the rest of the children? Someone find Kim, Annabel and Jemms." Harry clicked away with his new camera and Simon smiled benevolently from where he sat in the shade, his dog collar and jacket removed and placed carefully on a chair.

After about ten shots he called to his wife, "Kristin, come over. It would be good to take some pictures of you three girls. By the way, I forgot to tell you that you look lovely."

She looked delighted at receiving his compliment. Indeed, she looked stunning in a vivid blue linen dress with matching shoes and a chunky pearl necklace.

Hurrying over she stood alongside Celine and Samantha. The girls posed; relaxed in each others' company and Kristin quipped, "We must mark this day as the Saturday Afternoon Matrimonial."

Just as Harry had finished taking the shots the dogs began to bark as an unfamiliar car drew up outside. All heads turned as a diminutive figure wearing a pink suit and a navy blue hat at a rakish angle struggled out of the taxi trying not to drop what must have been presents. Bun's husband, a little older and greyer since Kristin last saw him, took two suitcases out of the boot and stood, bemused, as he viewed the scene.

Kristin was the first to react.

"Bun – you made it. Oh, how lovely to see you again." She rushed over and hugged her Australian friend before leading her into the throng. "I have someone here who you must be longing to meet."

Bun, looking flustered said, "I didn't think I was going to make it. The flight was delayed – but I'm here now. Wow, what a gorgeous house. Oh, it's good to see you again and looking so well and happy. Where's this sister of mine then? Have you told her that -?"

"No, I wanted it to be a surprise. You wait here and I'll get her."

Kristin had forgotten what a strong accent Bun had. 'This is just the icing on the wedding cake,' she thought as she looked for Veronica. She loved it when a plan dovetailed together.

Veronica was sitting in the shade fanning herself, in recovery mode after the fandango with Pedro. Kristin dashed over and took her hand.

"I have someone I want you to meet."

"Must I dear, it's so hot. It can wait. Who are that couple that've just arrived? They don't look Spanish."

"This can't wait – it's too important." Kristin insisted as she pulled a bewildered Veronica off her seat and dragged her, as if she was a reluctant child, towards Bun.

"I think it best that you introduce yourselves." Kristin beamed.

The two women searched each other's faces, one looking puzzled and the other with tears in her eyes.

"You must be Veronica. I'm Bun – your long lost sister." Her voice was barely audible.

Suddenly pale, Veronica held both hands up to her mouth and gasped. At first, Kristin thought she had made a mistake; that she should not have interfered. Celine was hurrying over to find out what was going on. Kristin had kept the secret from all but Harry, wanting the surprise to be a blessing to Celine as well.

Kristin held her breath, knowing that Celine's mother hated scandal of any kind. Then, to her relief, Veronica reached out to Bun as tears ran down her cheeks. They were not tears of sadness but genuine happiness to see her relative, all thoughts of her wayward father put aside. The two embraced amidst loud clapping and shouts from the exuberant wedding party.

Harry rushed forward, camera in hand, to record the moment.

When, at last, the guests had gone home, Samantha and Carlos retired to their honeymoon suite, an annex at the back of the house that was to be their new home together. Celine and Nick were alone and cherished each moment.

The moon shone brightly, lighting up the courtyard as they embraced. They held each other for a long time as the silence enveloped them.

"I've been waiting for this moment for a long time," he whispered.

"And I have as well. I never thought I could be so happy," Celine responded.

"I promise to love you forever," he said as he swept her into his arms and carried her to their room.

Much later that night Celine crept out of the huge bed that she shared with Nick. As he slept, she felt compelled to write a few words in the journal in which she had recorded the roller coaster of the past few years.

My heart is replete, my life restored and I am so grateful. Finally, the past is behind me, and the poison of betrayal a distant memory. The love of my life has returned and the future is a bright promise.

The End

Lightning Source UK Ltd.
Milton Keynes UK
UKOW051658020312

188229UK00001B/13/P